THE HOUSE WITHOUT A DOOR

AN INNER SANCTUM MYSTERY

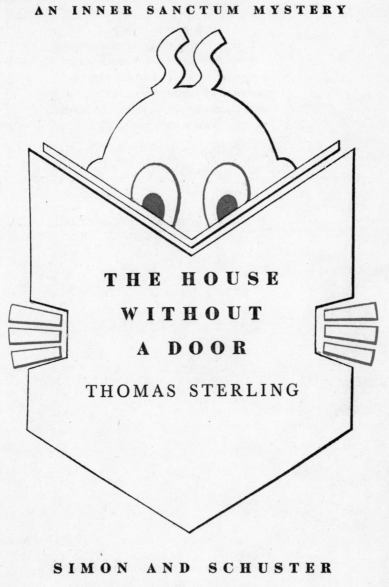

THE HOUSE
WITHOUT
A DOOR

THOMAS STERLING

SIMON AND SCHUSTER

NEW YORK

"I am the hunter here, and the hunted prey.
My own gunsight will seek me out some day
And though I plead, I will press the trigger and fire,
Ashamed to stare back into my own eyes
As I bleed, and die, and guiltily expire."
                                        —Paul Kresh

to whom this book is dedicated.

to whom this book is dedicated

THE HOUSE WITHOUT A DOOR

B O O K   O N E

Chapter 1

HANNA started down the last flight of steps. The lobby of the hotel loomed below her. She held tightly to the velvet railing with one hand and tested each stair with the toe of her tiny, buttoned shoe before she trusted it with weight. The hem of her brown satin dress trailed on the marble behind her.

She descended into full view of the lobby. Her massive body cringed at the unexpected attack of light and noise. Resolutely, she stepped onto the hard, broad floor and faced the host of strangers.

No one noticed her. Everyone was intent on his own business. No one laughed at her and no one pointed her out to his friends. No one advanced on her in a menacing way. These people were nothing more than strangers. They wouldn't hurt her—but they wouldn't help her either. She leaned against the cool wall next to the stairs and watched them hurry to and fro.

A woman in a silver fox cape rushed past her and threw herself into the arms of a mouse-colored woman in a cloth coat.

"Wonderful to see you again, Maggie! Let's have a drink."

Enviously, Hanna watched the two women hurry off to the little restaurant at the rear of the lobby. How nice it must be to have a friend, to have someone to greet you. She left the comforting wall and headed for the door. The

1

thought of Madison Avenue outside, with its darkened sidewalks and quiet trees, drew her on. She felt everyone staring at her back. She stepped down the old stone stairs at the entrance and stood beneath the blue canopy of her hotel, in the street at last.

The frightful noise came from everywhere. She had been prepared for changes, for the gleaming beetles in the streets and the great buildings and for the garish daylight coming from the shop windows. Even finding that there were no trees any more was not so much of a shock as the noise. The air rocked with it. The sudden crescendo of motors when the street light changed, the shuffling step of thousands of feet, and the constant undertone of talking all converged on her. She had forgotten how to choose the noises that she wanted to hear, the noises that were meant for her alone. She could not remember how it was to make her ears selective so that the distant screech of a brake didn't sound as though it were at her back. She walked slowly down the street, into the storm of sound.

Thirty-four years ago tonight, Hanna Carpenter had rented a small suite of rooms in the Hotel "38," a fashionable hotel on Madison Avenue. She had sent notes to her few friends and to certain old acquaintances of her father's who might worry about her, saying that she was going on a long trip and might not be back for several years. Having inherited her father's money, she could very well afford to do what she pleased. Also, this sudden decision had probably not seemed strange to anyone, since all of her acquaintances knew that her fiancé had recently left her; and her extreme action was considered to be the fruit of her great sorrow.

On receiving the notes, her friends agreed that she needed a change and went on about their business, soon forgetting the awkward young girl who had more money than she knew what to do with. Her father's friends clucked paternally in their beards and said that a change

2

of scenery wouldn't do Bert's child any harm, but that they hoped she wouldn't marry some European crook on the rebound. With this, they felt that they had fulfilled their obligation to an influential man, now dead and no longer influential, and promptly forgot that Hanna ever existed.

Hanna had intended to keep her rooms only for a short time, feeling that what she needed most was a time of complete rest and seclusion before she decided what to do with her future. At that time, what she considered her future entailed many responsibilities. Her father had left her a great deal of money, more than she needed merely to be comfortable, even on the most extravagant scale. Whatever her future was to be, it would require large decisions.

And so she lived quietly and serenely for a year, and then two years, never leaving her little apartment. Only gradually did she begin to face the fact that she did not intend to leave. Even later, she had to admit that her seclusion was no longer a matter of choice, but of dreadful necessity. She *could* not leave. She had pulled her door shut and it would not open.

She had tried to explain this to herself by saying that she had left the world because of a disappointing love affair. This appealed enough to her sense of the romantic to satisfy her for a while. But slowly, she had to admit to herself that this marriage, which had been more her father's plan than her own, had really meant nothing to her at all after her father had died. It was not so much that her fiancé could be said to have run away from her: he had merely stopped pretending that there was anything between them.

No, if anything, she had used the loss of her lover as an excuse to leave a world she had never known very well, a world which had been the exclusive province of her father. He had owned so much of that world, outright. He had made it do anything he commanded it to do. Throughout

3

her motherless childhood this world had stood tamely outside the windows of her father's house, like a huge wild beast which had been brought to heel. Her father had protected her from this beast, perhaps too well.

She had not been "spoiled," however. Her father would not have allowed that. For every luxury she received she had to pay full measure in the only coin she had—in gratitude and appreciation for what she had that others did not. Her father had never ceased reminding her that she was a fortunate girl and that all she had was hers only on sufferance. Perhaps she could have understood this, even as a small girl, if her father had bothered to tell her what *was* hers—what was truly hers to keep. But being a man a long way away from his own childhood, he did not think it was necessary to explain that he loved his daughter very much.

But as the years began to pass she recognized something else which kept her to her rooms. There was some other more violent, less logical reason why she could not leave her hotel. Somehow the beast outside, the tame reasonable animal of her childhood, had broken loose and was raging in the streets. She knew that it was there, a gray, cold, relentless monster which would one day find her and destroy her. She had tried to reason it away and to assure herself that nothing of the sort could exist. And yet she knew it was there. She felt it always, outside her doors and windows.

To protect herself she ordered heavy metal shutters placed over all of the windows. She installed an electric refrigerator in her kitchen so that she could be independent even of food.

But if she could have faced it squarely she would have admitted that it was useless to hide from a force as invincible as this, that one might as well live outside in the world, take chances with streets full of automobiles, fly in airplanes, ride in subways. She would have agreed that no effort she could make, nothing her money could buy,

4

could help her avert the inevitable catastrophe. And yet she hid, hid night and day from the world outside, living in fear of the thing which was coming to get her.

During the first years she read a lot. Arthur, the waiter who brought her food on days when she could summon enough courage to open the door, was commissioned to get books for her. She had not gone to a university when she was a girl and had no idea of the kind of thing one was supposed to read. At first, Arthur was given authority to choose anything he liked. Perhaps it was fortunate for her, therefore, that his choice was so catholic. He would bring her selections of every kind of book in the library. She read all of them and gradually came to know how to direct him in his choice.

Her mind became a large, disordered trunk into which she piled tidbits of indiscriminate knowledge. One day Arthur brought her a book of poems by Emily Dickinson. She learned that this woman, who, the introduction told her, was the greatest woman poet since Sappho (an author Hanna had not yet read), was a "recluse." She read the poems ravenously, trying to find in every line allusions to herself. Often, late at night when she could not sleep, she would pick up the book and read her favorite poems, finding in them a separate and particular message for her.

> *This is my letter to the world*
> *That never wrote to me . . .*

Hanna always cried when she read this, her great body breaking with sobs.

She was not long content with the books of fiction Arthur brought. They gave no real satisfaction. She could not be happy with these poor imitations of life. The more she grew away from life the less she could bear make-believe in others.

Outside of a few favorite books (chosen because of a fine description of something she would like to see, or because of a passage which she took to be directed to her), she began to prefer factual accounts of life as it was lived outside in the world. She subscribed to newspapers and political journals of all colors. She read all of the "inside" books and made Arthur go twice a week to Brentano's to buy the memoirs of presidents and statesmen. She became a minor authority on the first World War, the Revolution in Russia, the League of Nations, the rise of fascism, the great depression and the bloody second World War. She believed everything she read implicitly, even though half of what she read contradicted the other half. For her the world of men and their struggles was as distant as Mars. She read the reports of congresses and conventions as other people read fictions, and in the tales of uprisings and suppressions of peoples she found a way to share the world's life without endangering her own.

Her favorite publication, one which she began to look forward to as early as Tuesday of every week, was *Life* Magazine. This was almost like living in the world itself. She could step through these pictures into a college sophomore picnic, a New York secretary's vacation on Cape Cod, a coronation in Holland, a Papal blessing in Rome. With its help she knew what Texas oil men looked like, what unmarried girls in Bali looked like, what were the newest sports in Florida waters, and how a New York politician named Vito Marcantonio looked when he made a speech.

In time, Hanna became intimately familiar with practically all the large-scale suffering in the world. However, she lacked completely the desire or the ability to take any action based on her knowledge. She read about the massacres of Moslems in Hyderabad and the slow starvation of Navahos in the Southwest with profound sorrow, and yet it never occurred to her that she could do anything about these things. The thought that she might affect the course of the world's destiny in even the smallest way was fantastic and would have frightened her. Even though she sometimes mailed great amounts of money to relief

6

agencies—Italian relief, Russian relief, dumb-animal relief —she never wanted any accounting of how that money was spent.

It would have distressed her to know that ninety-eight dollars of the twenty-five thousand she had sent to rehabilitate a town in France after the first World War had been spent for flypaper. To know exactly what had happened to the money she contributed was too much for her. It brought the world too close. It destroyed, somehow, what little security she had found in her rooms in the Hotel "38." Once, a Jewish relief agency in Poland which trained refugee Jews in manual skills had gratefully sent her an itemized account of how her check was being spent, an account which listed the *names* of the distressed people who were being helped. She burned the letter, closed the shutters on her windows and wouldn't allow Arthur to bring her food or books or any other communication from the outside world for days.

Hanna wanted to belong to the teeming life outside her rooms, but only in the most limited sense. She wanted to know what was going on but on no account did she want to feel what was happening. She was excited by the works of Lenin, but the barest suspicion that these ideas came from a living, breathing, feeling man caused her to close the book in horror. There were parts of Lenin which she could never read; parts which were too much felt, which belonged to the world of the living.

If anyone had suggested to Hanna that she was selfish she would have denied it indignantly. How could she, who had nothing, who had less than any other living creature, be selfish? Wasn't she an outcast on her own planet? She had given up every form of human contact. Was there any greater loss than that? How can a pauper be selfish? She would have laughed if she had been told that her several million dollars didn't exactly entitle her to call herself a "pauper." She would answer that money, after all, is only worth what it can buy. Could she buy a friend? Could she buy safety? If she preferred not to hear the names of the victims of a war she didn't start, what difference did that make to them? Was it necessary that she bear *their* suffering on her shoulders as well as her own unhappiness? If there had to be revolutions and murder and pillage, did she have to smell and feel and hear it all, when she had not caused it? She could not have understood the rather too philosophical assertion that she was perhaps more responsible for these things than she knew, or that, in wanting to know what the men and women in the world were doing without wanting to feel, she was, like everyone else, trying to have her cake and eat it.

Therefore she continued to read, with the greatest equanimity, of the bombing of Belgrade, the death factories in Germany and the blinding, desperate starvation in China—sending off her checks in moments of Olympian sympathy—while a single article on the back page of the *Times* about a father who had lost his daughter in a furnace explosion froze her blood and caused her to sit rigidly in her chair all day and half the night, fighting off the cold fear of her impending doom.

Besides reading, Hanna had one other major activity. An activity which, for her, was entirely useless. She became a dressmaker. She could have spent these thirty-four years entirely naked for all the difference it would have made to anyone. She could have reverted to quiet barbarity, prowling through her modest rooms like a cave woman, lank hair down her back, white flesh gleaming beside the bric-à-brac. She would have been most profoundly shocked at this suggestion. Perhaps it is because a body cannot be alone and unlooked upon for a long time without becoming obscene even to itself; but, for whatever reason, Hanna clothed herself as demurely and as fashionably as she possibly could. From her current magazines she took patterns for dresses in the latest style and spent long hours hand-stitching them to fit her slowly expanding body. Many of her dresses had been torn apart and remade five or six times. Several times a year Arthur's wife would go out and buy materials for the "crazy old woman in the hotel." These materials were always specified by Hanna from advertisements in her magazines.

Hanna's closet was filled with dresses of every kind and for every occasion. She always dressed for her dinner and often, when she sat down—with no one to hold her chair—it was in the identical gown that some other woman was wearing in an excellent restaurant not four blocks away. And sometimes in the afternoon when she watered her philodendrons she wondered what other women, who were wearing copies of her green chiffon dress, were doing and whether they were alone or had some company.

In this manner the years passed; slowly at first and then more quickly, until Hanna began to find herself pressed for time. Each day she had to bathe herself, prepare her own lunch, dust the furniture, read, sew, do her hair in a new way. Her day was filled with little duties—duties which might seem unnecessary to anyone else, but which were most important to her. Several times a week she cleaned her silverware, especially between the tines of the forks, which were always collecting particles of food. She discovered that her fingernails grew at a prodigious rate—it was almost as if her entire vitality had gone into them—and had to be filed almost every day. Her toothbrushes collected bits of paste and had to be scrubbed. Her comb was always dirty, although she washed her hair constantly. Her carpet was wearing out in spots and she had to school herself to walk in other pathways as she went about the house. Eventually the duties she made for herself kept her so busy that she would be exhausted at bedtime and would finally have to rest completely for several days.

Twice a year the manager of the bank near her hotel would come to see her. During the months of May and October this patient man would alert himself for Hanna's call. He had learned from experience that his invitation would be good for no longer than twenty minutes after the

9

specified time. If he arrived later than this he always found the door locked and, though he knew his client was standing on the other side of the panel, nothing he could say would make her open the door. When she called he would grab a prepared folder from his desk and his hat from the rack and run in a most unbankerly way up Madison Avenue.

Once inside her rooms, their meetings were most pleasant. In spite of his twice-a-year sprint Mr. Howard wished more of his customers were like Miss Carpenter. She never asked foolish questions and went over her accounts by herself quickly and efficiently. He had the power to pay all of her debts under one thousand dollars. She ticked off his check stubs against the duplicate bills without ever making remarks about his beautiful handwriting. She never said that there was a mistake on page two of his financial report when there was no mistake or told him how dreadfully poor she was and how expensive everything was getting.

Between Miss Carpenter and himself there was always the strictest formality, a relationship he rather liked, and her occasional instructions for investing her money were almost invariably sound. She had got out of the European bond market a good year before the last war was declared, and she even bought a little piece of a uranium mine before the atomic bomb exploded. Altogether, he respected Miss Carpenter and she paid an excellent fee.

During all the time that Hanna spent alone in her rooms she never ceased to think that one day she might go out. At first she used to imagine adventures that would occur to her if she were to leave. She would have fantasies of meeting a friend—in a restaurant perhaps—who would talk to her. This friend would be kind and polite (sometimes it was a man, sometimes a woman) but no more. They would talk about all the special things that Hanna knew, about dresses and about the situation in Spain or China, about the latest correspondent's book from Ger-

10

many or about *Life*'s article on Midwestern homes. At the end of their talk the friend would rise and say, "I must leave now but I will be back here at this time next week. Will you meet me?" Hanna never carried this fantasy further. The very lack of intimacy in this friendship, its very casualness, made it seem more likely to happen. If she went further with it and imagined a real friendship, which would require her paying visits or having people come into her rooms, the dream would immediately dissolve. She was content to leave it alone. As time went on it even became unnecessary for her to think of meeting a friend; the very thought of going out on the street was excitement enough.

And then, she decided to leave.

Why had she made up her mind at last to go out into a world she had hidden from so long? Whatever the answer to this question might be, it is certain that it included many things. One can put off what one has to do for a long time but eventually it must be faced, the door must be opened and the step must be taken. Time changes nothing; an act might be put off for two hundred years (though not by one person) but at last it will be done. If the intervening time had any function at all it was to soften the reality until it appeared to be no more than a dream. Perhaps Hanna found the courage to walk out into the world because she had dreamed of doing it so often and now the doing was a dream itself. She had forgotten that even dreams can lead the dreamer to disaster.

Chapter 2

As Hanna joined the other people in the street she was relieved to see that she was going to be taken for one of them. People passed her without turning around to stare, just as if she had walked past these shops every evening of her life. She was protected in her cloak of anonymity and felt the same kind of excitement a child feels in a Halloween mask, secure in the knowledge that "they"— the parents, the friends, the "others" in the world— couldn't recognize the person underneath.

"All late!" She dodged past the man selling newspapers from a little stand, trembling because she thought he had been speaking to her. ". . . as I see it, we have to put our best foot forward tomorrow. That old man's a tough baby. Get Jenson to . . ." Voices. Yes, that was the strangest thing after all of the years—human voices. They rose out of the evening, came toward her and disappeared again, each one different, each one taking conversation for granted. Talking—talking—talking with an inexhaustible supply of words. More words in a minute than she had heard for months.

A bell rang beside her in the street; a little, tinkling, insistent bell.

"Good Humor, lady?"

Was it a question? What did he mean? Perhaps a way of saying good evening. Should she speak to him? He was a little, wrinkled man in a white suit and he sat on a bicycle which had a large, white sidecar. She stared at him and opened her mouth to speak, to speak words like other people on the street.

"Name your poison, lady. Chocolate, vanilla, pistachio, maple cream—what'll ya have?"

Hanna backed away and hurried across the intersection with the crowd.

She came to an immense window set into the side of a building. From it came a light which was whiter than day and made everything look as if it had been coated with flour. Inside, on the walls, were great tropical trees and vines. Wild orchids grew in their branches and parakeets and monkeys perched among the heavy leaves. It was

12

painted to represent some clearing in the jungle, filled miraculously with tables and chairs. The people in the clearing might have come out of that jungle. At one end of the clearing, beneath hanging creepers and luxurious palms, stood an immense counter of glass and silver, with people crowded before it, gathering food in trays. A tropical steam rose above the counter and disappeared in the thick green of the painted jungle.

This was a restaurant, she knew, and yet she'd never seen one like it before. Her eyes ached from trying to see it all at once. Just as she had forgotten how to hear the sounds that were meant only for her, so she had forgotten how to look at one thing at a time. She could never have imagined such color and such movement and such blinding lack of privacy.

Seated at a table just in front of her, before the window, was a man with his chin buried in a bowl of soup. A spoon raced the few inches between the level of the liquid and his mouth, again and again. Occasionally he withdrew his chin and, with his free hand, crumpled a cracker into the bowl. Hanna moved on toward the center of the window. She was hungry. She had told Arthur not to bring her meal this evening. She went to the door and allowed herself to be pushed through by the crowds.

"Check, lady."

She turned. A short man with a bald head was looking at her impersonally. He was wearing a greasy jacket. She stood dumbly before the little rail that protected him.

"Check, lady—*if* you don't mind."

The man didn't like her. How had he let the others go through and stopped her? Was there something about her which others could notice?

"What—what do you want a check for? I—I don't have any with me anyway," she finished lamely.

"I don't *want* a check, lady. I want for you to *take* a check. There!" He pointed to a tall silver box. From the box peeped a notched edge of cardboard. "Take it!"

13

She took it and jumped away from the machine as it whirred and sounded a loud gong. She remembered now that the gong had sounded when the others had passed the box. She looked around. No one was watching her; even the man at the desk had turned back to his work.

"Get the silverware, Hanna. Daddy's gone for the food. I'll hold the table."

She watched a twelve-year-old Hanna walk away from the table and suddenly she felt a great tenderness. She wanted to help the other Hanna; wanted to give her a present. The little girl moved efficiently through the crowd. No, she thought, sadly, I could give her nothing.

She followed some people who had just come in, to a place beside a coconut palm. She took a tray as they did and took a spoon and knife from a common metal box. She started to take a fork, but seeing the yellow flakes of egg between the tines she put it back. Perhaps she could find something to eat with a spoon.

She went to the counter and stood behind the crowd as they begged for plates of food from unhearing men in white coats. Someone jabbed a tray in her back and suddenly she realized that she was a part of the crowd. On one side of her a heavy, sweating man rubbed his body against her arm. She was pushed against the back of a bony, starving woman who was yelling, "Gimme the franks and beans!" A little man with an angry red face was banging on the counter and saying to one of the men in white coats, "No, no! The *porched* egg. I want a *porched* egg!"

Now, all of their faces and their arms and their legs seemed to push and undulate beside her until she felt that her own hands and feet and head were not hers any longer but a part of this mass of hungry men and women. A fat man cried, "Where are my muffins?" Hanna held her tray flat against her like a shield and, fighting against a growing panic, she turned and ran back into the clearing. All around her people were putting food in their mouths, some greedily, some primly, some missing the mark altogether.

14

Hanna felt she would never be able to eat again. She dropped her tray on an empty table and ran to the door.

"Check, lady."

The bald man looked up from his figures and held out a dirty hand. She stood before him once again, fixed.

"The check, please."

"But I took a check."

"No, lady. Now *I* want the check."

"But I don't have it. I lost it. If it's to show what I ate, I didn't eat anything."

"It don't matter if you never even smelled anything. I want the check."

"I told you it was lost. I had it in my hand and now it's not here any more." She would surely suffocate in the light and the noise if the man wouldn't let her go.

"That check's worth two dollars. Suppose somebody else found it. I ain't going to pay for it. I . . ."

"Oh, I have two dollars. I can pay two dollars. Here!" She pulled two bills from her purse and threw them on his desk. She ran toward the door. A man in a soiled shirt, who was coming in, held the door open for her and smiled. She rushed out into the street and then stopped, realizing that she hadn't smiled back.

How nice it was—how really *nice*—to be smiled at. Especially by a stranger who had nothing to ask. He smiled just because he wanted to smile. Perhaps that was the way things went in this world outside. Everything changed so fast that you didn't have time to be upset or grow panicky because the very next minute something nice had happened.

Out here on the street, with the impersonal crowds again, Hanna was amazed by her own exhilaration. She felt a certain sense of triumph. She had gone into a horrible place where people pushed and mauled her and had managed to leave it without running or crying or losing control of herself. She had paid the man two dollars—just paid money at the desk like anyone else—and, to the others at

15

least, she had acted perfectly normally. Now she could pretend to herself that she had gone in and bought dinner and paid for it—actually she had paid for it—and, when she left, someone had held the door for her.

Hanna continued walking in a direction away from her hotel. She was becoming used to the street and its sounds: the horns of automobiles, the noise of coughing, the sudden, strangled barking of small dogs who meet and hate each other; all of these noises seemed to blend together in a sound which she now recognized as the voice of this street. Even the faces which bobbed past her were blurred and became a part of the big face of the street. She began to understand how these people all lived so packed together and so lacking privacy. The trick was to make yourself alone no matter where you were; setting your mind, like a clock, to go off when a light went green, or a corner turned, or someone called you by your name. The rest of the time, though you walked and dodged lamp-posts and stopped to buy a newspaper or a magazine, you made yourself be asleep, lulled by the eternal noise of your street. It was not so different, really, from locking yourself in a room.

But she would be careful. She wouldn't go to sleep like the others. There was too much for her to see. Besides, if something nice were to happen, like smiling, she would have to be ready for it. She began to watch carefully the faces of the people coming toward her. Maybe someone else was out tonight who needed to be happy, who needed a friend if only to . . .

There, coming toward her, was a man, a tall young man. He was laughing, not a loud laugh, just quietly to himself. He was looking at the people who passed him and when they didn't look back, didn't wake from their sleep because their clock hadn't been set for him, he just laughed to himself and went on. Hanna was frightened by her own audacity. She was going to smile at him—perhaps even say hello. Maybe this was her friend. She screwed her face

16

into what she immediately knew must be an idiotic mask of pleasure.

The grinning, empty face, with eyes which looked at her without seeing and a mouth which gurgled words which were no words, hung before her like a wet moon. For terrible seconds she couldn't move, and the blind, unseeing, uncaring face before her preserved its stupid smile. A small and quivering "Hello," which had been shaped long ago, came from her mouth and fell dead to the street. With the sudden perception of horror she realized that her own face, with its stiffened grin, was a callow imitation of his. She pushed past him and ran, not caring any more what any of the other people thought.

It was only after she'd run a block that she dared to look back and there, more frightening even than the idiot, was a man she knew. It was the man who had held the door for her. She waited a moment to make sure she was not mistaken. It was the same man, with the soiled shirt and the brown, uncombed hair. From the distance of half a block she could see that he was watching her. He stopped for a moment in the light of a shop window and then came on. She wanted to run again, run back to the hotel where she could lock the door and be safe, but he was between her and the way back. If she were to cut off on another street she might get lost, and the side streets were dark.

Suddenly, her panic disappeared. She began to reason. Why should this man be following her? As soon as she asked the question she knew. She had forgotten that she had what thousands of people coveted. She had her father's money, a great deal of money. If someone had recognized her, or had seen her come out of the hotel—if Arthur had pointed her out to this man—wouldn't he follow her until she came to a deserted street where he could grab her? Perhaps he would knock her out or hold a chloroformed handkerchief to her face and then take her away so she would have to pay money to be free. Her mind imme-

17

diately rejected the thought that she might go up to him and offer him money to go away. Such men are never satisfied by peaceful methods. They think that if they can get so much without trying, violence will get them even more.

Hanna turned and began to walk in the midst of the crowd. At least here she was safe. Among people who didn't care for her and didn't even see her she was safe. They were her friends, almost because she had never spoken to them. They had never smiled at her, they never said hello to her, but they were her friends. As she walked she made a plan. Twice she saw him, reflected in a window, keeping always a little behind her. Perhaps he didn't know that she had seen him. She planned to walk with the crowd as much as possible until she found a policeman. She knew that would frighten the man away and she would demand that the policeman take her home.

It was Arthur, of course. Arthur, who had brought her meals and whose wife had bought the materials for this very dress she was wearing, had told the man in the soiled shirt about her and together they had planned to kidnap her. She regretted the large tips she had given him every Christmas. They had made him greedy, so greedy that he was willing to destroy her to get more of her money. The one person she had allowed in her room had betrayed her. It was almost useless to fight against such odds. Was there no one in the world she could trust? Perhaps she couldn't even trust the policeman. If the man were to offer the policeman some of her money wouldn't he help too? Oh, but she had to trust someone; that was the trouble, you always had to trust someone. It wasn't possible to escape— ever.

Hanna saw a policeman standing in the middle of the street. She looked over her shoulder, into the eyes of her pursuer, only a few feet away. She stepped out into the street, forgetting the cars. Maybe the man would try to overtake her before she could call for help. Car brakes screeched and a driver began to swear.

"Officer! Officer! That man . . ." Suddenly, the man loomed beside her.

"What's the matter?" said the policeman.

Hanna didn't answer. She looked fearfully at her enemy; her expression told the story better than any words.

The man spoke. "There's a BMT subway entrance around here somewhere, isn't there?"

He looked at Hanna and smiled pleasantly. She knew immediately that he thought he was seeing her for the first time. His cordial smile was entirely professional and contained not the slightest bit of personal feeling. It was merely an attractive display which he switched on and off like a neon light.

The policeman took off his cap and rumpled his thick orange hair with hard, dirty fingernails.

"One block up—one over. West side of Fifth. Are you with him, ma'am?"

"Oh, no. I just . . ."

"Thanks!" The man flashed his fine, white teeth once more at Hanna and strode off.

"I just wanted to know if you could tell me a place to eat around here."

"There's a Schrafft's in the middle of the next block. That the kind of place you mean?" His eyes were a darker color of orange.

"Oh, yes. I think so. I think I've heard of Schrafft's." She hurried off in the direction he had indicated.

A hostess, dressed in black, spoke to her sternly:
"Are you alone, Madam?"

It was a question Hanna could not answer. It was such a mocking and unnecessary question and she wondered, for a moment, whether the hostess were making fun of her. As Hanna followed her guide, whose clothes and manner

19

were so somber, she remembered a time when she had walked in terror behind her schoolteacher to the principal's office. The hostess drew a little, polished, wood table from the wall and somehow Hanna felt like apologizing because this little work she had done was too ignominious a thing. Hanna sat dutifully on the green leather bench and the table was pushed up to trap her. She was handed a menu and she had the curious feeling that it was a lesson that she was required to learn.

Hanna looked around her. Here were no hanging vines, no parakeets, no tropical steam; here were only tinkling glass, subdued voice, and surface of varnish and leather. There was a faintly luminous quality to the room as if its atmosphere were not air at all but pale water. It was hard to imagine that the food could have any taste. In the other restaurant, plates had been wreathed in the pungent steam of broccoli and cabbage; here the tiny casseroles hid their flavors under silver covers. A faint odor of watercress filled the room.

Hanna sighed and opened the chaste menu. It was a sigh of peace. She had found refuge from the storm. In here, the elements of color and smell and sound were tamed and reasonable. They did not tear at the senses and force themselves on you as they did outside. Here, people seemed to be eating, less because they had to, than because they wanted to. They talked, not to make themselves heard, but to amuse. The odors didn't assail you, they were managed. The savagery was extracted from everything, leaving only the essence; unless, of course—and this is a thought that Hanna would not have until later—the very essence of all things *is* their savagery.

"Your order, Madam." The waitress was not stern and unbending like the hostess. She was tall and pale and very young and looked like a stalk of wilted celery.

"Oh! Now let me see. Vichyssoise, I guess; and—ummm —leg of lamb, if you have mint jelly; and a roasted potato; and—ummm—what vegetables do you have?—Oh, string

20

beans." Hanna found herself tearing off the edges of the little paper doily on her table.

"Thank you, Madam." The waitress took the mangled place-mat from Hanna's hands and brushed the shreds of paper from the table. "I'll get you another." There was no reproach in her voice. She fitted her order book into her serving apron pocket and walked away.

Hanna sat before her little table, hands clasped on her lap. She looked approvingly at the silverware. The hostess brought two young men and seated them next to her. There was something splendid about them. She caught a glimpse of gleaming bluchers, argyle socks, and rich, tweed trousers as they were sitting down. Beside the restrained and lofty hostess they seemed almost Byzantine. Hanna noticed that the hostess' black dress was decorated at the throat by a gold-framed cameo, nothing more; whereas the two men seemed to be literally covered with jewelry, jewelry which for the most part pretended to be something useful. Even their glasses, surrounded by thick horn, seemed to take the place of veils from which they watched the world with Oriental eyes.

"He told me I could take any record in the album I wanted!"

"Oh, wonderful! Which did you take?"

"Well, I wanted 'Get Yourself a Geisha' but 'Marvelous Party' is so grand and . . ."

Suddenly, both of them looked at Hanna. She realized she had been staring. She tried desperately to pretend she was looking over their heads but they continued to regard her hatefully. She felt her face growing red and wondered what terrible thing she had done to make them despise her so much. She wished the waitress would come with her food so that she would have something to do.

The young men returned to their conversation but Hanna found that her eyes continued to stumble across them, absolutely against her own will. Whenever she so much as looked at the back of the head of the blond one

21

she would find herself caught in the haughty stare of the dark one. She could not know, of course, that her neighbors were as frightened of the world as she, or that they detested her because they thought she detested them. Within a few hours she would learn that there is no cruelty like that of the weak and the vulnerable.

Hanna was pleased with the food. The portions were meager and a discouraging amount of white plate showed, but the lamb was tender and the potato had a crisp brown crust on the outside. She ate the mint jelly separately and the sweet, pungent taste gave a special intoxication. The waitress gave her a hot fudge sundae for dessert. She drank her coffee slowly and looked at all the new people coming in. This was what she had dreamed of doing for so long. Year after year, a few blocks from her quiet rooms, Schrafft's had been serving lamb and mint jelly and hot fudge sundaes to others; and now, miraculously, *she* was here, behind her own little table, ordering her food and acting just like anyone else. The reality of her accomplishment struck her for the first time. She had done it. She didn't have to dream any more that someday she would do it. Hanna felt like a successful explorer who has just come out on top of a mountain which everyone had said couldn't be climbed. Below her lay the impossible terrain she had crossed; which, from this height, looked mild and peaceful. Its dangers had been exaggerated.

She was amazed to see that many of the people who came in were women of about her own age—alone. She watched the hostess guide each of them to a solitary table, like her own, and leave them sitting majestically before the polished silver and the empty glassware. They gave the impression of exiled queens from tiny and usually impoverished countries, forced to seek asylum in the friendly land of Schrafft's. How peculiar, she thought, that not one of them seemed to notice the others. They looked up from their menus only to signal the waitress, and if

22

the waitress didn't come right away they didn't connect this with the fact that another queen had called her first.

There was something about their features and the soft sag of their shoulders which made them look alike, as if they had come from the same family. When Hanna looked closer, of course, she could see that the women were quite different. A careful examination showed that their eyes and mouths and ears and noses were entirely distinct, not even vaguely related; but who, Hanna thought, will ever bother to look carefully?

And then Hanna knew why they had all looked the same, why even their dresses had seemed alike (though her practiced eye could see that they were different models entirely). It was because each of these women was alone. In the morning when they got up and at night when they went to bed, only one pair of eyes saw them. When they went shopping they bought their clothes for their severest and only critics—their own mirrors. In these reflections, perhaps, they saw traces of favorite characters in books or fashion models or movie stars, but in everyone else's eyes they might as well be dressed in flour sacks. The penalty for pleasing one's self is pleasing no one else. Hanna looked down at her own brown satin dress. She knew instantly that she looked as lonely as the others. She was a good dressmaker, she could follow a pattern and perhaps the dresses she made would look good on someone else—someone whose life was involved with other people—but on herself, no one would see them. No one would ever see what she saw in the mirror.

Suddenly, her whole adventure seemed profoundly unimportant. How could it possibly matter, even to her, if she left her hotel rooms or didn't? Her disappearance from the world had caused no comment, not a ripple of excitement among any of her friends. Her return to that world made even less difference. Perhaps if she had come out sooner—if she had given to someone else what she had

23

wanted to be given to her—things might be better. But the time for that had passed. What she had left to give, no one wanted.

Even the money she had somehow didn't count any more. It had stayed too long hidden, like herself, and had lost a certain essential part of its value—its connection with human beings. She had become like these other women who ate alone and whose lives made a difference to no one but themselves. She had grown to look like them without ever intending to. Like them, she had isolated herself from the world, from other people; and now the world and its people did not care. The best that any of them could do was to purchase a mechanical attention from waitresses and salesladies. What punishment did the world have to offer that was worse than this? Perhaps even rape and murder would be preferable. But would anyone care even to perform this violence on one of these ladies? Hanna seriously doubted it.

She paid her check and left the restaurant. The traffic and noise of the street assailed her again, but she knew now that there was no possible chance of her joining this stream of life. Not only were the joys of this life closed to her but its dangers and terrors as well were nonexistent and quite imaginary. The policeman on the corner was there to protect other people, not her—people who had something to lose. The traffic light was there to allow men and women who had some place to go to cross the street. She had at last accomplished what she had dreamed of doing only to find reality vastly overrated. The dream was much superior. She had even thought that she would find a friend if she went out, not a good friend—she didn't want a friend who would demand anything of her—but someone who would miraculously appear to talk to her about the things she knew, someone who would leave when she was tired, who would come back when she was lonely.

She realized now that this "friend" was no one but

24

herself. To this friend she had offered a devotion unparalleled in life or literature. She made new dresses, she washed her hair, she brushed her teeth and filed her nails—all for the sake of this person. She had eaten, slept and talked with her friend all her life and to her she had given all of her energy and kindness. And now perhaps, like these other women, she would learn to meet her friend at Schrafft's for lunch or dinner and confidentially discuss her most intimate thoughts and feelings. This friend of Hanna's was kind and thoughtful as no other friend could ever be. She was a disappointment in only one respect. She would not leave when Hanna was tired.

Hanna crossed the street against the light and paid no attention to the dodging taxis. They could not want to run over her. The policeman with the orange hair blew his whistle but she paid no attention.

On the corner, beneath the light of a street lamp, stood a newsstand. A man was unloading fresh copies of *Life* Magazine from a truck. Hanna smiled and took twenty cents from her change purse. This was Thursday night. Tomorrow, when Arthur brought her subscription copy she could say to him that she had already seen it. He would wonder how she got it and perhaps she could make up a story to tell him. He would be surprised. Perhaps he would even tell his wife about it. She took a copy of the magazine from a pile the man had left beside the stand and put it under her arm, dropping her twenty cents on top of some newspapers. She would read it tonight in bed. The cover had a picture of Marshal Tito that looked like Hermann Göring and there would be an interesting article inside all about what was really happening in Yugoslavia. She felt a little better. Tomorrow there would be so much to do and to think about that she wouldn't remember that she was alone. She walked on, stopping occasionally in front of shop windows to get new ideas for dresses.

A block before her hotel she passed a door and heard

25

music. She came back and looked in. Hanna did not have
a radio but she guessed immediately that this music was
jazz. From descriptions she had read she had always
thought she wouldn't like it, but this had a sadness which
touched her immediately. It was as if someone were pity-
ing himself in music and it cheered her to think that other
people could feel this way too. Inside the door she saw a
liquor bar. Both men and women were seated on the bright
yellow stools. Hanna had never been in a bar in her life
but she knew that it was now considered all right for
women to drink in the company of men.

Perhaps she would never have gone in if it hadn't been
for the music, which seemed to offer so much solace;
which said, with its muted brass tongue, that she had a
right to be unhappy and that there were others in the
world who were unhappy also. Perhaps the music also
suggested to her that she could find someone inside who
knew how she felt and would comfort her.

If Hanna had gone back to her hotel she could have
gone peacefully to bed and read her copy of *Life*. She might
have dreamed that night, her usual vague and transient
dreams of terror instead of finding them unbelievably
translated into reality.

Chapter 3

DAVID HAMMER usually came to the Hardwicke whenever
he was uptown. It was not much different from any other
bar on Madison Avenue, but it had a kind of underplayed
elegance which he liked. Most of its clients were exceptionally well-to-do. Though they gave no outward sign

of their affluence, it was possible, for David at least, to feel their wealth in the very air of the place. He knew that the occasional frayed jacket or scuffed shoe to be found here was not an evidence of poverty but of carelessness or a love of comfort. Most of these men and women had no need to make a display of their comfortable physical position in the world and some were positively afraid to do so.

David collected wealthy people. Particularly unhappy wealthy people. Part of this was snobbery. He liked to be with people he considered superior. Another part was business. Among other things, David was a blackmailer. Unlike most people of this profession, however, he was not crude or shortsighted in his work. Working with the very wealthy, as he did, he had come to realize that his clients demanded service, even when they were being robbed. Often a "friend" would bask in the sun of David's attention and sympathy for several years before the blow fell and the check was ruefully signed.

The top man in his field is usually amazingly endowed by nature. Champion runners have low pulse rates, supersonic test pilots have 20/10 vision. David was born with a truly remarkable ability to make friends. There was a quality in him which reached out to other people as easily and naturally as breathing. He could make his friends feel that he alone shared with them their most secret aspirations. They were always saying of him that he was much like themselves and all considered themselves authorities on what he really felt. The truth was that human feeling was almost completely dead in David and he never really felt anything at all, except a kind of overwhelming sympathy for himself.

In spite of this, some of his victims, even after they knew what he was, could not help feeling warmly toward him. He had, after all, given understanding and often an exceptionally good counterfeit of love in exchange for money. Among his female victims there were a few who

27

would have been glad to continue paying for these valuable intangibles.

By now, many people knew that he was not very principled; but the word "principle," in its moral sense, has a dreary sound and most people forget that it was invented to describe a real and valuable concept. A man might first meet David with suspicion, but the sight of this slight, dark young man, whose face was not officiously handsome and whose manner was so open and natural, soon dispelled all ugly doubts.

In addition, his position was protected because most people never saw their actions through David's keen eye for blackmail. The maritally unhappy executive of a tobacco company never felt that he was doing anything particularly wrong when he set the redhead up in an apartment on Fifty-fifth Street. Still less did he think it peculiar that David had introduced him to his "friend." When the blow was struck, David never struck too hard. He did not demand an impossible sum. In a surprising number of cases the executive quietly returned to his nagging wife in Mamaroneck and treasured his few weeks on Fifty-fifth Street forever, something he could never have done if the affair had gone to the point where the redhead had begun to nag too.

Part of his success was due to the fact that David was uncommonly sensitive to the unhappiness and misery of other people. He could detect, almost miraculously, the one or two people in any room who needed help, although this need might be disguised under an insulting manner or a vicious tongue. The nervous tic, the uncalled-for laugh, the senseless gesture, were all signs to David of the pitiful and cringing creature underneath who was crying for assistance.

The amount of aid these people asked was usually, considered quite coldly as an investment, ridiculously small. It required, at most, only three or four hours of listening to them talk each week; perhaps a walk of ten

28

or fifteen blocks at three o'clock in the morning; an occasional gift of flowers, if they were women; an inexpensive wallet or an introduction to one of the women, if they were men. He couldn't foretell, of course, exactly what would be required but, in all, the total outlay in time was never excessive and no money was spent, since David's companion had all of that that was necessary for both of them. Also, because he was unencumbered by any personal feeling for them, David could deal out love and affection in exactly the right amounts—never too little and, perhaps more important, never too much.

He had just ordered his second drink when he saw the old girl with the funny shoes. She was standing inside the doorway looking around the place as if she thought she wasn't allowed to come in. She was scared. Funny, he thought, the rich don't even have the same way of looking frightened as the poor. The woman was afraid, but not the way anyone in his family would have been. She wasn't the least bit afraid of the waiters who rushed past her. He could tell, from the way she ignored them, that she hardly considered them human—not maliciously of course, but all her life she had never seen waiters or gardeners or nurses doing anything but what they were hired to do. It was just the opposite with him. All his life he had lived with the people who waited on the rich. His father, his Uncle Arthur and Aunt Cora—directly or indirectly they were all servants.

As the woman was about to turn and leave, David beckoned to her and pointed to a chair beside his. Though he did not know it then, it was a tribute to his enormous attraction for all people that she came, hesitantly, but for the first time not afraid.

"It's not so noisy in here when you get used to it," he said, smiling warmly at her but without any suggestion of further intimacy.

The woman returned his smile—a little too eagerly, he thought—and sat down on the high bar stool.

29

There was something about the awkward way she moved that intrigued David. It was as if something were wrong with her physically, and yet there was nothing he could point to. Also, he realized now, she was not merely timid. Timid people had a way of effacing themselves which this woman did not do. Timid people tried to conform to what others wished them to be, but this woman, though he could see she was intensely self-conscious, could not conform to anyone's opinion, no matter how conspicuous it made her. There was something defiant about all her movements as if everything she did was a deliberate act of courage.

"What will you have?" The bartender had placed a small napkin on the bar before her and was waiting for her order.

Her face began to grow red. She looked desperately at David's drink and then, facing the bartender, said, "I'm afraid I don't know the . . ."

"I believe she wants an old-fashioned," David said to the bartender.

She turned to him and David knew by the look of panic in her face that if he were to assume too much friendliness at this point he would frighten her away. Why? he thought —why is she so afraid? He was suddenly determined to answer this question.

"Please excuse me for butting in. It was just an impulse. You obviously wanted the drink I was drinking and I thought you had forgotten the name."

Without waiting for a reply, David turned back to his own drink and sipped it quietly, indicating that the matter was closed and that he did not expect the conversation to continue.

He could feel her watching him. In a moment she said, as if she had at last made an important decision, "It was really very kind of you. You were quite right. I didn't know the name."

David stared into his glass, meditatively, as though he

30

were solving some weighty problem. He paid no attention to the woman beside him. The bartender brought her drink and placed it on the napkin before her. From the corner of his eye David saw her fumbling in her purse. She took out a coin and put it on the bar and then, quickly sensing that this was not enough, she added a ten-dollar bill to it. They could charge her four dollars for it and she wouldn't know the difference, David thought.

She tasted her drink and then turned abruptly to David. "I hope you don't think I was angry that you ordered my drink. I really do appreciate . . ."

"Nothing at all," said David. "I know how it is. Sometimes I forget even my own name."

"Oh, but I'm afraid I didn't forget. It's just that I never knew the name. I recognized it when you said it, of course, but I just never saw one before." She took another sip. "It's very strong, isn't it?"

"Depends on how much you drink. You don't act as if you'd ever been in a bar before."

For a moment she didn't answer and David felt her eyes searching his face for some sign that would tell her to be afraid again. He had evidently touched a sensitive place. It pleased him to realize that she would find nothing but the most open-hearted friendliness and warmth in that face. He was not a vain man but, in a special way, he was particularly proud of his physical appearance. It had been designed by a scheming nature to invite confidences.

"You seem to know so much about me," she said, at last. "Can everyone tell that much, just by looking at me?"

"I wouldn't worry about that," he said. "They all have too many worries of their own to bother looking closely at anyone else."

When he spoke the word "they" he indicated with a gesture all the people at the bar, implying that he and she lived in another world, exclusive of the others.

"They," he continued, "almost never see anyone but themselves."

31

"Oh yes, yes, that's so true!" she said, eagerly.

The bartender brought her the change from her ten-dollar bill. She seemed delighted at the transaction which gave her so many more bills than she'd started with. She put the money in her purse carefully, but without counting it, and there was something about the smug, overefficient way she acted that reminded David of a little girl playing "store."

"Yes," David said, "I can understand your not liking bars. They are usually very unpleasant."

She looked at him anxiously. "But it's all right, isn't it? I mean, before—long ago—it wasn't considered proper, but now it's acceptable, isn't it? These women in here are *nice* women, aren't they?"

Beyond his surprise at the question, David had the feeling that she wasn't so much worried about the possible immorality of her situation as she was about the danger of her having been mistaken or misled. But why had she asked in the first place?

"Of course they are. It's perfectly all right."

"You're wondering why I said that, aren't you? You're wondering why I don't know all of the things that anyone else would know."

"Yes," said David, "I am. But you needn't tell me if you don't want to."

"But I will tell you! I want to tell you!"

She finished her drink and her large, brown eyes sparkled with the trusting gaiety of a person who has never been drunk before. David ordered two more old-fashioneds.

She told him everything; sometimes adding details which seemed to David irrelevant, such as the average length of time it took her to make a blouse or a skirt for herself or her personal opinion that the Mohammedans were plotting world conquest. Sometimes, also, she would skip what seemed to David very important parts of the story, such as how her money was handled and how much of it she had.

32

Her name, she said, was Hanna Carpenter and she had
lived for thirty-four years in the Hotel "38." David interrupted here and asked if she had anything to do with the
Carpenter mining company. She told him that she hadn't,
that it had been her father's company and that he had
sold it just before he died. He quickly calculated that a
company worth one hundred million now couldn't have
been sold for pennies even thirty-five years ago, when her
father had died.

She told him about coming out tonight, about the man
she'd thought had been chasing her and about her dinner
in Schrafft's. David then said that he understood very
well her fear of leaving her room and that he had often
felt the same way. What sensitive person, he said, could
live in times like these without realizing that every
stranger was a potential enemy. He said he didn't want to
frighten her but the man she had thought was chasing her
might really have been doing just that. She mustn't forget
that she was a wealthy woman. It *might* have been her
imagination, of course, but just to make sure he would see
that she got home safely.

David also remarked that it was something of a coinci-
dence that he had been born on the same year that she
had gone into her rooms. Was she sure it had been 1914?
Yes, she said. It had been the spring of the year 1914 when
she had written to all her friends to tell them that she was
leaving. She remembered it was spring because the trees
on the Avenue were just beginning to get that new-green
color. In what season of that year had he been born?

"In the spring," David said, simply.

"April?"

"April."

"Oh, goodness!" She reached over and touched his arm.
"It's almost supernatural, isn't it?"

"Very strange."

They sat silently for a while, deep in their own quite
different thoughts. Suddenly, Hanna spoke.

33

"Aren't the Russians terrible?"

"They certainly seem to be making things as difficult as possible," replied David.

"Sometimes I think that we should just drop the atomic bomb and have it over with," she said.

David was surprised that she could use the word "we" so easily, considering that she had been locked inside a hotel room for over thirty years.

"Maybe they have an atomic bomb too," he said.

"Oh yes, I read that they did have it. The process for manufacturing atomic energy is no secret, you know."

"That's what they say."

"There's no doubt that they have it." Then she added, somewhat inconsistently, "I think they're perfectly terrible."

"Do you think Stalin is as bad as Hitler?" David asked, cautiously.

"Oh, there's no comparison. I think Stalin looks so nice too. Of course Lenin was always my favorite."

David was startled. "Lenin?"

She smiled nostalgically. "I almost feel as if I knew Lenin. He was so much in the news at the end of the last war. You know, when I read that the Russians called him 'little father' I knew why I liked him so much."

"Why was that?" David was not exactly certain now but he had always thought that "little father" had been a diminutive for the Czar of Russia.

"He looked just like *my* father."

"Oh. Then you are in favor of Communism."

David showed not the slightest bit of confusion. He never allowed his personal opinions to interfere with being a good listener.

"Good heavens, no! I think it's dreadful. It's unthinkable that we should become communistic. Do you think we will?"

"The Communists are a very well-organized minority."

David didn't think it was necessary to tell Hanna that,

34

among his other activities, he wrote a column called "Inside Communism" for a daily newspaper and that, at one time, he had been an active Communist and a member of the seaman's union.

"Of course I think Molotov is right when he says that Wall Street is deliberately creating a lot of this feeling against Russia because it has lost a lot of markets in Eastern Europe." Hanna spoke with a sudden assurance.

"Oh, well—Wall Street—you know that phrase is overworked."

David couldn't make up his mind whether his new friend was pro- or anti-Communist. He didn't care if she was either, but he did want to know in which direction she was tending.

"I know what you mean. But, you see," she said, roguishly, "*I* had quite a few investments in Eastern Europe before the war. Fortunately, I saw what was coming and got out in time."

"And just what did you invest in after you 'got out'? "

"Uranium," she said, happily.

Hanna had finished her second drink now, and she began to speculate what her life would have been like if she had got married. She might, she said, have had a little boy who would be about David's age now. Was his own mother alive?—Dead, replied David, softly—Where did he live? Did he have his meals inside or did he go to a restaurant?

When David told her that he lived in Greenwich Village she said that she had read that it was not a very nice place to live any more, in the sense of its not being very clean or healthy. She hoped he took good care of his health because that was the most important thing.

"Why did *you* come here?" Hanna said at last, and David was startled to realize that in this woman's mind everyone had to have a specific reason for every action he performed.

He looked up, gravely. "I suppose you could say, a

35

little, that I came here because I was afraid." Then he smiled a reassuring smile that told her not to worry but did not succeed in being too convincing.

Hanna leaned forward and touched his arm. There was an urgency in her movement which transcended her usual awkwardness.

"Oh, forgive me. I should have known—I was so eager to tell you all of my own troubles that it never occurred to me that you could have been afraid of anything."

"Well, now you know. Let's talk of something else."

"Oh, but you must tell me what it is. Perhaps I can help."

"I'd rather not. Just let it go at that." David's voice was a shade harder than he usually allowed it to be with women.

She looked into his eyes and gripped his arm, recklessly. "Please, David. I want to help you."

He was silent for a moment. Somehow this eager face staring into his, so ready to suffer for him, annoyed him. "Someone wants to murder me," he said, coldly, knowing the effect it would have on her.

Hanna drew away. She stared at him with large, fearful, brown eyes.

David continued. It was not like him to allow personal feelings to enter into his relations with a prospective client, but he suddenly felt a resentment toward this woman and all the people like her who so calmly asked for help but were afraid to give it if it cost them anything. The years of careful control suddenly disappeared, and he told her the simple truth.

"I'm having a party tonight. I was on my way home to prepare for it. I just stopped in here for a minute. Someone coming tonight wants to kill me. You see, it's quite simple and there's nothing you can do about it, is there?"

Hanna sat dumbly on her stool. She seemed to have lost the power of speech. She picked up her napkin from the bar and began to tear it to tiny shreds.

"I think you'd better let me take you home. I'll have to leave soon."

She shook her head but did not answer.

"But you can't stay here," David said, trying to keep every trace of annoyance out of his voice. "Finish your drink and let's go."

Again she was silent.

David shrugged and asked for the check. "I know you'll understand," he said, "I'm late already."

She nodded.

He held out his hand and said, "Would you mind if I called you tomorrow? Perhaps we can meet here and have a long talk. Would you like that?"

Hanna was still silent but her large eyes caressed every movement he made. She took his hand, not as one accustomed to shaking hands but as the first man must have shaken hands—in a desire to touch, to feel another person.

David paid the bill, smiled beautifully at Hanna, and walked out into the street. He saw a cab coming with its top lights on and waved to it. He was sternly advising himself that he had been very foolish and that he might have lost a very good contact simply because he had given in to a personal irritation. The cab stopped. He had his hand on the door handle when a small voice behind him called his name. He turned to wait for Hanna.

She was out of breath and her face reflected her decision. "Take me with you! Let me come to the party too. Don't you see, I'll help you if I come! I'm not afraid—really I'm not afraid. You tried to frighten me so that I wouldn't come! Please, David!"

Partly because the cab stood waiting with its door open and partly because he was not at all prepared for her onslaught, David hurried her into the taxi. There was probably a stronger reason than this for bringing Hanna to his party. This, at any rate, was one of the few times in his life when he had taken anything more than money from an acquaintance. This time he was taking courage, and

37

from Hanna who had so little of it—for he really was
afraid.

Chapter 4

DAVID gave the address and Hanna sat stiffly in her seat,
refusing to lean back against the soft cushion. They
started suddenly and surged out into the traffic. Hanna
gripped the yielding red leather and forced down her
nausea as the sidewalks began to rush by. She concentrated on the cabman's driving, and for a while it seemed
to her that only her mental pleadings for less speed or for
a sharp right turn were saving them from disaster.

David had said that someone wanted to kill him. Hanna
had lived too long with just such a fear as this not to
recognize it in someone else. In spite of his pretending it
was nothing at first and then trying to frighten her away
for her own safety, she knew that he was terribly afraid.
Strangely, when she knew that she had become less afraid.
It had been the sight of the back of his neck when he was
leaving the bar, so vulnerable and fine, that had made her
realize she must go with him. Even with her own terrors
crowding around her and urging her to run home she had
known that she had to choose between this and the silent
years ahead—alone.

And now as she sat here in the taxi beside David, what
she was doing seemed no longer impossible or even dangerous. She was with her friend. She was going to help
him, and somehow her store of courage, which she had
believed so small, was big enough for both of them.

38

David spoke. He suggested that she change her name.

"Some of these people coming tonight may know of your family or may have heard of you," he said. "Anyway, let's leave Hanna Carpenter back in the Hotel '38.' "

"You mean change my name and pretend I'm someone else?"

"Yes, be a new person."

The taxi was hurling itself through the traffic. The faces of people on the sidewalks were blurred by speed and the only people who looked as if they were quite motionless were the occupants of the other cars which kept pace with them.

"Who shall I be?"

"Why not—Margot Case? That sounds just artificial enough not to be made up."

"Margot Case. Oh, goodness. Margot Case!" Hanna leaned back in the red leather seat for the first time. There was a look of wonder in her face as if she were witnessing the actual transmutation of her flesh into another body. "I believe," she said, "that I know just what Margot Case is like."

"Then you like the name?" David seemed rather proud.

"Oh, *like* is hardly the word. You wouldn't believe it but everything seems so much different already as Margot Case. I'm not afraid of this taxi, for instance."

"Good, then that will be your name."

"You knew I was afraid of this taxi?"

"Yes. You should see a subway."

"Perhaps someday I will!"

They rode in silence for a while. Margot began to get the feel of riding in an automobile. It was hard to get used to the idea that she was just to sit in it and not contribute at least some effort to the car's movement. You just had to think that everything else was moving and you were standing still. It was only tiring if you tried to push it along yourself.

"What kind of work do you do, David?"

"I'm a newspaperman."

"Oh."

For years she had thought of newspapermen as being wild and adventurous personalities, carrying the mark of their trade boldly in their manner. In spite of her fondness for David it was a little disappointing to think of him as one of the people who had been writing these stories which had excited her for so many years.

"I write a column."

David began to tell her about his guests. They would arrive about ten, he said. That would give them half an hour to get prepared. One of the guests, he told her, was Barton Zimmer.

"Is he the one whose profile was in *Time?*"

"Yes. He's head of U. S. Marine."

David said this rather proudly. He often mentioned his friends' occupations or claims to wealth in parentheses behind their names. It made him feel as if he had a share of their greatness, a share he always made a concrete attempt to take, later on.

"He's in some kind of trouble with the government, isn't he?"

"It's a kind of trouble I don't think he minds. He's in trouble because he owns too much."

"Yes, I read all about it. It's an anti-trust suit."

Their taxi swerved dangerously around a truck. Margot paid no attention. She had already conquered her fear of riding in taxis and this fear, having nothing to do with logic, could not be easily revived by a little reckless driving.

"Then there are Peter and Sandy Coburg-James. They own something like thirty million dollars between them. You'll like them very much."

"Are they brother and sister or brother and brother?" she said.

"They are married," he said, and appeared greatly amused by her question.

40

The other two guests, he told her, were Theodora Dennis, a sculptress, and Vivian Boleyn, a Communist.

"A real Communist?"

"Real enough," he said. "He's an officer of the seaman's union."

"They're in all the unions, aren't they?"

"Not always," David said. When he wasn't writing his column, David was quite mild in his political views. He saw no reason to waste his vituperation on people who weren't paying for it.

"And who is Theodora Dennis? You didn't explain about her."

They were reaching Greenwich Village and David leaned forward to give instructions to the driver. As they slowed to pick their way through the maze of little streets, Margot realized that she would never be able to find her way out without help. She had always pictured Greenwich Village to be a place with narrow alleys crowded with dirty, starving artists. Instead, she found that the streets were quite clean and prosperous and looked, in spots, more like the New York she had known thirty-four years ago.

"Theodora has just done a sculpture of my head," David said, proudly.

"Does she live down here?"

"Oh no, she's not a Village artist, if that's what you're thinking. She was very wealthy once."

David seemed to be rather saddened by the fact that this woman was no longer "wealthy."

"Is that all?"

"Yes."

"And which one of them is it, David?" Margot said quietly.

"Which one what?"

"Which one of these people wants to—wants to kill you?"

David looked at her and seemed to think that what she had said was funny. He was going to pretend it was a joke. "Oh, all of them, I guess."

41

"All of them!" Margot felt suddenly sick as she realized that he was not lying.

David laughed. "It's not quite as bad as that. Only one of them has the nerve to try it."

"Which one, David? I could . . ."

"Forget it."

Margot reached out and touched his arm. "But which one is it? If I knew I could help."

David removed her hand. "A neighbor of yours—now forget it, we're here."

The taxi stopped and David helped her out. They stood before a large, low frame house.

"I have the top floor," he said.

They entered the house and Margot found herself in a small foyer, from which a flight of carpeted stairs led to the upper floors. For a moment she felt panic again. Then she told herself that she had no right to be afraid for herself any more. David needed her. He had told her about these people because he had been afraid. He had said that someone wanted to kill him because he wanted her help. Knowing that David needed her made everything different as she had never imagined it could.

It was easy to be brave for somebody else, for someone who wanted your courage. It was only when you were alone that you could be really frightened. Being with David and taking care of him, though she didn't know exactly how she could take care of him, made all of the shadows she had been frightened of distant and implausible. She was here to help David. Nothing could hurt her as long as she remembered that.

Margot started up the steps. Her small, pointed shoes creaked with the agony of old age. She heard David on the steps behind her. She mounted two flights and was only slightly out of breath when she reached the top. David opened the large, polished, oak door with his key, and when he turned on the light she walked calmly into a house to which a murderer had been invited.

42

Chapter 5

DAVID had taken great pains to furnish his home with exactly the right amounts of taste, comfort and luxury. He really had no feeling for the place he lived in. In his earlier days he had lived entirely in hotel rooms and often hadn't even bothered to transfer his clothes from his luggage to the big, ugly bureau drawers. He liked to live in a place as if he were going to leave it tomorrow and disliked any kind of decoration or mark of personality in his living quarters.

When he began to meet people to whom these things mattered he quickly saw that he would not be able to invite anyone to visit him unless he took an apartment and furnished it according to their tastes. As with all other things for which he felt contempt he succeeded very well. Since he didn't care about decoration he was able to plan the total effect of his apartment far more effectively than many more emotional people could.

He did not make the mistake, for instance, of furnishing his rooms too lavishly. He knew that there was supposed to be something cold and unhomelike about this and he forced his decorator to economize here and there for the sake of warmth. A fine old table in the living room had an ugly scratch on its surface which David made no attempt to conceal. His carpet was secondhand, and the nap was worn off in one spot. It had been an exceptionally good carpet once. In general, David found that the secondhand shops supplied him with much that he wanted. In order to give his own place a warmth he used things other people had already warmed.

In some portions of his apartment David spared no expense. The living room was dominated by a great fire-place which, when lit, imparted a kind of studious, pipe-

smoking cheerfulness to its surroundings. David had torn
out half of one side of the house to have this put in. Its
effect was one of casual ease and down-home comfort and
it had cost a great deal of money.

He had also covered some big, roomy chairs and an
enormous divan with worn, old leather and had placed
before the divan a large, modern coffee table with a two-
inch-thick glass top, to show his independence of period.
He had a powder room for his women guests filled with
perfumes and scented make-up which he had carefully
selected himself, though he detested artificial odors.

His study was lined to the ceiling with books, and his
large, mahogany desk carried a disordered rack of pipes,
though David seldom read books and never smoked pipes.
His bedroom was furnished with a Chinese feeling, though
nothing was actually Chinese except for bamboo blinds
and a few discreet prints. The furniture was neo-Oriental
and several people had recognized the rug as a copy of a
Hiroshige print in gray and blue.

The decoration of the bedroom was the only effect in the
apartment that David had intended for himself alone.
When he was by himself he lived in this one room and
never used any other. Far back in his bedroom closet, behind the row of excellent suits, there hung an authentic
Chinese robe. It was black and it hung to the floor. Its
entire surface was embroidered in purple, gold and orange
and was as prodigal of beauty as only something Chinese
can be. No one had ever seen this, although David wore it
often.

When Margot came into the room, David brought her to
one of the big chairs near the fireplace.

"Sit here for a moment while I get some ice and a few
other things."

"But you live in such a beautiful place! It's just exactly
what I expected."

David turned at the door. "Is this what you really expected?"

44

"Oh yes, it's just like you."

Margot got up. She could hear David collecting glasses in the kitchen. She walked over to a tremendous picture on one wall, more than six feet wide and at least her own height. It was a picture of a hillside in the country and she was surprised to see how perfectly she remembered what trees and grass looked like. If she stood off a little way it was like looking out of a window in the country, and she wished she could have a photograph like this in her own rooms.

She walked to the doorway and could see, at the end of a short hall, a part of the kitchen which appeared to be large and had a cheerfully painted breakfast nook in the corner that was visible to her. She could hear David moving about. On either side of the hall, between the kitchen and the living room, were doors almost exactly opposite each other. She went forward and turned the knob of one of the doors. Perhaps she should ask David first, she thought, but the door was already open and as she entered into the darkness she realized that she wanted to see it without David. She wanted to find out about him by herself.

She found a light-switch beside the door and when the room was lit by the lamp on the desk and by several concealed lights near the bookcases she could see that this was his study. Margot went to his desk and automatically began to arrange the pipes neatly in their stand. On the desk near an old portable typewriter was some typescript. She began to read:

"The Commies are up to their old tricks, this time in the seaman's union. Word is going up and down the waterfront and in the powerful Communist cells on each ship that the good old gravy train is coming now that tough, ruthless Vivian Boleyn has captured the post of treasurer in the seaman's union. Boleyn has been one of the red-haired boys of the Party since 1935. . . ."

Margot shook her head. "Terrible," she said, aloud.

45

And this man Boleyn was supposed to come here tonight. Is he the one? He might very well be. "Tough—ruthless." She decided she would keep her eye on him.

At the other side of the room, near the door, she saw a bronze head set on a high wooden pedestal. She knew immediately that it was the one that Theodora Someone-or-other had made of him. It looked like David and yet there was a quality in it she didn't like. Perhaps the eyes were too close together or the chin was too short. It made him look mean and a little hard. Of course, she thought, the fact that it was cast in metal had something to do with its looking hard, but it was not like the David she knew and she felt she disliked the woman who had made it.

She went over to look at it closely and was surprised to see that it wasn't smooth-surfaced, as it had appeared from a distance, but covered all over with little flakes of metal which looked as if they were about to fall off. Around the mouth, particularly, the flakes were very small and covered every portion of the bronze lips. She knew that sculptures like this were originally made in clay and guessed that these particles must represent thousands of tiny additions to the basic lines of the head and had been pressed in, layer upon layer, by the sculptress. Yes, even up close she could see something unpleasant in David's expression— something . . .

"There you are!"

Margot jumped. She turned from the metal David to the flesh one, who smiled at her genially. He had an empty tray in his hand.

"I just thought I'd look around. I should have asked you. . . ."

"Of course you shouldn't. I want you to see everything. What do you think of it?"

"It must have taken a long time to do."

"You can't tell with Theo." David came into the room and stood before the head. "She started it several years ago. I only got it last week but sometimes she lets a thing

46

alone for a year or two." He smiled at the metallic counterpart of himself, almost fatuously.

"Are the eyes too close together?" Margot said.

His smile faded. "No, I don't think so."

He took her into the bedroom and she admired everything excessively, to make up for what she had said about the head. She even noticed that the rug was a kind of large drawing, although she didn't know who had done it.

A two-toned gong rang. Margot looked at David and caught a look of fear in his eyes. Was this the one he was afraid of? She would watch carefully when he opened the door. If this was the person, she would know.

David turned out the light and walked out of the bedroom. He seemed to have forgotten that Margot was behind him. She followed him into the living room and got as close to him as she could when he swung the door wide.

"Theo! Good to see you."

Margot stepped back as the woman entered. When the door had first opened, the woman's face had been set in a hard line which softened a little, in spite of itself, when David took her around the waist and brought her over to meet Margot.

"This is Theodora Dennis, Margot. This is Margot Case, an old friend of mine."

Margot thought she saw a pained look on the woman's face, as if she were envying her title of "old friend." Theodora was also a large woman but there was something wasted in her look, a kind of cadaverousness which was not hidden by the careless, even sloppy, elegance of her tweed suit. Her face was young—in the late thirties at most—but somehow her character best expressed itself in her body, which looked old and stringy, but very strong. Margot could see no sign of the fear she had seen before in David's eyes.

"Do you want a drink, Theo? You ready for another, Margot?"

David strode to a big table behind the divan and began

47

to make drinks, without waiting for an answer. He knows what each of us drinks, thought Margot. David had become particularly gay and cheerful and Margot wondered if he was hiding what he really felt. Theodora sat on the edge of one of the big chairs and emptied her glass, which was filled only with liquor and ice, at one swallow. She handed it back to David. Margot sat down and sipped at her old-fashioned.

"Margot was just looking at the bust you did of me. She said the eyes were too close together."

"Whose eyes?"

"The eyes in the statue, of course."

Margot looked at David in embarrassment and discovered suddenly that his eyes *were* too close together. "I don't know anything about sculpture," she said, and realized that Theodora didn't care what she thought of it.

"I'm lucky to have it," said David. "Theo usually tears her work to pieces before she'll let it be cast. I bet she's sorry she cast this one. She doesn't like people to see her work."

"I like it as much as anyone." Theodora swallowed her second drink and held it out again. She spoke to Margot, although she was answering David. "It's just that very little I do is good."

Margot noticed that the fingers on her left hand were stained brown. When she took the refilled glass her hand trembled a little. She said, "Thank you," without looking at David. Theodora leaned back in her chair and Margot knew that she was looking at the big photograph of the hillside which was on the wall behind her own head. She wondered if Theodora saw it as she had, as a window looking out into the country.

The gong rang again and David jumped up. Theodora continued to look at the photograph, refusing even to glance at Margot; but when David's voice rose in a hearty, "Peter! Sandy! Good to see you," Margot caught the woman's expression of pain and anger, as if she could see

48

David advancing across the room with his arm around the waist of each of his new guests.

David introduced Peter and Sandy Coburg-James, who, Margot remembered, had thirty million dollars. They nodded easily to each of the older women. When Theodora got up, Peter shook her hand politely and with just the right degree of enthusiasm.

They seemed quite young, no more than twenty-seven or twenty-eight, and looked startlingly alike. They were both of medium height—Peter a little taller than his wife— and they both seemed to have been expressly designed to meet the ideal standards of the world. They had the easy grace of athletes, of the kind which, being sure of itself, does not attempt to exhibit itself before others. Their blond good looks in no way displayed an unnecessary robustness. When they sat down, they did it in one movement, with the perfect timing of champions, without the use of hands; and once they were seated they did not surrender to the sudden comfort of the chair, but maintained a kind of relaxed poise which made them seem taller than anyone else in the room. Margot felt immediately the extraordinary bond between the two. She had noticed Sandy's lithe, full-hipped body and Peter's slim one, and she could not imagine these two being married to anyone else but to each other. Even David, who had seemed to her so young and fine-looking, appeared rather tired and haggard as he handed the radiant pair their drinks.

"Here y'are, Pete. How have the happy couple been getting along?"

Behind David's cheerfulness there was a note of sarcasm and Margot saw Peter's arm stiffen as he took his drink. On Sandy's face there was a look of profound distaste. Surely these two would not be capable of committing a murder or of harming anyone. They had everything in the world they wanted. One could tell that by looking at them. And yet . . .

Suddenly, Margot realized that everyone in the room

49

disliked David except herself. No one was enjoying himself. No one pretended it was a party.

"It's surprising how much alike you two look," Margot said.

Both Peter and Sandy turned and looked at her angrily.

"Yes, don't they," David said. "Don't you think so, Theo?"

Theodora looked at the young couple. She lay back in her chair with her head resting on the cool leather. She appeared exhausted in the way a person is after a toothache has stopped. Her hands were clenched tightly around her empty glass. She ignored David's question.

"I think I've met you two before. In Poland."

Both Peter and his wife leaned forward. "Before the war?" Sandy said.

"Yes, in 1938."

"Did you—did you live in Warsaw?" Peter asked, intently.

"I did, for a while. I had some property there."

"Are you Polish?"

"My mother was. I met you when you were both quite young. You were living with your parents."

"They were Sandy's parents. They were my aunt and uncle," said Peter, quietly. "My parents died when I was a child."

Theodora looked as if she were about to say something else, then lost interest and looked at David. "May I have another drink?" Her voice was unnaturally calm and Margot felt that it was an effort for her to speak to him.

David stood up and took the glass. From the tone of his voice Margot knew he was speaking to her. "Peter and Sandy are not just cousins, Margot. They are what you might call double cousins, but they can explain it to you better than I can."

She knew that she was expected now to ask them what he meant. That was her job, to act as David's foil. She turned to them, wishing the whole subject could be

50

dropped. The room was quiet and she felt extremely uncomfortable.

To her surprise the girl, Sandy, smiled at her as if she knew what she had been thinking. "What he means is that my father and mother were the brother and sister, respectively, to Peter's father and mother. That makes us just twice as close as ordinary cousins."

Peter's hand fell gently on Sandy's shoulder, as if it had just slipped from the back of the couch, but Margot saw the white showing around his fingernails.

Theodora leaned forward to take her fresh drink and said, "Doesn't that make a eugenics problem?"

"I don't think so," said Peter.

David returned to his seat beside Peter and Sandy. "I should think it would," he said. "It's almost like being brother and sister." The room was embarrassingly still.

The next guest was a tall, stout man of about fifty. David introduced Barton Zimmer. He smiled coldly, apparently feeling that one smile was enough for them all to share. He did not appear to notice when David pushed up a chair, but after he had polished his pince-nez and put them on his long, sharp nose he sat down where a chair had not been before without hesitation as though he were daring it not to be there.

"I won't be able to stay long," he said, as if to indicate to everyone that his time was valuable even if theirs wasn't.

"I'm glad you came," said David. "There's someone coming whom I particularly want you to meet."

Barton Zimmer raised his thin eyebrows and his glasses rode precariously on the knife edge of his nose.

"Who?"

"The new treasurer of the seaman's union, Vivian Boleyn."

Margot tried to catch a changed note in his voice. She was sure that David had been referring to this man Boleyn when he had said that only one person at this party was capable of killing him. But was he a "neighbor" of hers? She decided she would try to find out where Vivian Boleyn lived. If he lived near the Hotel "38" she would know that he was the one she must watch.

"Ridiculous!" said Barton Zimmer. "I can't waste any more time. . . ."

As he started to get up David said, quietly, "I think you had better stay, Barton."

The tall man stopped, halfway out of his seat, and sank back heavily. He smiled broadly, as if the whole thing had been a joke.

"Well, David, if I'm going to stay you might give me a drink. Not too strong, please."

He drummed his long, pale fingers on the arm of the chair and leaned back with a sigh of comfort. His face was excessively white and his light blue eyes surveyed his companions with chilly contempt.

"How are you, David? I hope I'm not late."

They all turned. Vivian Boleyn closed the door behind him and came on into the room.

"It was partly open," he said, "and I didn't bother to ring."

David stood up quickly and Margot could see that he didn't like people coming in without ringing. He walked over to Vivian and shook his hand, formally. His new guest was not impolite but there was something in his manner which set David off balance. He had lost the initiative and his planned speech of welcome was dropped. Margot was sure now that this was the man who planned to kill David tonight, and yet, looking at him, she could hardly believe it.

Vivian Boleyn was short and slight. When he walked across the room to meet the other guests he almost bounced as if the power of gravity were not sufficient to hold him down. When he was introduced to Barton Zimmer, Margot noticed that he hesitated only a split second,

52

although it was clear that he had recognized the name. Zimmer didn't bother to rise and his blue eyes flicked nervously behind his glasses.

As Boleyn was introduced to Margot he gave her a quick smile and she wondered if it were possible that he had seen her before, but when he approached the others he smiled in exactly the same manner. He sat down in a straight chair, a little apart from the others, and she noticed that his fingernails were cut off close to the flesh. His hands were slender and moved about constantly and Margot felt that they would be hard and calloused to touch. Even though his face was exceedingly boyish and delicately made, she knew that he was older than he seemed—perhaps a little older than David. Tough—ruthless, she thought. Yes, it was possible.

Theodora spoke to Peter and Sandy. "Are you Polish?" She picked up their former conversation as if it had not stopped. Unlike the young couple, she lay back passively in her chair, her whole muscular body collapsed in apparent exhaustion. She did not seem relaxed, however. There was a tenseness in the angular lines of her shoulders and in her tight, fleshless hips.

"Our mothers were Polish," said Peter. He seemed grateful for someone to talk to. Margot suddenly realized how young they were. "At least, they were part Polish," he added. "Coburg is a German name."

"And you use your father's and mother's names together?" Theodora said. Her voice was flat and void of emotion, purged of all feeling.

"It was a custom. Father and Mother used it together also."

"Did you know my aunt and uncle?" asked Peter. Both he and Sandy seemed accustomed to speaking as though they were one person.

"No, not very well. I was invited there once, to a party they gave."

53

"I'm afraid we don't remember. You see . . ."

"I was very busy," said Theodora impatiently. "I didn't have time to see many people."

"We have heard of you, of course," said Sandy. "We saw some of your work in the Whitney several weeks ago."

"Oh, *that*." Theodora closed her eyes as if they had brought to mind a vision of something monstrous. "It was very bad."

"We thought it was wonderful. Really, we liked it better than anything else there."

Theodora frowned. "You don't have to say that. I know my own work."

"I think you don't understand," said Peter. "We are not trying to flatter you."

"There are two kinds of art—good and bad, creative and imitative—mine is the last!"

Margot felt that the woman's anger was not directed against any person in the room so much as against something large and intangible which she had been fighting for a long time.

Barton Zimmer spoke to Theodora, amused by this woman's vehemence. "I agree with you there, Miss Dennis. Some of these modern painters and sculptors should be made to do something useful."

Theodora answered him as though she were still speaking to Peter and Sandy. "There is no modern art or any classic art, only good and bad art. But there are people like you, Mr. Zimmer, who have an unerring faculty for picking out anything that's second-rate."

"Oh, come," Barton said, comfortably, "suppose we leave personalities out of this. I was merely inveighing against a certain pretentiousness in the modern art world."

He was amused. In his own world there were few people who would contradict Barton Zimmer. This was a pleasant change, a good intellectual exercise. Barton was

54

proud of his clear, precise mind and it was proud of him.

"Modern pretension," said Theodora, "is not confined to the art world."

"What about you, Vivian?" said David, pleased with the turn of the conversation. "Haven't you people banned 'decadent' art?"

Vivian smiled pleasantly. He appeared used to being called on to represent the opinion of the Communist Party in almost any discussion. "I haven't banned anything yet, but if Miss Dennis' work is an example of 'decadent' art, I like it." His voice, like his body, was light and vigorous.

"Do you know her work?" said Peter in some surprise. He and Sandy had never met a Communist before and they somehow imagined they were different—not likely to spend their time in museums, at least.

"Yes," he said, reading Peter's mind. "If we dress properly they allow us in museums. I think Miss Dennis' work is very fine."

Theodora scowled and Margot wondered what she would say if someone agreed with her and said her sculpture was bad. There was a feeling of animosity in the room and Margot felt that it was all directed toward David. She wondered why he had invited these people together if they disliked him so much.

"You know," said Barton, "the thing I don't like about you Communists—and I'll be frank, I don't like you—is that you're always hollering you're hurt even though no one's laid a finger on you."

"I think I should be the one to say that about you, now," said Vivian.

"Would it surprise you to know that I agree with a great deal that Marx has to say?"

"It would not surprise me."

"What do you mean by that, young man?"

"I think we have areas of agreement. Please go on."

"I believe that Marx was merely restating the age-old

55

struggle of the ordinary man for a fuller life." Barton spoke distinctly, as if a stenographer were taking down his words. "There is nothing wrong in that."

While Barton was talking, Margot noticed that Peter was staring at David. She was startled by the intensity of feeling in that look. His hand lay lightly on his wife's shoulder and Margot realized that, just as she had found that it was easy to be brave for David, so Peter might be capable of anything if he felt that he was protecting someone else.

"This immemorial struggle," Barton continued, "is the very life's breath of our civilization. It gives us the drive to go on and on. It gives us our medicine, our arts"—he nodded to Theodora—"our government, our machines. But though Marx was a seer—perhaps not a giant like the old philosophers and theologians, but a seer nevertheless—his followers have made the human mistake of taking him literally and setting him up as some kind of god. That function of a god properly belongs elsewhere."

Vivian Boleyn's face was expressionless. David was smiling and seemed a little drunk. The others listened respectfully. There was a quality of authority in Barton's voice which commanded that respect.

"Now I know men and I know how gullible they can be, especially if someone promises them a house and plenty of food and tells them they don't have to work for it. As you probably know, I own a large business and employ many thousands of men. The Communists hate that." He looked at Vivian for confirmation. "I am not one of those men, however, who takes his responsibilities lightly. I feel that it is my duty to give something more to my workers than money. The Communists have accused us, and justly I believe, of being soulless, of placing profit above everything else. I have seen the truth of this charge and have taken steps to correct the situation."

"What steps?" said Vivian, rather grimly.

"I have established a seaman's rest farm," Barton said,

56

simply. "It is not merely a place for the men to enjoy themselves, however; and in this way, perhaps, it differs from anything else of its kind in the world. It is primarily a refuge from the storms of life where a man may be spiritually rehabilitated. It·is nonsectarian, of course, and has no connection with any existing church. It is merely a place where a man may commune with his soul. The men live simply, with only the barest of material comforts, and each of them is assigned to a Teacher who guides him in the way he wants to go. They are free to arrive and depart as they choose."

"Sounds pretty dull to me," said David.

"Oh, but that's where you're wrong, young man. The farm has only been running a short time but already it is a great success. Men hunger for the spiritual life more than you know. You would be surprised how many tough oilers and wipers have taken to the Upanishads for comfort. I said that the farm has no preference for any religion but I have seen to it that the Teachers possess a broad knowledge of the Oriental beliefs, which I consider to be superior in many ways to our more empiric Western religions. I have withheld information of this farm from the press until I was sure it would be a success. You have not heard of it, Mr. Boleyn, because my first candidates were very carefully chosen. Now I am about to tell the world of my experiment and I am confident that other refuges like it will spring up over the land, and indeed, over the world. This is my answer to Communism, an answer which, I believe, cannot be taken lightly."

Vivian spoke. "For over five thousand years men like you have been worrying about the souls of other men. Whenever they get hungry you tell them to feast their souls; when they can't afford a place to live you point out the advantages of the spiritual life—for them. If men have souls—and I don't see why they shouldn't have— they certainly have been more of a burden than a blessing."

"I expected some such idiocy."

"When are you going to release this information?" said Vivian.

"Next week."

"About the time your anti-trust suit is scheduled, isn't it?"

"I cannot tolerate this implication."

"That's quite natural," said Vivian.

"You shouldn't talk so much, Barton," said David.

"Oh, I don't care in the least what the Communists say about this, either before or after I make the announcement."

"I didn't mean that. You have forgotten why you came here tonight. It certainly was not to give me more information than I already have." David turned to Margot and spoke to her as if she were his only audience. "You see, Margot, Mr. Zimmer is a very intelligent man but he has one fault. He has been on top for so long that he has forgotten to be cautious. Consequently, he talks too much —and writes too much."

He winked at Margot drunkenly, implying that this was a private joke between them. She could see Barton Zimmer, behind David's back, staring at them calmly with his cold blue eyes. He looked like a large, fierce bird.

David swung around and walked over to Vivian's chair. "And you, Vivian. You are cautious. There is no one in the world who is more so, except me." He patted him on the shoulder in mock friendship.

Vivian didn't move but Margot felt that he was within a second of jumping up and hitting David.

David blandly turned his back on Vivian and walked over to Theodora's chair. He sat on the arm and let his fingers lightly touch her shoulder. Margot saw her shrink from the touch and watched her body tense in a struggle against herself.

David looked toward Peter and Sandy and smiled. "And you youngsters haven't forgotten why you're here,

58

have you?" He turned to Margot again. "Do you know why they're here, Margot?" He paused and Margot suddenly began to feel sick. "They don't seem to want to tell you why they're here. None of them want to tell you, Margot, so I'll have to. Is that fair enough?" He looked around the room and appeared surprised when he didn't find approval.

The room was silent. Every person was watching David, and Margot felt that this was the moment the whole evening had been building up to. Now, one of them would make a break. One of them would jump from his seat and hurt David. She was surprised that she could face this so squarely and yet she knew that this was what she had come for. She had come here to help him. She must divert this now or it would be too late.

"I don't want to hear, David. Sit down and behave!" As he wavered before her she said it again. "Sit down!"

David took his seat and grinned foolishly. The tension of the room collapsed and the absolute silence gave way to the sound of regular breathing and the tinkle of ice in glasses. Barton Zimmer cleared his throat.

Margot spoke to Sandy. "Have you been in the United States long?" It was the only neutral question she could think of.

"Since the beginning of the war. We were born in Poland but we spent a great deal of time here when we were children."

"Do you expect to go back to Poland?"

"We can hardly do that now. Poland is a Communist country and I believe we represent everything they now profess to despise."

"How could they despise you? Your situation was not your fault."

"During a war no one has time to stop and assess personal faults or virtues," said Peter. "We are the only survivors of a once very powerful family. That, in a way, is our fault."

"What has happened to your family?" said Margot, feeling that every question she asked was likely to lead the conversation back to David.

"My mother and father were killed when I was a child, in an automobile accident. Sandy's parents disappeared during the war, and we have almost positive proof that they died in an air raid."

"Were you in this country during the war?"

"Yes," said Peter. "Perhaps Mr. Boleyn thinks we should have stayed in Poland and fought the Nazis."

Margot was surprised at the mention of Vivian's name. She had meant to keep watching him. Without being at all modest or timid he had a way of retiring from the group, of putting himself outside of their attention.

"You're the one who brought the subject up," said Vivian. "I think you've already answered your own question."

Margot was sick. It had started before when David was talking, but now she could no longer ignore it. She felt hot inside and she couldn't focus her eyes. This was being drunk. It was not the intoxicated feeling she had read about. It was more like lying alone in bed with a fever, and aching all over. She knew that she would have to lie down quickly before she fainted.

She looked at David. His eyes were closed and he was chuckling to himself. She knew that she should not leave him. She made an effort to sit up straight in her chair. She tried to force the people in the room into focus again with her will but the effort made her even sicker. Barton Zimmer was watching her. She felt that he was waiting for her to leave the room. She realized that he knew she was protecting David and that nothing could happen to him as long as she was there.

Suddenly, she felt an arm around her shoulder. She looked up and could dimly make out the features of Vivian Boleyn. I must watch him, she said to herself. Tough— ruthless, I can't let him take me away. But somehow she

60

did go away. Even as she struggled against it she felt grateful for the arm around her shoulders and the calm voice in her ear. Barton Zimmer preceded them and opened the door. They were going to take her into the bedroom. She could lie down for a while. If she could lie down she would feel better and then she could come back and take care of David.

Just before she left the room she turned around and looked at David. He was sitting on the couch, his head back. He reminded her of a little child. She wanted to cry. It was such a fine face. No one would ever know—no one would ever know. She had needed a friend and he had been her friend. A fine face.

Shortly after Margot was put to bed, she got up again and went to the bathroom, where she lost her Schrafft's dinner. When she stumbled back again—loathing herself—she heard quiet voices in the living room. She went to the door and opened it partly. She wanted to hear what was going on. She fell into bed and, soothed by the mumbling voices, went to sleep.

She woke to the sound of David's voice. At first she thought he was in the bedroom with her but she could see no one.

"One by one they come, and now you. You want to kill me, don't you?"

There was no answer. David's voice came from outside the door.

"You were the one I knew would try it. They all want to kill me but I knew you would be the only one with nerve enough. Step in here. You don't want everyone to see you, do you?"

His voice was taunting, like a child making an impossible dare. There was an overtone of complacency in it which showed that he was perfectly sure of himself. Margot heard them step into the study but they did not close the door and she could still hear David's voice. It was shriller

61

now and its tone was even more strikingly like that of a
boy's, contemptuous and certain of victory.

"How do you intend to go about it? You aren't armed."

Margot did not move. She repeated the word "No" to
herself, and by this simple negation she tried to wipe out
the catastrophe she knew was coming. Her body was suddenly cold and she felt dead. Her hands and feet were like
wax objects which someone had thrown upon the bed, and
only the terrible weight in the center of her stomach
made her aware that her body still belonged to her.

"All of you are cowards," David said. "Not one of you
is worth all the suffering you claim to feel. You are the
worst of all—a sniveling . . ." David's voice broke off on
a sharp note of terror. There was a thud, followed by a
metallic crash, and some heavy object fell to the floor.
Before Margot descended once again into the whirling
dreams of nausea, she heard footsteps in the hall.

She came to consciousness again, slowly. She did not
know how long she had been out. Her body began to
waken and she felt the blood tingling in her cold hands.
The first thing she heard was the murmuring of voices in
the living room and somewhere, from her receding dreams,
she heard David's voice calling for her help.

She sat up on the bed and tested her legs, sincerely
doubting that she would be able to walk on them. The
sickness and nausea had gone and had left in their place a
kind of lassitude which ruled her mind as well as her body.
She sat dumbly in the half-dark for a while, trying to
remember her dream of David. Finally she rose and walked
unsteadily to the half-opened door. She smoothed her hair
and brushed the front panel of her dress.

When she stepped into the hall she saw a light in
David's study. His door was ajar. Then it came back. Her
dream and David's young voice came thundering into her
mind. With one step she crossed the hall and flung his door
open.

David lay on one arm. The entire side of his head was

crushed. As she stood there her mind fed her the tiniest details of the scene. It wanted to make sure she would never forget. She could see the delicate little splinters of bone which had broken through the flesh; the velvet flow of blood, welling from the wound; and the matted, bloody hair, pasted to his forehead. A red lake was creeping across the dry carpet, and beyond it lay David's bronze portrait, its temple dark with blood.

What terrible joke was this? How could God have stooped to be so cruel and so malicious? It seemed to Margot that God had always held a grudge against her and that he had always destroyed everything that was hers, leaving her safe and protected from every evil but solitude and fear. Irrelevantly, she remembered a kitten she had owned which someone had slammed a door on and a little dog who had eaten poison. They were not classed in magnitude with the horrible thing which had happened to David, but it seemed to Margot as if they were part of a general plan against her which had culminated so brutally in David's murder.

Once again the terrible fear of being alone descended on her. She had been brave enough to come here to protect David, but now that he was gone the whole panic of her life returned, this time greater than before; because she had known, for a few hours, something different. And she had meant to protect David. She had meant to help him, and she had failed at this too. It was almost as if she knew she was going to fail. Even at the last minute, while she lay on the bed listening to David talk to his murderer, she could have saved him but she had not moved. What terrible hungry thing was this which destroyed everything in her life and would finally destroy her? How could she escape, when to relax for one minute meant that she lost?

In the living room she heard the faint hum of conversation. Why hadn't they missed David? Why hadn't someone come in to see what had happened to him? Margot turned toward the hall. But of course! Someone had come in to see him and was out there now, pretending that nothing had happened. One of those people out there had murdered David!

Vivian Boleyn, could he have killed David? Or Peter James, he had hated David—or the other man—or even one of the women. Was there any end to what any of them would do? What difference did it make now, who had actually done it or whether any of them had? They all wanted to kill David. They were all murderers and evil people. And now that he was dead and she was alone, they could kill her too.

Remembering it later, Margot never knew how she had gone through with it; how she had gone out in the living room and told them that David was dead. They had appeared surprised. She remembered that two of them, she thought it was Barton Zimmer and Vivian Boleyn, had gone into the study to see if she were telling the truth and how they had come out with solemn hypocritical looks on their faces and told the others that she was right. She'd watched them all pouring themselves drinks in a kind of ritual of forgetfulness and then, sitting in a chair, trembling and afraid of them all, she'd seen their pitiful attempts at gravity while, all the time, she knew that they were happy.

She remembered, also, how she had jumped up, not afraid of them any more, and accused one of them of murdering David.

"This is a very serious charge," said Barton Zimmer.

"He knew someone was going to kill him! He told me so!"

"Do you know who it was?" said Sandy.

"Yes, I know!"

Margot looked at each of them in turn. She wanted the murderer to be afraid. She wanted them all to be afraid. In her near-hysteria she was convinced that they all had done it. The room was absolutely still. Everyone was looking at her coldly and no one—no one wanted to help her or understand her as David had.

"What is his name?" said Sandy.

Suddenly, Margot knew that she had to run away from these terrible people. If she could get back to her rooms everything would be all right again and she would have time to think of what had happened. She must not stay any longer.

"I don't know," she said. "I don't know anything at all! I have to leave."

She ran to the little end table, beneath the photograph on the wall, where she had put her bag and her magazine.

"Do you know the name of the person who killed David Hammer, Miss Case?" Barton Zimmer's voice had the ring of authority.

"No. No! I don't know."

No one tried to stop Margot as she ran to the door. Perhaps they should have done this, but each one of them was thinking of something much more immediate, and the one person who might have wanted to keep her could not risk showing it.

A few minutes later, with a unanimous, if unspoken, consent, they all decided to leave. No one mentioned calling the police, as if it could be automatically assumed that the police would not be interested. They said good night to each other politely, the way people do after a party, and turned out all of the lights in David's homelike apartment except for the light in the study, which burned all night, lighting the scene of David's death.

Vivian Boleyn closed the downstairs door when they all left and managed to switch the night lock so that the door could be opened from the outside.

An hour later, Vivian returned and went upstairs to David's apartment. He was about to walk in when he heard a noise inside and stepped back into the dark hall. A few minutes later Barton Zimmer walked out and hurried down the stairs. Vivian went in and repeated Barton's fruitless search. During the night three more people came to David's apartment. Two came together and one came alone. They found nothing.

Chapter 6

WHEN Hanna walked out on the street in front of David's house it was about one o'clock. She had noticed the time on a clock inside, just before she left. She wished that she had wound that clock. It would have been like doing a favor for David. She had lived so long with inanimate objects that she knew, as few other people know, that they are really not dead at all. Objects take on the life of the people they live with. Clocks run, toothbrushes stay damp, clothes keep the shape of the person who wore them. All the little things a person uses keep their life for a short while after that person has left them, and then they too die. It would have been one thing she had done for him.

Hanna thought of her own rooms. All her things were waiting for her and they would still be alive, with her life, if she could only find her way back to them. She stood on the sidewalk and could see street lights at either corner. She started toward one of them, hoping to find another taxi and wondering if she would be afraid of it now, without David.

The street was lined with houses like David's, and she saw lights in some of the windows. Were some of these people friends of David's? Would they care if he had died?

Suddenly, she realized that she didn't know what was going on in these other houses. She had been thinking that other people were happy and peaceful in their houses, but what if they weren't? What if there was some kind of violence going on in that house with the light showing in one window on the top floor? She had seen one murder and she hadn't been outside before that for over thirty years; perhaps in every one of these houses, in apartments and rooms all over the city, something terrible was happening. The darkness seemed to move around her when she walked and she knew, suddenly, that she was right. Something evil was going on right beside her, behind that wall or under that roof.

A woman stuck her head out of a window on the other side of the street and cried: "I'll show you, you lousy bastard! You can't treat me that way. I'll jump!"

Hanna could see the woman framed by the light in the window. She had no clothes on. A man dragged her back into the room. At the same moment she thought she heard some people come out of David's house down the street. She began to run, and when she looked back she saw that someone was coming in her direction.

At the corner Hanna found that the adjoining street was just as dark as the one she'd been on. There were no cars at all and she did not think that she would be able to recognize a taxi in this dim light even if one came by. She looked back again and saw that the person behind her was now beside the house where the woman had screamed. She had to go somewhere. She must not meet any one of those people she had been with—one who was the murderer. She turned the corner and ran. When she came to the next corner she saw a little lighted place with steps going down into the sidewalk. This was a subway. She looked back again and saw the figure of a man leaving the circle of the other street light, coming toward her. She ran down the steps.

"TO EIGHTH AVENUE SUBWAY." A black arrow,

67

painted on the tile, gave her no choice. She found herself in a forest of steel beams which thrust up into a concrete ceiling and looked inadequate to hold the tremendous weight she knew must be over her head. On either side of her, spreading away at an angle, were white tile walls covered with advertisements. She recognized some of these from her own magazines, and it comforted her a little to find the familiar messages about gum and tooth-paste and automobiles. She was surprised to find that she recognized the little cage beneath a row of bare lights in the distance as the "change booth." She found, in fact, that a subway was more familiar to her than she had thought possible. Perhaps she had read about them some-where. In any case the journey she planned did not seem so difficult to her, and she was somehow comforted by the fact that she would be traveling underground, hidden from the street. She walked forward confidently.

"Take the 'E' train. Get off at Fifth," said the man in the booth.

She repeated this several times out loud, not being sure of its meaning but feeling confident that it was her key to a successful journey. She put her dime in the slot and jumped back when the machine snapped it from her fingers. She returned to it and pressed against one of the wooden arms of the turnstile and found herself inside. She stood between two stairways. One said "Uptown" and the other said "Downtown." With a feeling of exultation she took the "Uptown" stairs.

She saw a small, dusky man with a bald head, sitting on one of the benches. "Pardon me, could you tell me where the 'E' train is?"

"Take the next train that comes along this track." He pointed to the track behind him, without even looking at it himself.

Hanna was reassured by the note of confidence in his voice. Perhaps he works for the subway, she thought. He took a folded newspaper from his pocket and opened it.

68

"SUBWAY SLAYER TRAPPED IN CONEY!" Hanna turned and walked toward the other end of the station. She did not like the tabloids.

The platform on which she was standing was made of cement and it was divided down the center by a row of painted steel beams. On either side of her, below where she stood, were metal tracks which came out of the black mouth of a tunnel at one end and disappeared into a tunnel at the other end. Orange and white lights blinked in the depths of the tunnels and a soft, damp wind swept over the platform. On the far side of the station there stood an identical island of cement for "Downtown."

Hanna was ashamed of it later, but the excitement of a successful ride on the subway, all alone, had almost caused her to forget about the death of David Hammer. This might have been a natural reaction to the shock of seeing him dead. In any case, she had been insulated from reality for so long that she was not prepared to allow it to come rushing in all at once.

The station began to be filled with noise. It was the noise of wind and of wheels on metal tracks. As she watched, a line of gray, hooded cars emerged from the tunnel. The man had said this would be her train. She was not really frightened by it, although she kept to the middle of the shuddering platform until the cars stopped. She could distinguish the places in the sides of the cars which were doors and when they flew open she stepped in, feeling that she had already accomplished more than her share of the trip. As the train began to move out of the station, she thought she saw Barton Zimmer descend the stairs onto the platform she had just left.

Hanna walked almost gaily to one of the hard wicker seats and sat down, making sure that she was facing the direction the train was going. For a moment, while the train was gathering speed she felt afraid because she thought the driver was going to lose control. It seemed to her that he would never stop making it go faster, and it

69

occurred to her that maybe he had fallen sick or had died and that the train would continue to accelerate until it threw itself off the tracks. Just as she began to stiffen herself against the inevitable impact, however, the pressure on her back stopped and she knew that the driver was slowing down.

Outside her window she could see nothing but flashing lights and the blurred forms of steel pillars. Occasionally she saw through an arch in the wall of the tunnel onto another track. Once, she saw another train rushing in the opposite direction. It passed at such a speed that it was almost impossible to make out any of the figures in the other cars, but in one of them, alone and bending his head over a newspaper, Hanna thought she saw David.

They stopped at a station. No one got on her car. When they began to move again, Hanna found that she was urging the train on with her body. She wanted it to go fast again. As long as it didn't stop she could feel safe. Her feet on the floor could feel the clicking of the rails, and when the walls of the tunnel began to streak by her window she felt proud of her speed. The next station was Forty-second Street, and three or four people got onto her car. They took separate seats and paid no attention to her. The doors closed and she gripped the edge of her seat and stared out of the window into the dark tunnel.

The train hurtled through a station without stopping and Hanna sat very straight in her seat, so that the people waiting on the platform could see her. She tried to imagine how she must look to them. They would only be able to see her head and shoulders and she would flash past them in an instant. She was glad when they went into the tunnel again and left all of the people behind. It gave her a feeling of power to know that her train didn't stop at every station and that while she was rushing beneath the city streets nothing could touch her, nothing could stop her. They passed through another station, going very fast, and

70

Hanna looked around the car to see if the others were as excited as she was.

A man was looking at her. When she met his eyes he looked away toward a woman in a black dress who sat at the front end of the car. The man turned his head nervously as Hanna continued to watch him. Finally, he met her eye once again and then his glance fled, this time to the other end of the car, where a young man was sitting. Hanna exulted. The man was afraid to look at her. She had always been the one to be afraid of people and now somebody else was afraid. She felt free, as she had never felt before,

The train rocked back and forth on its tracks and she tossed in her seat. She wanted the train to keep going forever. It was only when you stayed in one place that things were frightening. When you move, she thought, you are different from everybody else. No one can touch you. She felt as if the train were part of her body. They stopped at another station and Hanna watched four more people enter her car. Two of them were Negroes.

It was only when they were picking up speed again that Hanna noticed that the station they were passing through was Fifty-ninth Street. It worried her that she was already so far uptown. If they went further up she would be past her own street. Still, she did not believe anything really wrong could happen as long as she was careful to watch for Fifth Avenue. The man on the platform, who seemed to know all about the subway, had told her that this was her train. Even more than that she *felt* this was her train. She was happy to see that they were now going very fast. She pressed her feet down hard on the floor of the car and thundered down the long track.

She found it hard to imagine that a few moments ago she had been standing, alone and helpless, in a street which was already many miles away. It seemed incredible that she could sit perfectly still and yet be moving faster than

71

she had ever gone before. Because she had spent so much time by herself she was accustomed to thinking of movement as something you did with arms and legs. She had never before had this feeling of moving all at once with no effort; her eyes and ears and shoulders cutting through space as if each organ were independent of the old rules of locomotion. She had, of course, traveled in surface trains and in automobiles but this was altogether different. The car in which she sat was a little world which was rushing through the bigger world outside, ignorant of any laws but its own.

The train roared on. They had passed through several stations without even slowing. At first Hanna had been pleased by this and had looked forward to the hollow, echoing sound the train made as it burst upon these open spaces in its tunnel; but in one of the stations she managed to read one of the enamel signs—"86TH STREET." At first she could not believe it. This was her train. It could not go so far uptown. Had they already passed the station which said Fifth Avenue?

The train hurried on, seeming even to increase its speed, as if it knew she had discovered its deception. Suddenly, she realized that she couldn't leave, that she had to go where the train was going. She had been happy before to think that nothing could stop it, but now she understood that the train was no more friendly to the people who were inside than it was to the people it left behind in the stations. They were all trapped, deep under the city, with no way to call for help and nothing to do but go where the train took them. Hanna had always meant to escape from the world and always this happened: The escape became more unmanageable than the reality.

She looked around fearfully. Perhaps someone could help her. The man sitting in the opposite seat, who had been afraid of her, was now reading a newspaper. Hanna got up and unsteadily crossed the aisle to his side.

72

"Where are we going?" She had to yell to be heard above the noise.

The man looked up. He did not smile and Hanna wanted to say something which would make him like her.

"Where are we going?" she repeated.

"Washington Heights." The man turned back to his paper.

Hanna knew, vaguely, that Washington Heights was a section very far away from where she lived, even further than Greenwich Village, she believed.

She touched his shoulder and he looked up again, angrily. "What is the next station?" The train seemed to be doubling its noise in order to drown out her words.

"Hundred and Twenty-fifth." He resumed reading and Hanna knew that he would not answer her again.

She returned to her seat. The train began to rock and she could feel the wheels underneath straining against the tracks. She looked up and saw that there were other people watching her. They had seen her crossing the aisle and they resented her moving in the train. Some of them hated her for it, especially the woman in black at the end of the train. She glared at Hanna. The two Negro people—a man and a woman—had not noticed her. They were talking to each other.

Hanna looked around desperately to find someone who would help her. There was no one. She knew that if she went to any of these people they would ignore her or deliberately give her the wrong answer, like the little man who had told her to take this train. Even more than the strangers she had seen on the street, these people were withdrawn into themselves. When they came on the subway they had suspended themselves in a vacuum from which they wouldn't withdraw until they arrived at their destination. When she had got up they had disliked her because she had disturbed them. Perhaps, with the woman in black, there was more to it than that, but with the rest

73

it was merely a matter of being brought out of their vacuum while they were still riding.

Hanna sat beside her window, not even bothering to fight the movement of the train any more. They had been riding for a long time and still the train showed no signs of slowing down. Occasionally, Hanna would have moments of calm, in the way that disaster brings a kind of peace. She would sit watching the countless iron pillars and strange-colored lights passing outside the window and feel that whatever was happening to her was inevitable and that there was nothing she could do to stop it. Then she would suddenly feel her stomach convulse with fear and every light she passed reminded her that she was being carried further and further away from her home. They passed through station after station until, when Hanna had ceased to care, the train began to slow and some of the people in the car rose from their seats.

Hanna got up and stood behind the Negroes. She steadied herself by holding on to an enamel pole beside the door. The doors opened and she walked out. She looked back into her car and noticed that the woman in black was still staring at her. The doors shut again and the train began to move away.

She turned around and saw that the Negro man and woman had moved to the other side of the platform. Hanna had read about the discrimination against Negroes and she was a little afraid to talk to them. They might decide that she had something to do with it and hate her. Also, they looked frightening because they were very black and she could not see their faces very well, but they were the only people she knew—they had been in her car—and she walked up to them, praying that they would help.

"I was told to take the 'E' train and to get off at Fifth Avenue. Can you tell me if there is another train that goes there?"

"You're a long way from there," said the man.

"Will you tell me how to get back?" The man was not

74

friendly, but Hanna felt that at least he didn't dislike her.

"You can take an 'A' train down to Fifty-ninth and change there to a 'D' train, which will take you to Seventh Avenue. You can catch the 'E' train there."

All her hope vanished. She would never get back. She hadn't even tried to remember what he had said. It was impossible.

"Are you lost?" said the woman. She took the answer for granted. "Why don't you take a taxi back, if you can afford it?"

"Where can I get a taxi?" she said, eagerly. "I wanted to take a taxi before but I couldn't find any."

The man pointed to a stairway which he said led to the street. There would be plenty of taxis there, he told her. Hanna thanked them and started toward the stairs. A train roared into the station and her friends got on it. She waved to them from the steps because they had been so nice, but they were talking to each other and didn't see her. A Negro woman who was standing beside them in the train saw her, however, and glared back.

Almost everybody going up the stairs with her was a Negro. She realized that she must be in Harlem. She had read about it in books and in the newspapers and knew that it was a place where horrible things happened, but she was so exhausted by now that she could do nothing but follow the black crowd out into the street.

She did not know exactly what she expected to see, but in her desperation she would have accepted almost anything. She had seen so very much in this one evening that she had achieved a state of stoicism which nothing new could penetrate. She was surprised, therefore, when she found that the street she was on was no different than Madison Avenue. It was a little wider and the shops were different, but the noise was the same and the stream of people was the same, except that they were Negro; a difference which was slight and became slighter as she walked through this crowd of disinterested strangers.

She no sooner stepped from the curb than a taxi drew up beside her and a black hand reached from the window to open the back door. She got in.

"Where to?"

"Do you know where the Hotel '38' is?"

"On Madison Avenue?"

Hanna sighed. "Yes."

The car joined the rest of the traffic and Hanna sat back in her seat, unable to be afraid. Not caring any more what happened.

She must have fallen asleep because a moment later the driver said, "Here we are." Out of the window she saw the entrance of her hotel, which she had left so calmly at the beginning of the evening. She looked at the black box which told how much money she owed and handed a five-dollar bill across the front seat, remembering David.

"Keep the change," she said, and remembered that she had read that in some book. She got out and closed the door.

The lobby was empty. Even the man who should have been at the desk was nowhere around. She walked quickly to the stairs beside the elevator and was grateful that no one had seen her. When she got to her floor she had difficulty finding her room. It was funny, she thought, not to recognize the place where she had spent most of her life, and yet she had seen it only twice from the outside.

She was surprised to see that her door looked so small and fragile. She had always thought of it as being so strong and protective. She reached in her pocketbook for her key and discovered that she still had her magazine clutched under her arm. It was the only thing she had to remind her that this night had really happened.

As Hanna was trying to find her key she heard someone coming up the stairs. The footsteps were slow and seemed to be those of someone who didn't want to be heard. She fumbled desperately in her change purse. She was terrified. She had traveled all over the city in the middle of the night

76

without being hurt. But now she felt, when she was outside of her own door, a few inches away from safety, that she was in greater danger than she had been all evening.

She found the key and worked to get it into the lock. The steps had almost reached her floor. She knew they were close, although they sounded even softer now than before. The lock turned and Hanna rushed inside. She locked the door behind her and slipped on the night chain. The steps were in the hall now. Someone was going to pass her door.

Then she heard a knock.

B O O K   T W O

Chapter 7

DETECTIVE-LIEUTENANT Kevin Corelli walked every morning from his home to the 169th Street station of the Independent Subway in Jamaica. The distance was more than a mile. The last few mornings had been chillier than usual, he was thinking. Soon he would have to be wearing a coat. Kevin liked walking, especially in the morning. He had an idea that half the sickness in the world would never occur if people walked enough, and he attributed his own splendid health to this exercise. It gave him a justifiable feeling of righteousness.

Also, on this particular Friday morning, he was thinking, as he strode along beneath the elms on Hillside

Avenue, that when his kid came he would teach him how to walk correctly. Of course, there would be a time when he would have to stay indoors with his mother, but as soon as the boy was big enough Kevin would take him out in the open. He would teach him how the long, easy strides ate up the distance even better than running and how important it was to breathe deeply and swing the arms for balance. It wasn't only exercise you got from walking. You learned to see what was going on outside and how to see yourself as others see you.

Words like "self-reliance" and "man-to-man" were going through Kevin's mind. His wife had learned to pardon a good deal of this fatuity in view of the fact that her husband had never been an expectant father before. For her own part, she was convinced that the child was going to be a girl.

When Kevin arrived at the subway entrance he turned and looked longingly at the broad, tree-lined avenue. He hated to leave Jamaica. It wasn't exactly like the country but compared to the city he considered it so. He had grown up in the city and to him this suburb was a paradise. Perhaps he wouldn't have had such strong views about the city if he were in any other kind of work, but he saw New York at its worst and when he thought of "his kid" growing up in a place like that he shuddered. Fortunately, he was not too well acquainted with the Jamaica precincts.

He walked down the stairs, struggling for change in his pants pocket. He took the proper number of steps to the first landing without looking and followed his private path on the concrete floor as he had done several thousand other mornings. He found a dime and crashed through the turnstile as he heard his train in the station. He ran to the stairs along with ten or twelve other people who had appeared from nowhere. He did not recognize any of them, although he had seen them all hundreds of times, running wildly down these same stairs. Before he got to the train he almost dropped his book and did drop his newspaper.

78

By the time he took his seat, his face had assumed that alert and noncommittal expression by which his fellow workers identified him. As usual, there was no need to hurry. The train waited patiently, with its doors open, while other people sprinted down the stairs. The trouble was that when you took your time the door always slammed shut in your face.

He opened his paper and gave the front page a quick going over: The Russians again, the ERP, the Chinese war —was there ever a time when the Chinese weren't in a war?—the report of the Secretary of State. He read one paragraph of a feature story at the bottom of the front page about a little girl from Oklahoma who had been cured of meningitis at Lourdes. He folded the paper again and took up his book. If nothing big happened today he could read the paper at the office. He could never get away with reading the book there. The Department liked the idea of his studying law but it didn't like any practical demonstration of it. The train doors closed on a silent, struggling man and when he had managed to force his way in they snapped shut with a bang. The train jerked forward and the eight-fifteen crowd started on its long journey to the awakening city.

Lieutenant Corelli stopped to talk to a group of men outside the door of his office. Most of them were older men. They had been on the force for a long time and were sweating out their pensions. They were privileged characters around the place and the biggest part of the work was given to the young fellows. Kevin didn't mind this—it was the way it should be—but sometimes they would get him into a conversation about the old days and before he knew it the whole morning was gone.

They usually started off with "Do you remember Pat Mulroony? Great big bruiser, he was. Used to be up in the Thirteenth Precinct when Molloy was there." This was the opening for a couple of stories about Pat Mulroony and then a few more about what Molloy did to the rookies who

79

came to his precinct and then a whole string of stories about tough precinct captains. Kevin liked these stories as much as anyone but, after three or four, he would begin to wonder how late he was going to have to stay after the old guys had left, to get his work cleaned up. He could always walk away from them, of course, but it didn't do a man any good to get a reputation for being unsociable, especially if he brought a book in with him every day. He had to be careful to steer a middle course.

"How's the bookworm doing today?" one of them said. "You any smarter today than you were yesterday?"

"I'm never going to be as smart as you, Mike, but I'm working at it."

"Don't let them kid you, Kevin. These old bastards haven't even read a parking ticket for the last twenty years."

"Smartest man I ever knew couldn't read."

"Well, there's something in that. Old Joe Hoffstedder who was down here at Centre Street for thirty years couldn't read a word and no one ever knew it. He had a memory like a steel trap. You was here then, Mike. You remember him."

"That's right, he had a photogenic mind. I remember one time when . . ."

A messenger came across the hall.

"Lieutenant Corelli. Call for you. I was sent up here to get you to answer it. Inspector Dayton says for you to follow it up."

Kevin walked into his office and shut the door. When he lifted the phone the police operator told him a man by the name of Barton Zimmer was calling. Kevin took a piece of scrap paper and told the operator to connect him.

"Yes, I can take the information. Go ahead."

Kevin drew a picture of a fish on his paper.

"What was the man's name? Do you know his address?"

He placed this information below the fish and started making a cow.

80

"What time last night?"

Kevin wrote the time in the middle of the cow's stomach.

"Did you see the murder committed? . . . How did you discover he was dead and why do you think it was murder?"

Nothing in the world was so uninteresting as the details of a man's death. Also, the person who called to report a murder was usually either drunk or a crank or completely inaccurate. Chances were, this guy Hammer had died in bed.

"May I have your name and address, please? . . . And your telephone number?"

Kevin wrote down, "U. S. Marine—President." He was certain he was a crank.

"Now, suppose you come down here and give us some more of the details."

The man said he would and Kevin knew he was a phony. Big-shots like that didn't come to the police—the police went to them.

"Well, thank you very much, Mr. Zimmer," Kevin said sarcastically. "I'll expect you at about eleven this morning."

He hung up. The guy would never show. He looked down at his notes. The story would have to be checked anyway. He picked up the phone and asked the operator to call Zimmer's office. He also called the precinct near the address he had been given and asked them to send a patrolman to Hammer's apartment.

He had just got started in his newspaper when the phone rang again.

The operator said, "Inspector Dayton says all these calls about this stiff in the Village are to go to you. I got two of 'em. A man and a woman, which do you want first?"

Kevin took a clean piece of paper. "Give me the woman."

"By the way, I got this fellow Zimmer on the phone and asked him if he just called and he almost took my ear

81

off. Says he'll report the whole thing to the Mayor. Big-shot, I guess."

Kevin took the information more carefully this time. It was the same story as Zimmer's. Some guy got his head smashed in at a party. He asked the woman to come to his office and give him more information. She said she'd be glad to. He told her to come at eleven.

He got the story again from the man. He almost knew it by heart now. When he wrote down the fellow's name he thought he'd seen it before in the papers. Another big-shot maybe. Kevin asked him if he'd be kind enough to come to see him at eleven.

He sent a detail to Hammer's place, and asked them to call him back when they got there.

Another call came and a man named Coburg-James said that he and his wife wanted to report a murder. Kevin listened politely and suggested that they come to his office at eleven.

"Can you tell me how many people were at this party?" he said.

Kevin asked for their names and checked them against the calls he had received. One person had not called.

"Do you know where I can find Margot Case?" he said.

And so he began his long search for a woman who would have been more than glad to have him find her.

A short while later Detective Murphy called and said that they had found Hammer lying dead in his apartment and that the light was still burning in the room where he had been killed. Kevin said he'd be up at noon and told Murphy to put a guard on the apartment to keep out any reporters.

He typed up the notes he had taken and then, to kill time until eleven o'clock, he went out into the hall and listened to a couple of stories about life on the force in the good old days.

"Now then," said Lieutenant Corelli, when all five of his callers were settled in his office. "Will you please tell me

82

one thing? Why were you all so anxious to report a murder between nine and ten this morning when none of you apparently thought of reporting it last night?"

"I think I can explain that," said Barton Zimmer.

Kevin saw that he felt he had degraded himself by coming to Centre Street to talk to a young Lieutenant, and wondered what had made him nervous enough to decide to do it in the first place. In fact, none of these people appeared to be the type to go out of his way for anyone, particularly for the police. Why had they all agreed to come so easily, as if the greatest pleasure in their lives were to do him a favor? Why were they so anxious to tell him what had happened?

"You see," Zimmer continued, "normally I should have phoned the police immediately, but last night I was so upset by the unfortunate occurrence that—if you can understand this—it entirely slipped my mind. I have never before, I'm glad to say, been present at a murder and the impact of the—the event was too great for me to remember my social responsibilities."

Kevin thought that shock was the one emotion they didn't appear to be suffering from.

"Let's start from the beginning," he said. "I assume you all knew the murdered man well?"

"Certainly not!" said Barton Zimmer. "I met him recently and haven't seen him more than a few times. I hardly knew him at all."

"But you knew him well enough to be invited to his party."

"That was a business matter. I—I was thinking of hiring him for a project I had in mind."

"Did you hire him?"

Zimmer's long, plump fingers beat nervously on the arm of his chair. "No. As a matter of fact I changed my mind after I arrived."

"And you, Mr. Boleyn. Were you a good friend of Hammer's?"

83

"I knew him, casually, fourteen or fifteen years ago. I haven't seen him since."

"And have you any idea why you were invited to this party?"

"He was a newspaperman." He spoke these words as if he were quoting what someone else had said, as if he would have called David an entirely different name. "He was probably interested in my work."

"What is your work?"

"I'm treasurer of the seaman's union."

"He's an agent of the Russian government—that's his work," said Barton Zimmer.

"Mr. Zimmer is undoubtedly referring to the fact that I'm a Communist," said Boleyn.

Kevin affected complete disinterest, as if he met Communists every day. "You believe, then, that he wanted information from you in connection with your—work?"

"I'm sure he did."

"We didn't know David very well either," said Mrs. Coburg-James.

"What was your reason for going to his party?" said Kevin, wondering if all of these people had gotten together and made up a unanimous story for his benefit. One look at Zimmer and Boleyn, however, told him that this was impossible.

"Well, you know the way you go to parties"—Kevin didn't—"you go to almost anyone's party if they're not unbearable. Even your own worst enemy. . . ." She cut off short and smiled half-heartedly to show that she had just been using a figure of speech and that, of course, she didn't mean . . .

"I suppose, Miss Dennis," Kevin said, bearing down a little, "that you hardly knew David Hammer."

"I knew him rather well."

"You would call yourself a good friend?"

"I was, once. Recently, I hadn't seen so much of him."

84

"Did he tell you anything about this party? Did he mention the other people he had invited?"

"No, I received a note from him asking me to come. I didn't know it would be a party."

"That's a little unusual, isn't it?"

"Not for David."

Without asking, Kevin knew immediately what kind of relationship she had had with the man. There was an intimacy in the way she pronounced his name which was impossible to hide.

"Why not for David?"

"Because he liked to take people by surprise, to catch them off balance. It was a trick of his. David was very cruel in little ways, though most people didn't know it."

"But you knew it. Was he cruel to you?"

"It did not matter any more if he was cruel to me."

Kevin understood that she was lying. "Now, who among you arrived at the party first?"

"I did," said Theodora.

"You were alone for a while with David before the others came?"

"No, Miss Case was there before me."

"Do you know this Miss Case?"

"No, I'd never met her before, although David said she was an old friend." Her voice underlined the last two words as though it were some kind of unpleasant joke.

Kevin looked around. "Do any of you know Margot Case?" No one answered. "Have any of you ever met her or heard of her before?"

They shook their heads.

"Can you describe her?" he said to Theodora.

"She was middle-aged and very quiet," replied Theodora. "I believe she had brown eyes and her hair was slightly gray. Her face was very strong. Also, she was wearing peculiar old-fashioned button shoes—if that means anything."

"I understand that this woman discovered the body between twelve-thirty and one o'clock. Can any of you tell me exactly what happened?"

"Yes," said Barton Zimmer. He picked his pince-nez off and began to polish them. He forced Kevin to wait until they were adjusted again before he continued. "Miss Case had been ill and we had to put her to bed. Hammer was too drunk to take care of her so we had to do it ourselves."

"By 'we,' he means he and I," said Vivian Boleyn.

Zimmer paused a minute to underline the rudeness of the interruption. "A short while later, young Hammer got up and walked out of the room. He made no attempt to excuse himself, and since none of his guests knew each other it was unpardonable. I wanted to tell Hammer that I had decided against hiring him so when he didn't come back I got up and left the room myself. I found him in the study. . . ."

Peter James broke in, "Before that, however, I had gone back to speak to David myself. I wanted to see him because he . . ."

"Young man! I am endeavoring to remember these events exactly as they happened, as they seem to be of the utmost importance. I am speaking of a time much before you left the room."

"You are not remembering the events very exactly, Mr. Zimmer," said Vivian Boleyn, "if you cannot recall that almost immediately after David left the room, I went in to speak to him."

"I'm sure that's not true," said Sandy. "I remember when Peter left and I know it was before any of you."

Kevin remained quiet. If they lost their tempers he would get more information in two minutes than he could get normally in two days. Some extra sense seemed to warn them of this. They all grew silent and looked at Kevin.

"We seem to have hit a snag," he said, smiling. "Can anyone tell me who *didn't* leave the room?"

They remained silent.

"I went to the—the powder room during the time David was gone," said Theodora. "I saw the light in the study but I didn't go in." When she spoke, her voice had a dead sound as if she had been the one killed, not David Hammer.

"I left the room too," said Sandy. "After Peter came back. I—I could hear someone whistling inside David's study, so of course he was still alive then. Peter never left me after that."

"David couldn't whistle," said Theodora.

Wouldn't you know they'd mess things up, thought Kevin, grimly. "For the time being we'll leave the question of who left the room last, unsettled. Will you continue with your story, Mr. Zimmer?"

"Of course, Lieutenant. I should judge that it was about an hour and a half or two hours after our host left us that Miss Case came into the living room where we were all sitting and told us that David Hammer had been killed. She seemed rather hysterical and, of course, I went in to see for myself."

"Did you go in alone?"

"No, he went with me." Zimmer inclined his head slightly toward Vivian Boleyn. "The woman was right. Hammer had been killed with a statue which had hit him on the side of the head. All of this must have happened a short time before we went in because the blood was still flowing and had hardly covered as large an area of the carpet as it would if it had been flowing for any length of time."

"Did you examine him to see if he was dead?"

"Well, no. He didn't seem to be breathing."

"It's possible, then, that you left him there while he was still alive?"

"I don't have your particular kind of experience. There was no reason to think he was alive. He couldn't have survived that horrible wound."

87

"What happened then?"

"We came back and told the others. Shortly after that Miss Case, who seemed greatly agitated, said she had to go and before any of us could stop her she had gone."

"Did she say anything at all?"

"Yes," said Sandy. "She accused one of us of committing the murder. She said David had told her that he knew one of us would kill him."

"I suppose you didn't bother to ask her which one?" said Kevin, hopelessly.

"Yes, I did. She seemed to have changed her mind because she said she didn't know at all and then she ran out of the door as if she were afraid of us."

"She said nothing else?" Kevin wondered why it couldn't be just as simple as that. Someone told you who committed the murder, then you knew who did it. One, two—just like that.

"Nothing."

"Then what?"

"A little while after that we all left."

"Now," said Kevin, "there are just one or two questions which occur to me." He turned to Theodora. "Can you tell me if there is any other entrance to either the bedroom or the study besides the hall which leads from the living room?"

"No, there isn't."

"What about the fire escape?"

"Well, yes, that leads from the bedroom. Perhaps someone came in from outside?" Her face reflected Kevin's doubts.

"Now, about the time. You say it was between twelve-thirty and one. How do you know?"

"I saw Miss Case look at the clock just before she left," said Sandy. "I noticed that it was one o'clock."

"Yes, that is correct," said Barton Zimmer, in a voice which suggested that the question was now settled. "I

88

looked at my watch shortly after I left and it was ten
minutes after one."

Kevin wrote down the time in his notes and thought to
himself that, unless Zimmer was lying, this bit of information was likely to be as accurate as if it came from Greenwich.

"Would you be able to make a guess," he said to Barton
Zimmer, "at the weight of the statue which killed David
Hammer?"

"Sixty pounds," said Theodora.

"How do you know?"

"I made it."

"She is a sculptress," said Boleyn.

Kevin looked at her hands. They were trembling slightly
and they had that luminous, slightly puffy look which
comes from overdrinking, but they were strong and corded
with muscle.

"Could this statue have fallen accidentally and killed
Hammer?"

"No, it was exactly his own height and unless it had
fallen from a distance it couldn't injure him."

"The statue is heavy to lift, Miss Dennis?"

"Yes."

"Could you lift it?" He looked at her gaunt body and
answered his own question before she did.

"Yes."

"Do you think any woman could lift it?"

"No," said Theodora, "not every woman could, and
most women couldn't lift it high enough to do what you're
suggesting."

"Could you lift sixty pounds above your head, Mrs.
James?"

"I don't know."

"Do you consider yourself comparatively weak, physically?"

"No, I don't believe so."

89

"You are active in sports? Tennis? Horseback riding?"

"Yes."

"Now, do any of you have the impression that Miss Case would have been capable of lifting a sixty-pound statue over her head and smashing someone's skull with it?"

No one spoke.

"You described her as an older woman, didn't you?"

"Middle-aged," said Barton Zimmer.

"She was a big woman," said Theodora.

"I believe she could have done it," said Vivian.

"There was something deceptive about her," said Peter. "She seemed to be trying to act like a delicate little old woman, but when you looked twice you realized she wasn't so delicate and she wasn't so old."

"But she was a woman, I hope," said Kevin, exasperated.

He paused for a moment. Maybe it was just because she wasn't here, thereby gaining sympathy by distance, but this Case woman somehow struck him as the only human being in the lot. At least she had the decency to get hysterical when a murder had been committed. Every one of them, even this Dennis woman, was as cold as a fish. It was obvious that they were all here to save their own skins. He didn't know yet why they thought they had to work so hard at it, but if they were so worried it must mean that the answer was lying around for anyone to pick up. Kevin intended to pick it up fast and when he did he would see them again.

"One more thing. While you were all seated in the living room, after Hammer had left and before Miss Case came in to tell you that he had been killed, did you at any time hear a noise—the noise of a heavy object falling to the floor?"

"No," said Vivian Boleyn. "I have been thinking about that and I don't remember any unusual noise."

"The rest of you?"

They shook their heads. "When you're talking," said

90

Sandy, "it's usually hard to hear any other noises unless they're very loud."

"I think I have enough to work on now," Kevin said. "I'll come to see you all within a few days. Perhaps tomorrow or Sunday. Will you write your home and business addresses on this pad, please?"

When they had finished he ushered them out into the hall, past Mike and the boys. They were arguing about the proper pronunciation of the name "Costello."

"It's Cóstello, I tell you. Cóstello, that's the way a true Irishman pronounces it!"

Chapter 8

KEVIN went back to his office and flopped down in his chair. He pushed away the pile of notes he had taken. He thought about Mary and wondered what he was going to tell her. She had wanted him to ask for his vacation now so that he could be with her when the kid came. Now he was up to his neck in a murder case and when the newspapers got on to it he wouldn't have a moment's rest. Already he had a job to do on Sunday, and Mary would want him to spend the day with her. If the case dragged out, of course, Inspector Dayton and the District Attorney and everyone else would come in on it and then he wouldn't have a free moment. Everyone would be giving him orders and would expect him to be in twenty places at once. That would probably happen anyway with men like Zimmer and Boleyn mixed up in it. The newspapers would drag in politics the first chance they got.

Kevin Corelli made himself a promise; a promise he was

going to keep for Mary and his son. He was going to clear
the whole thing up in a week. With good luck, Mary
would hold off that long and if he solved the case he
would have no trouble taking at least a week of his vacation to be with her. "God damn it, that's a promise! For
Mary and the kid!" The more he thought of it the nobler
Kevin's feelings became.

At twelve-thirty Kevin arrived at the scene of the
murder. A patrolman was stationed outside the house. It
was one of those old private houses which had been con-
verted into apartments. There were three floors, with one
apartment on each floor. They were the kind of apartments which would have cost sixty or seventy dollars in
Queens but which rented for more than twice that in
Greenwich Village. There was supposed to be something
picturesque about living in the Village, but Kevin couldn't
understand paying that much for atmosphere.

He went upstairs. Outside of the door on the top floor
he met another patrolman.

"Hello there, Lieutenant. Remember me?"

"How are you, Jim? I thought you were uptown."

"I was, until this morning. I got transferred. I hear
you're going to be passing out cigars soon."

"In about a week, I think."

"Well, the first one's the toughest. After that you sort
of know what to expect."

"I suppose so. There been any reporters around yet?"

Jim ran a rough hand through his bright orange hair.
"None yet. The people downstairs have been asking questions, though."

"What'd you tell them?"

"Just that there'd been an accident. Is this your case,
Lieutenant?"

"It looks like it," Kevin said, gloomily. "How are things
going inside?"

"The doc's been here and gone and there's a couple of
detectives inside, going over the place."

Kevin walked into David Hammer's living room. In spite of the smell of stale cigarette smoke and the collection of half-empty glasses, he immediately felt that this was a place he would like to live in. He had always wanted one of those big, leather easy chairs, and he could picture himself sitting in one of them before a roaring fire in the fireplace. It was easy to see that this Hammer fellow had enjoyed his comfort and for a moment Kevin half wished he was single again so that he could afford the peace and solitude of a place like this. He reached in his pocket for the pipe he smoked occasionally, but he had left it at home.

He wandered over to the big photograph on the wall. Now there was something that made sense. It was just like having a part of the country right in the room with you. There was something about fields and trees, Kevin thought, that made you relax and take it easy. He wondered what kind of man this David Hammer had been. Probably just an ordinary guy like me, Kevin thought, who wanted peace and quiet and maybe a place in the country someday. How did he ever get mixed up with the bunch of fish that had been at his party last night?

He heard noises from one of the other rooms and walked through the living room into the short hallway. He could see into the bedroom through the open door and he heard Detective Murphy's voice.

"Jesus! Will you look what I found?"

He walked in and found Murphy holding up a black Chinese robe. Two other detectives, who had been searching other parts of the room, turned to look at it. The robe was covered with purple and gold embroidery and reached to Murphy's ankles as he held it up in front of him.

"Fancy dress, maybe," said one of the others. "Hello, Lieutenant."

"I just found this in the back of the closet," said Murphy. "Do you think maybe the guy *wore* this?"

"Belongs to a woman," said Cohen, from the corner.

"No other women's clothes here. Funny—what kind of

93

things a guy will keep. Yeah, and here's some Jap slippers. I seen them in Japan. Men wear them in the house."

Kevin walked over and took the robe in his hands. The silk was heavy as metal. The insides of the sleeves were lined with crimson and the entire robe was hand-stitched. Kevin wondered what Mary would say if he wore a thing like that around the house. He handed the robe back to Murphy and went into the other room.

On the floor lay a corpse. The head was completely caved in at the temple and looked like a smashed walnut. The blood had caked in the hair and had streamed across the gray carpet almost to the opposite wall. Bending down near to the floor, Kevin could see the features which had once belonged to David Hammer. By an effort of his imagination he managed to place those slack features in a living face and, in spite of the present unattractive state of the body, the imagined face was immediately likable. He went over to the metal portrait of David, which was also coated with blood. Here, he was confirmed, although there seemed to be something disagreeable about the eyes.

Kevin looked around the room. He noticed some pipes on the desk and wondered, idly, where the tobacco jar was. He went to the desk and picked up a sheet of typescript and read it. He didn't bother to go through the desk—that would have been done already. For a moment he stood in the room, alone with the man who was no longer alive: a man who would never read one of these books again, who would never sit before his fireplace on winter evenings, never talk, never laugh. Kevin imagined that he could feel the hate and fury the murderer had imparted to the atmosphere of this room.

All that afternoon he worked to give some sort of order to his knowledge of David Hammer and his friends. He found an address book choked with names. Among these names he found all the people who had been at the party the night before, except Margot Case. There was no trace of her at all and there was no woman with such a name listed in the telephone book. Among the names in the address book Kevin recognized many which were prominent. He gave the book to Murphy and told him to follow up all of them. He didn't envy him the job.

Kevin checked the bedroom window which led onto the fire escape and found it locked. He interviewed the neighbors below and found that at approximately twelve-thirty last night they had heard a loud thump on their bedroom ceiling which was exactly below David Hammer's study.

Before he left, Kevin tried an experiment. Leaving the doors of the study and the living room slightly ajar, he had Cohen raise the statue to the height of a man's head and drop it on the carpet in the study. He stood in the living room and listened. It was audible, plainly, but not as much as he would have liked it to be. Yes, he thought, during a conversation it was possible that it wouldn't be noticed.

Back in his office he found on his desk five special reports on the guests at the party. There was still no trace of Margot Case. The fingerprint report stated that, because of the flaky texture of the metal on the statue, no clear prints could be found.

There was also a preliminary medical report which stated that David Hammer had died at about 5:00 A.M. on Friday morning.

Chapter 9

THE corner street light went on when Kevin reached Apple Terrace. The sky was still light enough to throw the row

95

of trees and houses on the far side of the street into dark silhouette. He counted up three houses from the end and identified his own home. Like most of the houses on the street, it was two-family (divided through the center, front to back, so that two separate families could live in the same house). Kevin lived with his brother- and sister-in-law, George and Lily Shea. George was in the Fire Department. As Kevin approached he could see the miniature picket fence which he and George had built last spring. Kevin had planted morning-glories on the inside of the fence and had trained their shoots through the pickets, and now the white wood was almost covered with greenery and flowers. Within the fence there was a well-kept lawn, a good six feet deep.

Two steps took Kevin across this little Eden. He went up the stone steps and onto the small porch, noticing that there was a light in the Sheas' side of the house. He found Mary and Lily in the kitchen. Lately, Lily helped her sister as much as she could, and when George was on a duty shift and had to stay away from home she stayed with Kevin and Mary. The kitchen was warm and filled with the smell of cooking meat and spices. Kevin kissed Mary and held her body close to him longer than usual. It was strange, he thought, how he could go for two or three days without noticing what Mary looked like or how she moved and then it would hit him all at once how beautiful she was. She had the kind of hair and voice and eyes which all went together in a perfect harmony. Separately, her features were ordinary and could have belonged to any insipidly pretty girl, but together they transformed themselves into something as calmly beautiful as the frontispiece portrait of the heroine in an old romance.

"Don't. I've got work to do." Mary pushed away but her voice was pleased.

"Where've you been?" said Lily. "The roast is overdone."

"Where's George?"

"He's washing up. We're eating with you tonight."

"You mean he doesn't wash up when you eat alone?"

Kevin sat down in one of the chairs by the kitchen table. Mary hurried back and forth across the kitchen. Kevin had wanted to hire someone to do the housework and the cooking, but Mary had made it a personal point of honor not to alter her usual routine. As her body had become more ungainly, she developed a kind of pride in it and insisted on doing all the work she had done before, and some she hadn't. It was the sight of this miracle going on within her which had convinced her, beyond any doubt, that she was capable of doing anything.

"Kevin, please get up. I've got to get the silver. Go up and wash."

Kevin rose dutifully and went back through the dining room and living room, which were just as long but half as wide as they should be, and went upstairs to the bath. While he was washing he sang a song of his own making which went:

> *"Katydid, Katydidn't*
> *Let him die on a rug—*
> *Katyshould, Katyshouldn't*
> *Kick the bucket like a bug—*
> *Katywould, Katywouldn't*
> *Wait until his grave was dug."*

He wiped his face vigorously, put his necktie back on, and ran noisily down the stairs to find the dinner all ready on the table and everyone seated, including a clean George.

The two sisters looked much alike, except that where Mary was calm and quiet Lily was agitated and voluble. If they had both been struck dumb Lily would probably have died of frustration, and it would not have altered Mary's life very much. When Lily spoke her voice was clear and unmistakably explicit—she had once been a telephone operator—as if she were trying to make herself heard over some inner babel. When Mary spoke, her voice barely went above a whisper but rooms had a way of quieting, and salesmen always served her first.

The dominant expression on Mary's face was simple faith—faith in the promises of butchers ("Pick out a *good* steak for me"), lending library saleswomen, doctors ("Now we mustn't worry. Just let nature run her course"), and Kevin. The typical expression of Lily was doubt ("George, your glass is too near the edge of the table."—"Grind the steak out here where I can see it."—"But what is *in* the medicine. What will it do?"). Both sisters recognized, however, that these were superficial differences; merely different ways of achieving the same ends. Simply put, these ends were building a home and eventually populating the world with little Corellis and Sheas. Neither Kevin nor George was quite aware of these ends—of this grand project of which they were such an essential part—and each was privately convinced that the sisters were really very different and that he had married the better one.

"Now, take Klein's," said Lily. "You know that black with white lace I bought there last spring? It cost seven dollars and the very next week I saw this well-dressed woman wearing it on Fifth Avenue. I wanted to walk up to her and ask how much she paid for it. I'll bet she paid twenty-five, at least."

"May I have some more gravy on my meat, please?" said Mary. She was sitting in a big chair with a cushion behind her back. She looked pathetically awkward, sitting so far away from the table, but when Kevin took her plate she smiled at him with such bland confidence that his throat choked up with adoration. No, he wasn't good enough for Mary. He was a beast. He despised himself. When he handed back her plate, she touched his hand lightly and Kevin returned to his chair, grateful for her caress, while Mary turned ravenously to her plate of food.

"Look," said George to Lily. "You don't have to wear yourself out looking for bargains. If you want a dress that

98

costs twenty-five dollars, get it. You don't save anything that way."

"Oh, but I didn't need anything *that* much. I never would have paid twenty-five dollars for it. Don't eat so fast, George. You'll get a stomach-ache again."

George turned quietly back to his meal. He was a listener and seldom spoke an unnecessary word. Whether this disposition had been forced on him during his five years as Lily's husband or whether it was native to him, even he had forgotten. He managed to maintain his place of authority in his household by sheer reticence. He was one of those people who project a feeling of security and confidence, primarily because he said nothing to dispel this feeling. People always asked George's advice and went away thinking they had received it, unaware that they had done all the talking.

"Honestly," said Lily. "You should see how Mary runs around this house all day. You'd think having a baby was the easiest thing in the world. I don't think she's even the least bit afraid."

Mary helped herself to some more peas. "The doctor said that women often have babies without any trouble at all. Worry," she said contentedly, "can cause a difficult delivery."

"Have you made up your minds what you're going to call him?" said George.

"If it's a boy," said Mary—and she could feel the little girl moving in her—"we'll call it Kevin, of course."

"No," said Kevin. "Then everyone will call him Junior."

"And if it's a girl?" Lily knew perfectly well that her sister had planned for a girl.

"Then," said Mary softly, "I think Ann would be nice."

"What about a name like Marc?" said Kevin, suddenly.

"It's up to you, dear. Whatever you like best. May I please have some more meat?"

Long after the others had finished Mary was still eating. She made no attempt to hurry, savoring each mouthful

99

with a kind of sensual abandon. All of the images Kevin thought of in connection with Mary were so delicate and evanescent that he would have been shocked if anyone had told him that, for the past few months, his wife had been eating like a horse.

"Just a little dab of potato," she said, passing her plate to Kevin.

When she had finished her second dessert, Mary sat back in her chair and smiled benignly at her family. Lily began to collect the dishes.

"Now you just sit there, Mary, and we'll have this cleaned up in no time. Come on, George, you carry these."

Mary stood up. "No, I want to help."

Kevin piled the coffee cups in a precarious tower and followed the others into the kitchen. Lily moved about clearing the drainboard and distributing towels, but there was never any doubt that this was Mary's kitchen or that she was in charge.

Mary stood at the cupboard and put the dried dishes in their proper places, bestowing special smiles on her blue-flowered cups as she hung them on the little brass hooks. When they were finished Mary announced that she was tired and that she wanted to go to bed. She kissed George and Lily good night and proudly took Kevin's arm so that he could help her upstairs.

When Kevin came down a little later he found George alone in the kitchen.

"Lily's got a book she wants to finish."

"Glass of beer?" said Kevin.

"Sure. What've you got on your mind?"

"Does it show?"

"A little bit. I guess if Lily was having a baby I'd have something on my mind too."

"Why don't you have a baby?" Kevin felt that he was now sufficiently experienced to offer advice. He went to the icebox and took out a quart of beer and brought it to the enamel kitchen table.

100

"We wanted to wait a little, first. I've been trying to lay aside some money so that if I get sick or something we won't be stuck."

That was just like George, Kevin thought. He never took a chance on anything. He always thought out everything beforehand. That's why he liked to talk to George. It gave him a sensible perspective.

George leaned back in his chair and took two tumblers from the closet above his head. He tipped one of the glasses and began to pour. It was a familiar routine. They often talked like this. George always listened and nodded his head and asked leading questions. They usually went through a couple of quarts of beer this way if Kevin had something on his mind.

"Dayton put me in charge of a murder case today."

"Sounds pretty good. Maybe you're being groomed for a promotion."

"No, it's one of those situations where, if you do well, no one says anything, but if you mess it up you get hell."

"What's worrying you?"

"Well, the first thing is that if I can't break this case in a week I won't get any time off to stay with Mary."

"Can you do it in a week?"

"I don't know. I think I've got it narrowed down to six suspects, even though one of them is missing."

"When did it happen?"

"Last night, at about twelve-thirty. The guy didn't die until five this morning, though. Somebody smashed his head in at a party in the Village and they all left him lying there."

"Did they know he was alive?"

"The two that saw him say they didn't. There was a woman that saw him too, but I don't think she knew either. She disappeared and there's no trace of her."

"Do you think she did it?"

"Maybe. The weapon was a statue that weighs sixty pounds and it would take a strong woman to use it."

"Have you got a description of her?"

"A pretty vague one. First, they said she was an old woman and then when I began to ask who could have picked up that statue and bounced it off a man's head they all started to say that she wasn't so old after all. She's anywhere between forty-five and sixty—and big."

"Well, you can never tell about a woman's strength. I saw a woman carry her husband out of a tenement fire last year and he must have weighed twice as much as she did."

"Maybe she could have done it, I don't know."

"Did anyone have a motive for killing him?"

"I don't know. We didn't find anything yet but I have a feeling that something's going to show up there, at least. As a matter of fact, one of the suspects had a motive but I'd just as soon he didn't."

George filled their glasses and went to the refrigerator for more beer.

"This guy is a Communist," Kevin said, "and the stiff is, or was, the fellow who wrote this 'Inside Communism' column."

"You think the Communist Party decided they didn't want him around any more?"

"That's just what I mean," said Kevin, angrily. "If the newspapers get hold of that they're going to make politics out of it and then the District Attorney and the whole city administration will come down around my neck."

"Maybe it is a political murder. It wouldn't do any good pretending it wasn't."

"Not to me it isn't. A man or a woman did it, didn't they? If they drag in politics the whole case will get so fouled up that I'll be on it for the next two years—if I'm even on the force at the end of that time."

"You got any of those Mexican pretzels left?"

"No, I think Mary ate them. You know, there's one thing all these old-timers down at Centre Street always agree on—just about the only thing they agree on, too—

and that is never to get mixed up in politics. You may go up fast that way, they say, but you come down twice as fast."

"You don't think the Communists had anything to do with it, then?" George searched through the breadbox and came back to the table with a nearly empty bag of Mexican pretzels.

"Maybe they did and maybe they didn't. I don't know anything about those things. All I'm saying is that a man or a woman picked up a statue and caved in that poor fellow's head with it. I know something about criminals but I'll be damned if I know anything about political parties and I'll be damned if I want to. I'm going to catch the man—or woman. Then my job is through."

"What about the others?" said George. "Can you make out anything against them?"

"Well, that's the thing, George. They all called up this morning to report a murder they saw last night. Does it sound right to you that five people—I won't count the woman who disappeared—should completely forget about a murder for nine hours?"

"Did they say they forgot?"

"Yeah. Slipped their minds. Convenient as hell."

"Sounds as if they knew you'd catch up with them anyway."

"Right. But why didn't they remember that last night?"

"What do you think, Kevin?"

"I'll tell you what I think. I think that at least one of them went back again after everyone had gone. Murphy said the papers in the guy's desk were all messed up as if someone had already gone through them—some amateur, he said. And one of the men who was at the party—a bigshot named Barton Zimmer—said that when he first saw the body the blood hadn't spread very far. Not as far as it would have if he had been lying there a long time, he said.

"Now you know something about head wounds, George.

103

You know that sometimes they don't bleed at all and sometimes they bleed like hell and then stop, especially when the guy's alive, like this one was. I think he knew the blood was going to spread further because he saw it later when it had. Maybe I'm reaching too far for this, but it all ties in."

"You think they all came back to look for something and when they didn't find it they called you because they thought you would find it?"

"Maybe not all of them—though that's possible. But one of them did, and I think it was Barton Zimmer. It stands to reason, doesn't it, George? Why should they all be so anxious to help me out if they didn't think I had something on them? Well, I haven't got anything on them —yet—but they've as good as told me I can find something if I look hard enough.

"And this fellow Zimmer. What's a big-shot like that doing, running around the city after a lousy little police lieutenant? A guy like that probably calls the District Attorney by his first name."

"What does this Zimmer do?"

"You've heard of him. He's the boss of U. S. Marine— the company that's in trouble with the government now. Some kind of anti-trust suit, I think."

"What are your newspapers going to do when they get hold of that? Never mind the Communists."

"It's worse than that. This Communist is an officer in the seaman's union."

"Boy! Now go on and tell me the other three are the President, the Secretary of State and the Governor."

"No, they're just people"—Kevin smiled—"just folks like you and me. Two of them have twenty-eight million dollars and the other one is a lady sculptress and has only about a hundred thousand."

"What are you going to do, Kevin?" said George, letting his belt out a notch.

"I'm going to take a chance on getting a quick arrest. I

thought it all out, George—all the pros and cons, just like you would. If I call in Dayton and take a back seat I'm not going to get out of any of the work, and if the thing grows into a political murder I'll be on it until my first pension check comes.

"If I go ahead with it myself I may get burned—both Zimmer and the political party the Communists are supporting have probably got enough influence to send me out to Flatbush—but on the other hand, I may be able to make an arrest before the whole thing gets fouled up. If I can, I'm out of it and Dayton will see that I get time off to stay with Mary. More important, I'll still be in a position to go places in the Department. That means a lot to me, you know, George. What with the kid coming now, I've got to keep moving ahead."

"In other words, you're going to take a calculated risk," said George, levelly.

"That's it, George. That's just it!" He finished his glass of beer and got up. "Thanks a lot. I knew you'd help me out. I've got to turn in now. Plenty to do tomorrow."

"Good night, Kevin."

"Night, George, and thanks again."

"What about this woman who ran away? Where does she come in?"

"She's the one I've got to find. She either did it or she knows who did. I'm counting on her."

"What makes you think she knows who did it?"

"She told the others at the party she knew. And she was in the next room when the murder was committed."

"Then all you've got to do is find her and you've got yourself either a murderess or a witness."

"Or another corpse," said Kevin, as he left the kitchen.

Chapter 10

HANNA woke from a fine, light, cloud-flecked dream. She had been on a hillside in the country and the morning sun had been shining on the nape of her neck and across her shoulders. She had been sitting there in a huge flowered skirt and white shirtwaist, a young girl still, admiring the view of the surrounding hills with a fervor that few young girls could match. And then she opened her eyes and felt the terrible sucking weight in the pit of her stomach which accompanies the descent into a nightmare.

Nightmares are bearable because, when they are at their peak, the mind reassures by waking and saying to the dreamer: "It was only make-believe." The dreamer then experiences that great flood of relief which, in some cases, is almost worth the nightmare. After that, lying on the cool pillow with a delicious sense of gratitude at being awake, it is possible to check off—one by one—the events of the dream and say: "But that didn't really happen— I am safe—I can put that out of my mind—no one will knock on my door—no one wishes to kill me—no one at all."

Hanna had had such dreams often and had awakened to peace and her lonely security. She had been frightened many times by steps in the hall or by a sudden noise in the court outside her window, but always she knew that she was safe.

There is a point beyond which the imagination cannot go unless it takes the sanity with it. Until now Hanna had always had some reason to suspect that her fears were groundless and that her dreams were just dreams and would not trespass too far into the world of lunches and hand-washings and furniture dustings. But now, waking from a world which should have been her reality, she faced the vicious nightmare of her life. The night had become the day.

Her bedroom was dark. The shutters on all the windows had been pulled shut and were locked. She knew, however, that it was day. A faint luminous glow replaced the usual morning sunlight which had always come through un-shuttered windows.

Yes. The door too was shut and locked—and chained. There was nothing to do now but wait. The knocking would come again. That insistent, merciless knocking which rattled the wood of the door as if it were paper. The terrible, sharp, impersonal sounds would be repeated over and over until they drove her out of her mind. Some-day, if the knocking lasted long enough, she couldn't help but open the door to it.

Whoever had come to her door last night had known that this sound, like the beat of her own heart, would destroy her. That person—last night—had known that Hanna was standing just inside the door, hardly breathing, afraid to move, feeling in her body every blow on the thin, wood panel. That person had hoped to force her to unlock the door.

What had been most frightening was that there was something unhurried about the knocking as if it were perfectly sure of getting what it wanted. Long after it had stopped, Hanna had stood by the door listening to the unnatural silence of the hall outside. At first she had thought that the person was still standing there in the hall, waiting for her to make a sound, wishing that satisfaction, that small triumph as a prelude to a greater one; but then she had become aware that she had been left alone, wait-ing behind a door which defended her from an empty hall, and that this was even a greater triumph.

Hanna got out of bed slowly and put her feet into her knitted slippers. She drew her robe around her and turned on the bed-table lamp. She must begin this day as she had begun all the others. She went to the closet and picked out

107

a navy dress. She had seen it advertised in *Vogue* a month ago. It had a tight waist and tight sleeves to the elbow, and whenever she wore it it made her feel stronger and neater. It would press tightly against her body and that was the feeling she wanted most today; the feeling of being constricted, of knowing where her own body stopped and the outer world began.

While the bath was drawing she took toothbrush, nail-file, comb, hairbrush and deodorant from her bathroom cabinet. This was a ritual, never to be varied, never to be hurried; this was the way to conquer time—and fear. She felt the water in the bath and turned the cold knob a fraction. Then the teeth, the nails, the preliminary brushing and putting up of hair and the careful massaging of the face with cream. She turned the water off when it was six inches from the top of the tub and resolutely locked the bathroom door. She knew that coming out again would be a test of her courage. Someone might break into the apartment while she was in the tub but she could not, she simply could not, take a bath with the door open. Every door she locked against the outside eventually became a trap, not a defense, but she could do nothing else. She poured some eau de cologne into the steaming water and stepped into her bath.

The water rose almost to the edge of the tub. She remembered a time when it had not risen so high. Hanna seldom looked at her body, usually only when she was powdering it or adjusting clothing to fit it; but this morning she watched it tremble beneath the moving water and wondered how it was possible to know so little about it. How could the slim, young girl, whom Hanna recognized as herself, be buried in this mass of flesh? Was the girl still lying there, inside, sleeping her life away? If she looked closely could she still see traces of her? That sharp line at the hip, that was not the older Hanna, surely. But then she moved and the pure line was dissolved in a lake of flesh. Hanna looked away and shuddered. No, the girl was locked in. She had shut herself away and she could not come out. When one begins to shut doors on the world there is no end to it, until one is locked in one's own body, the most impregnable fortress of all, which only death can open. She washed scrupulously, starting with the feet, and when she had finished, the water was mildly tinged with the white of the soap.

She wiped the cream from her face, applied powder and a faint touch of lipstick. When she was talcumed and deodorized, she put her robe on again, stepped into her slippers, and stood before the door. Outside, her rooms were silent, but this could be expected even if someone were waiting there for her. She knew that no one could be there, and yet how could she be sure of anything any more? She unlocked the door quickly, with a loud noise, and walked boldly into her living room. Without stopping she went on into the kitchen and walked back through the living room into her bedroom. Yes, she was safe. For a little while longer she was safe.

She had put on her dress and was arranging her hair when the telephone rang. She stood quietly before the mirror in the bedroom, with her hands at her head. The telephone was in her living room (she could not have borne to have it in her bedroom) and its metallic voice called to her—pleaded with her to answer. It could be Arthur, she told herself, or Mr. Howard. But it went on ringing, long after the waiter or the bank manager would have stopped.

She walked slowly into the living room. The little black object cried to be picked up. As she listened, anticipating each ring to the second, she imagined she could hear her own name in the sound. Haaaaannnnnnaaaaa. Haaaa-annnnnnnaaaaa. Haaaaannnnnnnaaaaa. It continued. She placed her hand on the receiver and felt it tremble. She must not answer it. She must not allow even a strange voice to enter here.

Haaaaannnnnnnaaaaa. Each time it sounded she felt as if eyes were watching her, as if the instrument were en-

109

dowed with power to see as well as hear. Haaaaannnnnnnaaaaa. Haaaaannnnnnnaaaaaa. Would it never stop? It was
almost better to answer it and force it to stop. It went on,
and each ring tore at her nerves. It wasn't the ringing,
however, which was the worst. It was the silence in between, the waiting for the next ring, hoping it would come
so that it would be over. Now. Haaaaannnnnnnaaaaa.
And now. Haaaaannnnnnnaaaaa. Again. Haaaaannnnna-
aaaa. Now. But it had stopped. She waited, but it did not
start again and Hanna sank into a chair—exhausted. And
the day had just begun.

For a long while she sat quietly in her chair and stared
down at her own knees. This was the chair she used always
when she was in the living room. Its back was toward a
corner where there was no window and no entrance to any
other room. The springs in the chair had long ago come
loose and pushed up into the fabric, making uncomfortable
lumps. She had refused to have it changed or repaired. It
reminded Hanna of herself. Thirty-four years ago it had
had an air of upholstered elegance. Its lines were trim and
firm. Slowly, with the attrition of years, it had lost its
shape and become an almost worthless hulk. It sagged
wearily now with her weight and it embraced her with
the casual intimacy of an old friend.

There had been times in this chair when Hanna had
sat all day and half the night, staring at her hands or her
feet or watching the opposite wall with its doorway which
led out into the world. During these times she could do
nothing useful, she could not even read. They had not
been unhappy times, except that occasionally her face
would contort in a child's mask of crying while the un-
moved, unfeeling person inside would look on curiously
without the faintest idea of what the crying was for. Then
at two or three o'clock in the morning, after a day of no
feeling, no thinking, she would rise solemnly from her
chair and retire to her bedroom, as if she had done a full
day's work.

As Hanna sat here now she remembered that, after such days, she would fall into a deep sleep from which she would awaken the following afternoon, more exhausted than ever. Her body would ache with fatigue and her mind would seem barely able to direct her back into her clothes and out into the waiting chair again. There would follow days of excruciating drowsiness, when even the joints of her wrists pained with the effort of movement. At last, becoming aware of her state, she would force herself to some menial labor which would tortuously bring her back to "normal."

Now, Hanna realized—too late—that there was a kind of luxury in fearing the vague and the indefinite. It was the kind of self-indulgence which she could no longer afford. She could not allow herself to sit here and stare vacantly into the room, anticipating a disaster or encouraging self-pity. The thing had come now and she must be alert. In one way, perhaps, the final emergence of her fate gave her a sense of relief, as the commander of a fortress must feel relief when the threatened attack has begun. Her own forces were now consolidated against the enemy outside as they had never been before, when there was a reasonable doubt in her mind that the enemy even existed.

She knew now that the enemy did exist. She had no more proof than a prolonged knocking on her door and a telephone's insistent ringing, but calmly, without hysteria, she knew that someone wanted to kill her. She remembered David's poor, crushed face too well to allow any incredulity to enter her appraisal of the situation. Sooner or later—it was only a matter of time, and she was surprised how coolly she took it—someone would try to break in and kill her.

For the first time she wondered who that person could be. The question had not occurred to her before, merely because it had not seemed in the least important. She had for too long lumped all of the people who walked the streets

111

outside into one menacing identity to care what name or what sex her assailant would bear. In fact, this very nameless and sexless quality of her enemy had, until now, been one of its principal characteristics. However, the possibility of identifying the person who had stood in the hall last night and who had rung her telephone a few moments ago now seemed most important. It excited her to think that, at last, the fear she had lived with for the greater part of her life had a voice and a mind and perhaps brown or blue eyes.

It was clear to Hanna that one of the people she had met last night intended to murder her. It could be no one else. That person had first killed David and now wanted to kill her. But how did the killer know where she lived? Had she been followed home? No, that was impossible. There had been no one on the subway car she recognized. Even the woman who had glared at her from the end of the car had not got off at the station of 125th Street and she had been already on the train when Hanna had come into the car.

No. One of the people she had met last night must have known her all along. Perhaps she had been seen leaving the hotel earlier in the evening. Perhaps even David had told someone who she really was and where she lived. Yes, that was likely. David had told. Suddenly, she was angry at David, in the way one is angry at someone one loves who one knows is irresponsible and not to be trusted. David should not have told.

When she thought of David she was surprised that she did not feel more upset at his death. Perhaps it was because her own death was too imminent now for her to be very much shocked by the death of someone else. A person who is in the middle of a lake in a sinking boat does not mourn the loss of a drowned friend. She had not known David very well, he was merely all that she had, but even now she felt perhaps he was waiting for her in whatever place was given to people who had died.

In a way, she was glad that she had not known David

112

better because she felt that he was not as fine as she had
first imagined him. Remembering the looks on the faces of
the people last night, she realized that David must have
hurt one of them very deeply, if not all of them. She did
not blame David for this, she could not blame him for
anything since he had been her only friend. Still, in a way
she felt almost a sympathy for his murderer, even though
his murderer was likely to be her own.

Hanna got up and went into the kitchen. She checked
the kitchen shutter again. The metal cross-bar, which
swung on one end, was securely set in the brackets of the
opposite shutter. It would be impossible to force, even if
there weren't a straight drop of three stories to the cement
floor of the court below. With the hinges on the inside of
the shutter it was inconceivable that anyone could enter
here. Only one window, the one in the living room which
had its exit on the fire escape, was a possible danger, but
even that was so securely bolted that it was no more
possible to enter than the door.

She opened the door of her pantry. There were literally
hundreds of cans of food on the shelf, cans which she had
stored here in anticipation of the times she would not be
able to open the door to let Arthur in. Here was everything
from canned pheasant to canned bread. She had bought
the best vegetables and the finest fruits. For the past
thirty-four years, whenever she had seen something
particularly appetizing advertised in her magazines, she
had sent for it. More recently, as canning techniques had
improved, she had bought practically everything that was
possible to eat. Every few weeks she would ask Arthur to
pick up something new from a special store on Madison
Avenue, whose stock she knew almost by heart.

She picked out a can of crêpes suzette for her breakfast.
She put a pan of water on her little stove and began to
open the tin. She was almost cheerful. She had everything
here that she would need. She turned the bright red handle
of her opener and the squat tin spun around under the

knife. The room was suddenly filled with a thick, musty odor. The contents of the can crawled with green mold, and when she tipped it slightly a poisonous syrup broke through the surface of the mold and spilled to the floor. She felt as if a giant hand had grabbed her by the back of the neck and were forcing her to watch the diseased thing. She almost dropped it to the floor as she became aware of the implication of what she had found. She looked up again at the rows of canned foods which had given her such comfort before and was suddenly overwhelmed by the treachery of all things.

The bright labels on the cans were mocking her. There, that can of peaches, whose advertisement proclaimed a golden, succulent treat, was filled with the slimy ruins of a fruit which had ripened fifteen years ago. And the can of butter she had been about to open was not sweet and fresh as a country field at all; it was an acrid, fatty paste with no resemblance to the substance which had been sealed so negligently in fragile metal walls. All of these things, in which she had placed so much faith, things she had saved for this moment, had grown sour and rotten in their pitiful shells.

Hanna's hand trembled as she took down another can. She fastened it in the opener and turned the handle slowly—perfectly certain of what she would find inside. The can was filled with little new potatoes. They lay at the bottom of the can beneath a clear liquid. The odor was that of the freshly peeled, tart little potato which she sometimes had in the spring, boiled whole and sprinkled with parsley. Delightedly, she ran to her shelf and got an enamel saucepan. Then she busied herself with her Silex because the water was boiling.

Hanna had her breakfast in the living room. She did not mind at all having potatoes for breakfast. She had put them in a covered dish and soaked them with butter—it was as sweet as a country field in early summer—and sprinkled them with parsley. She drank her coffee from

114

a pretty white cup which glowed brown when the coffee was in it. This was the way she liked things, everything quiet and perfect and arranged like a little feast, to which she had invited only herself. She took two potatoes from the covered dish and put them on her plate. She split one of them open with her fork and lifted the smallest piece to her mouth. It was excellent.

She spent the rest of the morning cleaning, although it meant crowding a great many things she had to do into the afternoon. Actually, by the time she had dressed for cleaning and had moved furniture, she had very little time to do the work she had planned. She had felt uncomfortable about her walls for a month and wanted to give them a good washing.

She was able, however, only to dust them well before it was time to start lunch. This was the way her work always went, and Hanna was constantly nagged by the feeling that she was falling behind. She had to finish sewing the new dress this afternoon. Already the necklines on the newest dresses were changing and, at the very least, she must start a new blouse tomorrow. She was also anxious to get through her lunch because she had a great many things to think about and she had been saving all her thinking for then.

At last she was settled in her chair with the nearly completed dress on her lap and her sewing basket on the end table beside her. The day had been quiet, like every other day. Even Arthur had not called, but that was not unusual since he always waited for her order; otherwise he assumed that she did not want to be bothered.

But she was not fooled. She must go on as she had always gone because that was the only way to escape the fear; but she did not for a moment allow herself to believe that the danger had ended, that the murderer had given up. It would be so easy to do that. She had trained herself for a long time to meet this emergency. She knew what was coming and she waited quietly for it, conserving her strength for the time when she would need it. Long ago, when the murderer may have been an innocent child with no dreams of malice, she had begun to prepare for this time. It was even possible, she thought, that she knew more about these things than the murderer. The fox often knows more about hunting than the hunter.

One question which puzzled her was why the murderer wished to kill her. It was a question of secondary importance since she had been perfectly convinced for more than thirty years that someone would try to kill her someday—still, she realized that there must be a logical reason for it now. Immediately, she knew the answer. Someone had thought she had seen David murdered. She remembered that she had spoken as if she knew who had done it, just before she had left the party. She hadn't known anything, of course, beyond what David had told her, but the murderer thought she knew and that was enough.

It was a horrible joke. Someone was trying to take her life away and it was all a mistake. It would be a stupid, clumsy error and there was no way she could explain. She would have to wait and fight to keep someone out she didn't know just because that person thought she did know.

Her body froze at the sound of the quiet knocking on her door. Until it came she had not realized that her senses had been straining all day for some out-of-the-way sound or sight or smell which would tell her that danger was here again. The knocking came again, muffled but strong, as if it were being done by the meaty part of a fist. She stood up and went toward the door.

For a moment there was silence outside and then she heard a rustling of paper at the bottom of the door and a white square slid into her room. She bent down and could just make out the words "to live Forever"; the rest was hidden under the door. The letters were printed and Hanna wondered if they could have been clipped from some magazine and pasted on another piece of paper. She had heard that people did this so as not to leave a sample of their handwriting.

She could hear no sound outside now. Had the person gone away again or was he still waiting? She came very close to the door and pressed her ear against one of the panels. She could hear the noise of the elevator at the far end of the hall and something that sounded like laughter coming from one of the other floors. At her feet the paper waited for her. ". . . to live Forever." She leaned down and picked it up. It was a printed circular which began, "Learning to live Forever."

"Madam," said a sepulchral voice from the other side of the panel, "the Lord has said: 'I will not lie unto David. His seed shall endure for ever, and his throne as the sun before me. It shall be established for ever as the moon, and as the faithful witness in the sky.'"

Hanna dropped the paper from lifeless fingers and stood before the door, not daring to move, although she knew now that it was too late. Whoever had knocked had waited patiently on the other side until she had taken the circular. He knew that she was listening to him now.

"If you will allow me to come in I will give you the Lord's word as it has been made known to me in these troubled times. I do not ask anything of you but a moment of your time. Hear my words and Christ will enter your heart. I have prayed that you may hear me."

Hanna was shaking, not from fear now, but as if a very tight wire inside her had snapped and left her helpless in the face of this new onslaught. She did not even try to think who it was that was speaking to her or what was being said. She merely heard a high, male voice chanting some kind of argument which didn't seem to be directed at her at all but to a third person more important than either she or the speaker.

"And he has said in his wisdom, 'The friendship of the world is enmity with God; whosoever therefore will be a friend of the world is the enemy of God.' Can you say to

117

yourself truthfully that you have forsworn the world? Oh, we are sinners! Heed God. 'Love not the world, neither the things that are in the world. If any man love the world, the love of the Father is not in him. For all that is in the world, the lust of the flesh, and the lust of the eyes, and the pride of life, is not of the Father, but is of the world. And the world passeth away, and the lust thereof; but he that doeth the will of God abideth for ever.' "

The voice droned on, and in a kind of quietus of terror Hanna found herself thinking of a time when she was a little girl and had gone to a church with her father, where a man spoke like this. She remembered now that she had met the man after his sermon and had been frightened by the cold, fanatic, blue color of his eyes. He had looked at her without seeing her at all and had taken her hand into his cold one. He had smelled of sweet soap.

Somehow, she could not leave the door until he had finished and gone away. She knew now that this was not the one who had knocked on her door last night. In a way he was even more dangerous than that other one because he knew about locked doors and he understood perfectly how the person inside would be trembling and wishing with all her might that he would go away. He had spent as much time trying to get in to people as she had spent trying to keep them out. She remembered the cold fever in the eyes of the minister and realized that here was a pursuer who would follow even beyond the grave and that nothing, nothing in the world, was so horrible as this.

At last the voice subsided and she heard his steps going away from her door. She knew, however, that he had not left because he was defeated. He was not discouraged. He would try again and again at other doors and sooner or later he would get in. He was the enemy of everything and everyone and he would win because he could conceive of doing nothing else.

After her evening meal, which consisted of roast duck and asparagus and the rest of her potatoes, she washed

118

some stockings and some underwear in the bathroom washbowl. When she had finished this she went into the living room and picked up the *History of Charles XII of Sweden*, by Voltaire. This was one of her favorite books. She felt as if she knew Charles even better than Voltaire had. This young King had been afraid of the world too, frightened of everything in it; but instead of hiding as she had, he had gone out and attacked it and tried to tear it apart. It gratified Hanna to read of his amazing success, as if this would have been her success if she had tried such a thing.

She reread the part about his seeking refuge in Persia after he had been driven from Europe. The young man who had conquered more of that continent than Hitler, who even had England trembling in fear of a certainly successful invasion, had been defeated at last, most miserably, because he cared nothing for administering the countries he had conquered, only for the glory of winning battles.

Hanna liked particularly the story of his sojourn in Persia, for it was here that he first allowed himself to sleep in soft beds and to enjoy a life of comfort and ease. She understood so well why he had fought violently with his few thousand followers, to keep from being put out of that hospitable country; why he had built his camp like a fortress and faced the hordes of the Khan of Tartary to keep from being sent back to the bitter, warring north. She understood so perfectly how he had made a religion of being afraid of nothing because he was afraid of everything.

Hanna read the book like a novel, and as with a good novel she could never read the end without crying. She read how he was forced back to Sweden and to his ruin, and now it seemed like a personal lesson to her. He should not have left his fortress in Persia. He should have stayed there, no matter how great the odds against him. He shouldn't have gone outside into the world again.

She closed the book and wiped her eyes with a big

handkerchief which she kept tucked under the cushion in her chair. Why must she read a meaning into everything? Why couldn't there be one thing she could hear or see which didn't have some special significance in her life? Were other people like this? She was sure they weren't. If only her life weren't so full and so tortured always. She supposed that was the meaning of the word "sensitive," and in books it was always rather a compliment to call someone sensitive. It was not a compliment to Hanna, since she could not compliment herself on something which made her life a great, aching mass of feeling.

She got up and walked over to the table beside the door to get her *Life* Magazine. How safe, how really safe she had been when she had bought this, and now she mightn't be able to finish it before the violence came. Marshal Tito stared at her soberly from the bold cover of the magazine. He had looked the same early last evening and yet so much had happened since then. How could he not change his expression? Was he so lofty and so far away from the most important thing in the world—her imminent danger of being murdered?

She took the Marshal back to her chair. She wanted to read a part of *Life* before she went to bed. There was something comforting about contemporary history, quite unlike Voltaire's tragic work. Perhaps it was because the modern events were not quite so irrevocable as those which had happened hundreds of years ago; perhaps, also, it was because of the nice way the people on *Life* wrote.

When she read about a crucial battle in China in the magazine there was a certain understanding that everything would come out all right which Voltaire just didn't seem to be able to give. There was an undertone in the magazine which implied that there was information, yet to be divulged, which would give the victory to the good ones; which Voltaire, naturally, could not supply, since the battles he spoke of were long ago decided and almost forgotten.

120

More than this, Hanna had a pleasant feeling about modern history because it seemed so unreal, so unimaginably distant from anything she knew or cared about. Even full-page pictures of rotting bodies, while unsightly, were a necessary part of this fiction which was running, in serial form, in the magazines and newspapers. She opened the cover of *Life* with a sigh of relief, glad to escape that too-real world of Charles XII of Sweden.

Of course, it was impossible to find Marshal Tito inside. That was the way *Life* tricked you; a great big picture of something interesting on the cover and a little article buried somewhere in the back which you couldn't find until you had read everything else. She thumbed through an article on the marine life of Okinawa, which was embarrassingly full of pictures of women without any tops on their dresses. She stopped to read about a mayor of a town in the Southwest who used to be a circus acrobat and campaigned from a platform while standing on his hands. Finally she came to the disappointingly meager article on Tito which explained why he was having trouble with the Russians.

She was about to discard the magazine, intending to read it more thoroughly tomorrow, if she had time, when she found herself staring into the face of the murderer.

Chapter 11

KEVIN knew the U. S. Marine building well. During the summers, when he had gone to school, he used to be a runner on Wall Street. Somewhere along here was a basement hallway which cut directly through the building and came out on the opposite street. From there you could take a twisted passage under another building, and another, so that it was possible to walk from Wall, past Pine where he was now, and almost up to Fulton without stepping outside of a building except to cross the street. This was important when it rained, and Kevin remembered how he used to look with scorn at people who got wet. It showed they didn't know their way around "The Street," which was the term used for the financial district.

For a time, he had had dreams of becoming a great Wall Street trader, buying and selling millions, and when he had been put on a ticker he was sure he was on his way. By the time he had memorized the cabalistic symbols on the tape he knew that he was headed for great things. But six months after he had left school, when he read the ticker as easily as he read his own name, he suddenly woke up to the fact that he was still getting eighteen-fifty a week, so he had quit and joined the police.

He walked past one bank of elevators and turned into a narrow marble hallway. The elevators to the top five floors, he remembered, were on the other side of the building. This was one of the older buildings, built in the boom days of the last century when the new world was beginning to realize its importance and loved to show it in its architecture. Imported marble covered the walls, and the grillwork on the ancient elevators had been custom-designed. There was an air of well-to-do gloominess about the building which seemed to have been the style seventy-five years ago. Upstairs, there were hardly any windows, and those that were there were prevented from admitting any light by the Gothic gables and gargoyles.

The starter nodded. The old man had recognized him, just as if he hadn't been away from The Street at all. In his mind, probably, no one ever left. When you had been working at one job for forty or fifty years and Lamonts and Morgans and Whitneys knew your name and maybe

122

gave you twenty dollars for Christmas, then you couldn't
be blamed for thinking that the whole world was The
Street and that no man would be fool enough to quit a
job down here. Kevin said hello and got into the elevator,
feeling that he should have a leather envelope of bonds
under his arm.

Kevin got off at the top floor. He was directed by the
operator down the hall to a large glass door. He had
remembered that the top five floors of the building were
occupied by U. S. Marine. He had once delivered an obscene drawing by a famous cartoonist to one of the
executives on the floor below. It had been a present from
his boss, who drank DeWars and White Rock all day long
in the conference room and traded drawings with other
executives in other conference rooms. As he approached
the door Kevin found himself assuming a rather over-
respectful attitude. He told himself that he was here to
investigate a murder, that he represented the law and
must bow to no one; but the associations of the past were
too strong for him, and he found himself stammering his
reason for being there to an unsmiling secretary.

"Perhaps I can help you. Mr. Zimmer is busy."

Kevin could tell that she expected him to leave his
message and go. He wished he looked older. After all, he
was a Detective-Lieutenant and had risen in the Department in half the time it took most men. Some trace of the
reason for that rise must appear on his face.

His scowl was not all he intended it to be. "I'm Detective-Lieutenant Corelli and I'd like to speak to Mr.
Zimmer personally, if you please."

She picked up her phone but did not appear to be much
impressed. "Mr. Zimmer. There's a detective out here to
see you . . . yes, I will."

Kevin swore under his breath.

"Will you sit down for a moment, Mr. Minelli. Mr.
Zimmer will be out in a moment."

Kevin sat in a hard chair beside a long table and leafed

123

through a *Pacific Marine Review*. It was now 10:30 A.M. He wouldn't be able to get uptown until after lunch. That would probably mean he would have to put off his last two interviews until tomorrow. He reached in his pocket and took out his notes. With the information he had got this morning he might be able to break this case right away.

Perhaps Zimmer? Well, he would just wait and see. He had started out this morning with no motives. Now he had four, possible five. The thing was growing. If he could just keep on top of it maybe everything would break. Now, about Zimmer, he had to let him know who was running this show right from the start. The man was big. Maybe he had a lot of influence, but he couldn't buck a murder. . . .

"Come on in, Lieutenant."

The door had opened and Barton Zimmer was beaming at him. The smile sat so uncomfortably on the man's face that Kevin could see that it actually hurt him. He got up and walked into the inner office behind his host.

When he stepped into Zimmer's office Kevin felt that he had stepped back fifty years in time. Everything in it was designed to make the visitor think the twentieth century was still to come. Probably it was more exact to say that its original design had never been altered. At one time it must have been wired for electricity, but this was so effectively disguised in the body of the tremendous gas chandelier, all brass and crystal, that it could hardly be noticed. The walls were paneled wood and the ceiling was gold leaf. A fat, riduculous and golden cupid lurked in each corner of the room, near the ceiling, holding an impractical bow in its chubby hands. A huge fireplace, faced with highly polished malachite, dominated one wall of the room. Over it hung a portrait of a man in mutton-chop whiskers. On the mantel, below the picture, were a number of cups and medals, which seemed to have been awarded for no particular accomplishment of the person who had won them but just to indicate a general excellence in all fields.

124

In the center of the room stood a massive desk on which were placed no papers, no telephone, nothing at all except several expensively bound books, a green marble pen set and a clean, green blotter. Also, at one side of the desk lay an old-fashioned pocket watch attached to a heavy gold chain. Covering each wall were portraits of old gentlemen with mangy beards and excellent frock coats. Scattered among them were group photographs of what appeared to be the same gentlemen at business banquets.

"Quite a place you have here," said Kevin, feeling suddenly completely inadequate for his mission.

"It was my father's. I have tried to keep it exactly as he had it. It symbolizes to me a spirit which does not seem to be present in our time."

Kevin could not help feeling a little like someone who had come to ask for a job. Perhaps that was the effect Barton Zimmer had on everyone. Practically everyone who saw the man either worked for him or wanted to work for him. Kevin pitched his voice rather deeper than usual and began.

"Mr. Zimmer. I believe I have discovered why you did not call the police immediately after the murder was committed."

"Really. I was under the impression I had already told you why."

The man seemed not at all nervous now and Kevin felt almost as if he were speaking out of place, taking up an important man's time with something that might better be handled by one of his subordinates.

"We found a key to a safe-deposit box in David Hammer's effects." I must get on top of this, he thought, I must give this man a scare. I'll never break this thing if I don't. "In that box, Mr. Zimmer, we found some papers which give you a very good reason for murdering Hammer."

Barton Zimmer placed the pads of his long white fingers together and nodded his head peacefully. "Tell me what you found, Lieutenant."

125

"We found correspondence between you and David Hammer dating back several months. There seems to have been some agreement between you and him that he should write a series of articles on Communism in the seaman's union. It was understood that you should pay him a sum of money for these articles."

"I could have told you all of this if you had asked me. I cannot see how this makes me a potential murderer."

"No, except that David Hammer seems to have taken particular care to preserve all the correspondence he received from you and copies of all his own letters. As he pointed out to you in one of his later letters, it would not improve your position with the public to have it known that you paid, or offered to pay, for something which should have been spontaneous and objective in a newspaper column. This would be especially true if it were pointed out that you were doing this to distract public attention from your anti-trust suit."

At the mention of the word "anti-trust" Barton's face grew angry. The anger was not so much directed at Kevin as it was at a world which would allow such a disgraceful thing as this suit to go on without rising in wrath.

"Lieutenant, it does not reflect any honor on the Police Department to have one of its representatives go around mouthing the rabble-rousing opinions of Communist filth."

"I am merely repeating the substance of Hammer's letter to you. It was a letter written in reply to one of yours, and I'll be honest and say that I might not have thought of interpreting your letter in quite that way. But I know nothing of these things."

"In my letter to Hammer," said Zimmer, "I merely expressed an opinion that, instead of squandering government monies on political trials of innocent men, the administration might do better to attack the real threat to this country and its institutions, which is Communism."

"The correct interpretation of your letter is not my job, Mr. Zimmer. The fact that David Hammer was black-

126

mailing you for a considerably higher price for his series of articles is all that I am interested in, in view of the fact that he was murdered while you were present in his apartment. Also, there was one other thing, far more serious, on which he was basing his blackmail."

Zimmer did not speak. He watched Kevin closely, and the younger man thought he was waiting for some sign of weakness, some faltering step which would show him the course he should follow. He did not appear nervous or afraid, he was merely waiting to see what positive step he could take to dispose of this matter. Kevin knew that this man would consider any step, no matter how ruthless, quite proper and "positive" as long as it did the job without a disproportionate risk.

"In one of Hammer's letters to you he stated that his series of articles would be much more effective if he could promise the revelation of a scandal or something sensational enough to catch the public's interest.

"In your reply, you stated that the bookkeeper in the union office was 'your man' and that, through him, you would arrange for an amount of money to be withdrawn from the union treasury and deposited to the personal account of Vivian Boleyn, who was the newly elected treasurer of the union and a known Communist."

Zimmer nodded. "That is the letter, if not the spirit, of the truth, unfortunately. I was very foolish."

"Then you intended, through Hammer, to accuse Boleyn of a crime which, actually, you caused to be committed?"

"It was not done, of course," Zimmer said. "Hammer thought it had been and that he had me on the griddle. Probably it would have been done if our bookkeeper hadn't been fired shortly after Boleyn took office."

"Still, the existence of the letter you had written, proposing the theft, was incriminating enough."

"My dear young man, I wish you wouldn't use the word 'theft' so loosely. I admitted that what you had been

127

saying was the letter of the truth, but the spirit—oh, the spirit was quite a different thing. I have been very frank with you because I thought you might understand.

"What difference does it make if I, who have the good of the industry and the union in mind, simulate a theft which will take place in actuality soon enough. Oh, I don't think Boleyn is personally dishonest, though he may be that too, but from now on, the treasury of the union is in the hands of the Communists and will be used only for purposes of which the Communist Party approves."

Kevin interrupted. "Mr. Zimmer, I am a detective. Your political opinions are not my business. The only thing that interests me is that Hammer was blackmailing you and that he seemed to have a pretty good case. So good that the 'business' you had with him Thursday night might easily have been to kill him."

Zimmer smiled and Kevin had the uneasy feeling that the man had decided where the conversation would lead and was already three steps ahead of him.

"If you mean to imply that I had no intention of paying the young man a penny and that I would rather have seen him dead, you are quite right. However, I would not have touched a hair of his head as long as the suspicion could so easily fall on me. Furthermore, at his death all of this would have come out in the open and my distaste for that, as you correctly surmise, is exactly the reason he thought he could blackmail me. It is therefore absurd to think that I killed him."

"Suppose you had reason to believe that the correspondence was somewhere in Hammer's desk? If you had murdered him and come back later, after everyone had gone, taken the correspondence and destroyed it, you would have no reason to fear anyone."

"You believe that I did return later?"

"Yes."

"That is very acute."

"You killed him."

128

"Of course not. Young man, I find you extremely intelligent."

Kevin choked down an automatic thank you, but Zimmer had already seen it in his eyes.

Zimmer continued, "I was glad to see that a young man of your caliber had been put in charge of this case. It is gratifying to note that the Police Department has followed the leadership of modern industry in this instance and invigorated itself with young blood. I wonder if you know why I did not contact the Police Commissioner or my good friend the District Attorney yesterday morning?"

Kevin shook his head. He wished Dayton were here with him. The Inspector would be able to see through all this double talk. He didn't like dealing with suspected murderers who knew the Police Commissioner and the District Attorney. Somehow it didn't seem quite right. He felt himself outflanked. The difference between the big crooks and the little ones was that the big fellows had a way of making you doubt whether the law was meant to apply to them at all.

"Because," said Zimmer, "I did not consider them reliable. Generally, I do not believe in criticizing a man's superiors in his own hearing, because such remarks promote a feeling of anarchy—a feeling which is altogether too rampant in our age—but I feel that you are level-headed enough to understand when I say that these men are like straws in any political wind."

There was a note of sincerity in the man's voice which could not be mistaken. In spite of his long-winded speech, he obviously meant every word he said.

"My father worked all his life for this Company and I have followed in his footsteps as far as I was able. It has not been easy and you will not believe me when I tell you that I have fought battles for this Company which I would not have fought to protect my own life.

"The Company has grown until it is now the largest and most efficient carrier of cargo on the seven seas of the

129

world. Unfortunately, as it has grown, so have the forces of unrest grown in the world. Jealous little men stand on the sidelines and try with all their might to tear down what we have built. Communists incite the men to strike and venal politicians resurrect some obsolete anti-trust laws, hoping to extort liberal contributions to perpetuate their wretched political lives!"

Barton Zimmer picked up the watch from the desk and cradled it in his hand, letting the heavy gold chain dangle in the air. Kevin guessed that it, like everything else in the room, had belonged to his father. Zimmer held it tightly in his hand as a person would hold a charm or an object of sentimental value, gathering warmth and a kind of peace from it.

Kevin wondered what this all had to do with him or with the murder of David Hammer.

"Now, I consider you reliable. That is, I do not believe that you are a Communist or that you would be tempted to ride ahead in your career on a wave of political publicity. I am seldom wrong in my judgment of a man, and I find that I have judged you to be a man who will not be swayed from your goal. You, I am sure, will not be tempted to make unfounded statements to the press about my unfortunate involvement in this murder nor will you publish, or make known to the press, correspondence which has nothing to do with the case."

Kevin leaned forward angrily. "Now look here, Zimmer. I don't care who you are. If you committed this murder I'm going to charge you with it and nothing you can do will stop me. It doesn't matter to me how many important people you know, you're not immune to the laws of this state any more than I am, and if you think you've got hold of a dumb cop who's going to shield you and cover up for you then you're dead wrong!"

Barton Zimmer nodded sagely. "That's just what I hoped you'd say, Lieutenant. You are out to catch the murderer of David Hammer, and I'm behind you one

130

hundred per cent. It is the kind of approach to a problem that I like. Direct. Forceful. You have seen your duty to be that of apprehending a vicious criminal, perhaps a maniac, and no merely political consideration will turn you from your objective.

"You have perhaps reasoned that human beings are involved in this, not ideologies. I was merely trying to point out to you that some others would not be so scrupulous as yourself. They would join the pack in trying to tear down a great institution of commerce, hoping that they might salvage a morsel for themselves. You are not this kind of man."

Kevin was trying to fight his way back to a perspective of his situation. He had decided that he didn't like Zimmer but he wanted to keep his personal feelings entirely out of it. After all, Zimmer's fight with the Communists was not his business and he did not intend to allow any information about the correspondence between Zimmer and Hammer to get out. It was enough for him to know that there was a motive for the murder. The trouble was that the others had motives too. He was no further along than he had been before.

"Mr. Zimmer, you speak as though you were clear of the suspicion of murder. You aren't. I have every reason to believe that you are guilty and no reason to believe that you are innocent. You have admitted that you came back to the apartment after David Hammer was killed—he didn't die, by the way, until early the next morning—to get correspondence which had been used in an attempt to blackmail you. Isn't it possible that you also wanted these letters because, if found, they would throw suspicion directly on you?"

"That is exactly true. I knew that the police would be looking for a motive and that they would be so overjoyed at finding a reason for my committing the murder that they would stop short and not pursue their case. In a way, one might call what I did a conscious service to the cause

131

of justice, but I don't suppose that you can see it in that light."

"You suppose correctly. You don't appear to be interested in how we knew that you had come back to the apartment after everyone had left."

"Not at all interested. There was no reason to hide it after I couldn't find what I was after."

"Did you know that David Hammer was not yet dead when you came back?"

"I should like to say yes, Lieutenant, since that would prove that I had nothing to do with his—injury, but I believed he was dead. While I was searching his desk I saw no signs at all that would lead me to believe that he was alive. It was a most distasteful experience."

Zimmer's tone was almost petulant, and he implied that searching David's apartment was a dreadful imposition on him which might have been better handled by one of his junior executives.

"Now, will you tell me again, Mr. Zimmer, what happened after Miss Case became sick and left the room?"

"Certainly. I saw young Hammer leave the room shortly after, and, as I mentioned before, I remarked to myself that this kind of rudeness was unpardonable. I do not know how long it was after this that I decided to go in and speak to him. I went to the study and . . ."

"You say that you were the first one to go in to speak to him?"

"Precisely. I am absolutely certain of this. I went in and told him much the same thing as I have told you. I said that he would not get a penny out of me, that our contract for the articles was canceled, and that if he tried to put his threats into practice he would soon regret it."

"What did you mean by that?"

"He knew what I meant. He knew that if he persisted in his vile scheme I would surely record my objections to his criminal methods with the management of his paper.

132

I felt certain that the board members of the publication—whom I know well—would see the justice of my complaint and discharge him immediately. As a matter of fact I had decided to request his dismissal before he had an opportunity to do any harm. This was an extreme measure, of course. If he had been at all tractable it would have been safer to have him on the paper."

"How did Hammer take this?" said Kevin.

"He acted perfectly sure of himself and told me to think it over and said he would call me the next day. I'm sure he was bluffing."

"That was all?"

"Yes, everything."

"After you came back did you notice any of the others leaving the room?"

"I did. I believe that during the course of the evening all of them left the room for a short while, but that of course is not at all unusual and I couldn't attempt to remember the order in which they went or even how long they were out."

"The only thing you are positive about is that you left the room to see Hammer before any of the others?"

"Yes; that was because I was anxious to see him alone, as you can understand."

"Did you know any of the others at the party?"

"No one. As a matter of fact I didn't really expect it to be a party. Young Hammer had said that there would be one or two people there, but that he and I could find time to talk privately. I went only for that reason—because I thought he had come around to my way of thinking. I certainly would not have gone if I had known that Bolshevik Boleyn was to be there."

"What did you know about Hammer, outside of the fact that he was an expert on Communism?"

"I knew nothing at all beyond that. With hindsight, I should have been more cautious. I ought to have known

133

that a man who had once been a Communist, no matter how repentant he pretended to be, was already so morally disintegrated that he could not be trusted. I will be honest with you and say that I am extremely glad that another Communist—and I am convinced now that he was just that, that he was working hand in glove with them all the time—has been removed from the earth. That may sound harsh to you but sometime, somewhere, we men of peace must take to the field of battle against such creatures."

Kevin thought he had never seen anyone less warrior-like, less capable of taking to the "field of battle" than this tall, plump man whose whole being seemed to be centered in his weak blue eyes. And yet this man was what was known as a captain of industry. It seemed incongruous to Kevin because he had grown up to think of captains as hard-visaged men with weather-beaten faces. But the style in captains had changed. The quarter-deck and the battlement had given way to the executive office and the board room. The eyes behind the pince-nez had to peer no further than the typed sheet of bond paper and the well-modulated voice could be magnified to reach to Calcutta and back with the help of a telephone. This man was an Alexander, a Caesar, a Ulysses. Those old heroes would have laughed at him, but he could afford to let them. He had already achieved more than they.

Kevin made a move to go, but Zimmer motioned him to remain seated.

"I hope that I have sufficiently explained my actions to you, Lieutenant. I believe that if you will consider carefully all that I have said, you will come to the conclusion that I could not possibly have been mixed up in this business."

"It looks to me as if you are very much mixed up in it."

Zimmer laughed in a manner which was meant to be pleasant. "Well, of course it is your job to suspect everyone and I cannot blame you for wanting to do your job thoroughly. I admire thoroughness, and stick-to-itiveness.

These are American virtues and, in the end, they win through."

"I'll find the murderer of David Hammer, if that's what you mean."

"I know you will, Lieutenant. Tell me, have you given any thought to your future?"

"What do you mean?"

"Have you planned to stay in the Police Department?"

Kevin was about to answer that he was studying law until he realized that he was the policeman and that *he* should be asking the questions.

"Possibly."

"Well now, if you don't mind an older man giving you this bit of advice, I believe that would be a mistake. Modern industry is growing, as you know, and there is a critical shortage of intelligent young management personnel. You are married, I presume?"

Kevin nodded.

"Any children?"

Kevin could not help answering this one. "One, on the way."

"Grand. Grand! I will not pretend to know how much money you are earning now but I'd be willing to bet that any one of my offices—in Shanghai, for instance; or Southampton; or even in New York—would be willing to pay you two or three times what you are earning now. I have drilled into the heads of my employment managers the fact that good personnel is half the battle. When they see a good man they have orders to get him, no matter what the cost. I think you are such a man."

Kevin was witnessing a curious phenomenon within himself. There seemed to be two Kevins in him instead of one. One of the Kevins was listing all of the advantages to be got with two or three times his present salary—a new home, clothes and gifts for Mary, a good school for the child; the other Kevin was calmly telling him in a contemptuous voice that he was being bribed.

135

Barton Zimmer sat solemnly at his desk, dangling the great gold chain of his watch in the air. He watched his visitor intently, waiting to see some sign of acceptance in his face. Suddenly the telephone rang. Barton opened the door of a Venetian cabinet which stood beside his desk and withdrew the receiver.

By the time the receiver was back on its hook, Kevin had decided and was able to say in a businesslike manner:

"Now, Mr. Zimmer, suppose you tell me what you know about Margot Case."

Zimmer appeared surprised and his expression eloquently said that Kevin was acting a fool.

"I know exactly nothing about her. I never met her before and I've never heard her name."

"Are you sure she didn't say anything which might help us identify her?"

"Not a thing. I've told you as much as I know. Look here, young man. Perhaps you didn't understand. I was offering you . . ."

"I know what you were offering me. If you persist in it I'll make charges against you immediately for attempted bribery."

Zimmer leaned back in his chair. "Yes," he said, as if he had just asked himself a silent question. "I like you very much. Very much indeed. I'd really like to offer you some advice—though with your hot temper I'm afraid you'll say I'm trying to intimidate you, or something theatrical like that. This thing involves a lot more than the murder of a cheap little crook. You have probably seen that. If you don't watch out it will get way over your head and you may be hurt badly. I don't mean physically hurt, either. I'm sure you could take care of yourself that way. You know there are other ways of being hurt. There are large forces at work here, and for your own good I hope you don't get sucked under."

Kevin got up. "I'll manage all right."

Zimmer walked with him to the door. "Come back to

136

see me again, soon. Maybe we can have a longer talk next time. Good-by."

Kevin walked quickly out of the office.

Chapter 12

KEVIN prolonged his lunch hour as much as he could. His next interview was going to be extremely unpleasant. He hated to question women. They were never satisfied to give a logical explanation of their actions. They invariably forgot that he had come to investigate some particular crime and looked on his questions as an excuse to inform him about their emotional lives with a thoroughness which appalled him. To be flooded with information in this way was almost worse than to be given no information at all.

In addition to this, Theodora Dennis was an artist. She had given the address of her studio as the place he could reach her. Kevin had never been in an artist's studio before but he had already pictured it in his mind with horrible clarity. He saw the model, clad only in a filmy wrapper, and the bearded young men drinking Pernod. He anticipated the feeling of immorality which would somehow pervade the air and make the visit of a detective ludicrous. In fact, the word "studio" had, for him, such an ominous sound that he wondered if he shouldn't postpone the visit and see Theodora later at her home. If she had called the place an "atelier" he certainly wouldn't have gone.

As it turned out, Theodora's studio was in an ancient office building off Twenty-third Street on Fifth Avenue.

137

The elevator man took him to the proper floor and watched suspiciously as he searched for the right door. Kevin knocked, rather timidly, on the filthy panel of door number sixty-five. He strained to hear the laughter of a model.

A husky voice called, "Come in."

The elevator man banged the door of his cage irritably and began his slow descent. Kevin turned the brass knob and walked in.

Theodora Dennis stood in the center of a perfectly ordinary one-room office. She had a ball of clay and a cigarette in her left hand and she was working on a figure with her right.

"Sorry this place is such a mess," she said, pleasantly, but Kevin could see that this was what she said automatically to all strangers. She couldn't have cleaned it in months.

The room was a waste of old paper bags and empty coffee containers. In one corner was a forest of bottles: milk, Coca-Cola, and whisky. In a little alcove, next to a sink, stood a group of figures muffled with gray towels. Beside them were several ten-gallon tins of clay. All the objects in the room, a stool, a short ladder, several empty armatures and a coat rack, were streaked with the white of dried clay.

She did not stop her work. Every few seconds her hand would dart to the clay head. She would pinch a tiny piece from the clay in her hand and roll it between her thumb and forefinger until it was the size of a beebee shot, then her hand would stab again at the lifeless head.

"I would like to ask you a few questions," said Kevin, vaguely grateful that her studio was so little as he had pictured, and also strangely disappointed.

She nodded. "I hope you don't mind if I continue working."

"No. No, go right ahead," he said, uncomfortably.

"You're the first one to see it, you know."

"See what?"

138

He was suddenly aware of what he had been uncon-
sciously thinking since yesterday morning: he wished he
had been assigned to a nice, simple murder case where
some drunk had got himself knocked off in a fight in a
bar and no one involved had been a Communist or a
millionaire or an influential businessman or, God forbid,
an artist.

"This head, of course. It's David. This is my second
portrait of him. I suppose you've seen the other one, by
now."

"Oh—oh, yes. I saw it. Naturally, it was part of the
evidence."

Why in hell couldn't the woman sit down and talk like
a normal human being! What was he, anyway—a detective
or an art critic?

"Of course, I realize that," she said, as if he had apolo-
gized, "but I wanted a copy for myself. I was never quite
satisfied with the other one. There was something wrong.
It's never possible to tell just where you go off in a thing
like this, but the feeling was false. Oh, but I do think this
one is going to be all that I planned the other one to be!"

Her voice was tense and excited, except that all her
excitement seemed to be concerned with the statue she
was making and not at all with the fact that he had come
to question her about a murder.

The entire surface of the head was covered with tiny
wafers of clay. They had been pressed firmly into the
structure, one on top of the other, layer upon layer. He
tried to calculate how many thousands and hundreds of
thousands of clay beebees had been used to build up the
head this far. He understood now why there had been no
fingerprints on the statue which had killed David. The
final surface had been so scaly and uneven that there was
not one unbroken surface large enough to hold a good
print.

"That looks like a lot of work," he said, sociably. "How
long have you been at it?"

"Since early yesterday."

For the first time he noticed that she was still wearing the suit she had worn in his office yesterday morning. It was covered with white streaks where she had wiped her hands. She must have been working on this steadily since she had left his office.

Reading his thoughts, she said, "When I begin to work, I work without stopping for as long as I can. I haven't been to sleep since I saw you last. That accounts for my appearance. I apologize."

Actually, Kevin thought, she looked better now than she had before. Her hair was rumpled and her eyes were slightly red, but she seemed much brighter and more youthful and her hands didn't shake so much. For the first time Kevin could conceive of a love affair between her and David without feeling embarrassed.

"You and David Hammer were engaged to marry, weren't you, Miss Dennis?"

Her hands continued to place the little pellets of clay on the face which was to be David's, but Kevin could tell that he had all of her attention now, and all her distrust too.

"We are in possession of a file of correspondence between you and David Hammer which goes back a good many years."

What a pompous way to begin. He wanted to warn her, in the bluntest way possible, that he had read these letters. It was bad enough to read someone else's mail, but when that mail was full of the pleading of a woman who needed so much and needed it so pitifully, the only thing to do was to make it absolutely clear that all of this was in the line of duty, as if he were a doctor.

"Yes," she said, "we were engaged."

"And," he continued (this was the most difficult part to say, although he knew she was expecting it), "you were aware of why he wished to marry you?"

"For my money, naturally. While I had it."

140

Her hand began to shape the lips of the statue, drawing out sharply its ridges and contours with each movement. Then, with wafers of clay, she began to build up the body of the mouth, slowly and methodically, applying her shreds of whitish earth with as much patience as Nature herself was using to destroy the real mouth.

"How long had you known David Hammer, Miss Dennis?"

"Since 1939. I met him at a party." She kept her eyes on the image of David as she spoke. "He was the only person in the world who understood me. From the moment we met and began to talk I knew he was the only person I could tell things to who wouldn't laugh. Even toward the end, when I knew all about him, I still felt that way. David understood people. Everyone felt that."

"Did you first meet him after you came back from Europe?"

"I suppose your knowing all about this means that he kept all of my letters. I would have been very happy to hear that, once—but of course he didn't keep them for sentimental reasons. He merely thought they would be useful to him someday."

She gathered up scraps from around the base of the statue and kneaded them into the ball.

"Yes. I met him shortly after I came back from Europe. I had been in Poland, running my mother's property. I had inherited some mines from her and there was no one to take charge of them but myself. I hated doing it. I never wanted to own so much—to have so much responsibility. I would have given it all away if I had only known how."

She didn't look at Kevin. Her hand moved back and forth to the lips of the statue and she spoke in a low voice, as if she were talking to herself—or to this clay image she was making.

"There was more to it than that, I suppose. It was a kind of challenge. The managers of the mines were trying to cheat me, thinking that I wouldn't know the difference.

141

I had to show them that they couldn't do that to me. I would have given it to them gladly but I couldn't let them steal it.

"David understood this, as he understood everything. He seemed to guess it before I even spoke. He knew how tired I was of being both a man and a woman. He knew how awkward and stupid I was and yet he accepted me just like that and never asked me to make any changes. I knew that I had found the right person and that at last I could relax and be just quiet and myself and I could do my work and he would look out for things for me. I was going to give everything to him. I wanted to be rid of it and never have to worry about money or the businesses that make money again. No one would ever have a chance to cheat me again, I thought."

Kevin interrupted. "How long was it, after you first met, that you decided to be married?"

"Very shortly. Within a few months I asked him to marry me. I wouldn't have believed I could do that but it seemed so simple then because he and I were so close—or I thought we were.

"It is very hard to remember those times now because they were happy. I can't even believe them at all any more and it doesn't interest me to try to recall them. It isn't true that a few moments of happiness are enough. You can remember a second of unhappiness for the rest of your life but it doesn't work the other way around. . . ."

"No, I suppose not."

Kevin stood a few feet away from her, shifting in embarrassment from one foot to another. He had meant to have her verify the information he already had in the letters, and by this device, perhaps, to get her to tell him something new, but he hadn't expected this flood of reminiscence, given almost as if he were not in the room.

She continued. "When the war began and Hitler overran Poland, David postponed our marriage. It was as simple as that for him. Everything was always extremely

142

simple for David. No tickee—no washee. He didn't even feel that he had done anything wrong and so, of course, the deceit didn't show in his actions as it would with a more human person. He merely put the marriage off and gave some vague reason for it. That was all. He knew *I* would cover up for him so he didn't have to bother. He knew that I couldn't bear the truth and therefore would fight to keep it a secret from myself.

"Finally, however, I came to realize the truth: David wanted to marry me for my money. The realization didn't have the traditional effect, I'm sorry to say, no shock and revulsion, no proud rejection. No. Instead, I found myself praying that the Allies would win so that I could have my property and David back. It is strange now to realize that the whole massacre was, in my mind, merely a titanic struggle to decide whether or not I'd be married. Men froze to death and were blown to pieces and families were torn apart for no better reason than that I should have enough money to buy a husband."

Slowly, the mouth and chin of the statue began to take shape. Under Theodora's relentless thumb the features were narrowing down to the likeness of one particular person. That chin could no longer be just anybody's chin. Some other chins would be longer or wider or they would have deeper clefts. This clay on the board had first been nothing but a solid mass; then it became a head, anybody's head, everybody's head; and now it was becoming one head, one particular countenance—almost nothing again.

"Perhaps," she said, "I would have been successful in buying David. If he had all the money he needed I don't think he would have known what to do with it. He didn't care anything for me but then he didn't care for anyone else either so it wasn't competition I had to worry about. There is a limit to everything, even dishonesty, and if he had finally got all my money perhaps he would have been as miserable with it as I was. Then he might have needed someone. He might have needed me. At least that's the

143

way I thought then. Unfortunately, I didn't reckon with the Communists. David did. In matters like this he planned far ahead."

In spite of her unhappiness, Kevin couldn't feel completely sorry for this woman. With all her talk about hating her money, she still had more than enough to live on. Enough to buy nice clothes and rent this office for a studio and to buy whatever kind of food she wanted. He had seen enough of suffering to know that people can be completely unhappy even though they have all the material things they want, but none of these people knew that there was something even worse than unhappiness.

There was misery. There was deep, unrelenting misery which comes from poverty. It was a feeling having nothing to do with pain or disappointment or even fear. It was just dead, monotonous, humiliating, reasonless misery. It went so deep that the person caught in it could not even afford to be aware of it. Kevin had seen dead men and killers who came from backgrounds like this. Perhaps, if the law would allow it, there was some excuse for them; but if this woman had killed a man because she was unhappy or because she wanted to be loved or for some other stupid reason, he had no sympathy with her.

"So, when the war ended, David offered to go to Poland to protect my interests—by then we both understood that they were his interests. He said he was certain that Poland would go Communist but that he would try to save something before the mines were expropriated. I gave him my power of attorney. He came back with nothing and said, quite simply, that he thought we ought not to be married. David was exactly the beginning and the end of everything I ever wanted."

There was something about the mouth of the statue which Kevin found very familiar. He could already recognize the sculpture as being a copy of that blood-stained one which had lain on the floor next to David's body, but it was not quite the same. Even though he had only seen

144

the first statue once he knew that something here was different.

"As you know, Miss Dennis, most of the story you have just told me was explained in the correspondence which David Hammer kept. I merely wanted you to verify it. I think you must realize that the whole story gives you a direct motive for murdering Hammer. You felt a strong attachment for him. He had promised to marry you and then he refused. You had an opportunity to do it, a reason to do it, and you were physically capable of doing it."

She looked up from her work. "The way you put it I can hardly do anything but be graceful and admit my guilt. However, there were others who had an opportunity to kill him and were physically able to and, if I know David at all well, they probably had reasons to murder him also.

"I know that David cheated everyone, and if you look hard enough you will find that he cheated, or was trying to cheat, all of the people who were there the other night. Perhaps you've already discovered that. If you found out about me I suppose you must have found out about the others too. I knew David better than anyone else, after all, and I know that every friend he had was his friend only because he thought he could get something out of him. No, I don't suppose you have a better reason to suspect that I killed David than to suspect any of the others."

This was all so true that it made Kevin angry. She was working calmly on the head again as if he were no longer there. This infuriated him more. They were all perfectly secure because each of them could have done it. By their mutual guilt they protected each other. There was nothing he could do.

"You say you did not go in to see David after he went into his study on the night of the party?"

"No, I did not. I went to the powder room. Going to and from it I passed David's study but I didn't go in. I had nothing to say to him and I'm sure he had absolutely nothing to say to me."

145

"Do you remember who was the last person to leave the room before Miss Case came out and said he was dead?"

"I have no idea. People leave the room and come back usually several times during a party and I'm not in the habit of keeping track of their movements."

"You say that you had never seen Margot Case before?"

"Never."

"And yet you were a good friend of David's and had known him for a long time."

"Yes."

"And you told me that Hammer introduced Miss Case as an 'old friend.'"

"Yes, but I'd never seen her and never heard of her before. She was a complete surprise to me."

Suddenly Kevin stared at the clay head with a flash of recognition. He remembered now where he had seen that strangely slack mouth. It was David's mouth, but not the one he'd seen on the original statue. It was the soft, yielding mouth he had seen on the face of the man with the crushed head. There was no mistaking it. Even incomplete as it was, it was evident that the new statue had not been modeled on the living man but on the dead one.

"In your original story," he said, "you told me that you had not seen David Hammer after he left the room on the night of the party. I believe you were lying. I *know* that you saw him later."

Something in his voice made her drop her hands and step away from her work. She looked at him in wonder.

"You saw. You saw the face! And now you can recognize it from the little I've done!" She stopped and smiled sheepishly. "I don't know whether to be very happy or very unhappy. You see, it is rather flattering to realize that I have caught the right expression but of course I've given myself away completely." She looked at the statue proudly.

How batty can you get? Kevin thought. He said, "Then you admit that you saw Hammer after the murder was committed?" He felt as if he were the one sane man in a world of babbling idiots.

Her face sobered. "Yes. After everyone had left I went back. The door was open and I went right in. I had to see David again."

"That's your only explanation for coming back?"

"What other would I have?"

"I believe you came back to look for the letters you had written David. You said yourself that he never threw away anything which might be useful to him. Letters from a wealthy woman would fall in that category."

"I came back to see David."

Kevin ignored her. "That's the reason you didn't call the police about the murder until the following morning. You knew that these letters would throw suspicion on you if we found them. You wanted a chance to look for them yourself first. When you didn't find them you realized that the police would and you decided to be co-operative, hoping to divert some suspicion from yourself in that manner."

"Was that why the others didn't call? Did they come back also?" She looked at him and got her answer.

"Did you kill David Hammer?" Kevin said, feeling that this was rather like asking a waiter if the roast beef was overcooked—there was only one answer you could expect.

"No."

"You had been in love with him. This meant everything to you and when he gave you the brush-off your love turned into hate. . . ." Kevin knew immediately that he had phrased this all wrong. She was laughing at him.

"Isn't that just a little too dramatic for a Saturday afternoon? I think you've been reading the wrong class of books."

Suddenly, Kevin was angry. He wanted to break something. If only he could throw this God-damn statue out of the window or toss the can of clay through the glass door.

147

"Now you look here, Miss Dennis! You're up against a serious business of murder. Every one of your actions since the evening of the murder has been suspicious and you have the best motive in the world for hating David Hammer. You're one of the chief suspects and—by God—if you did it I'll see that you're caught and I'll make sure that you go to trial and that you're convicted!"

Theodora Dennis returned to her work and began tenderly to apply all her skill to re-creating the face of the man who, more than anyone else in the world, she hated.

Chapter 13

SUNDAY morning Hanna woke at half-past eight. Before she even looked at the clock she knew that something had gone wrong. For years she had wakened at exactly half-past nine, not a minute sooner or later. There was a particular combination of noise and odor at nine-thirty which was not duplicated again during the next twenty-four hours, and this was her alarm clock.

As she lay in bed now she heard a *full* garbage can being dragged across the court beneath her window. At nine-thirty there would be the noise of empty garbage cans and usually the deep, comforting voice of the cook repeating an order. She heard steps across the court and they were strange, not nine-thirty steps at all. Also, there was a kind of tender crispness to the air which she wasn't used to and she could smell water. She turned on her side to look at her clock. She had wakened to the world an hour earlier than usual. Why?

148

Then she became aware of the noise. The sound which had called her from sleep was so faint it could hardly be heard. It too was unfamiliar, though she had imagined it many times. It was the small, metallic searching of a key in the lock of her door.

She lay in her warm bed and the instinct was to pull the covers up over her head and shut out the noise. For a moment she almost succumbed to the desire to sink back again into that sweet world of sunlight and warm words and joyful, little-girl fantasies. Her body ached for that other world and ridiculed her fears. She imagined so much, she had always imagined so much. That was the way she had always been. Better to forget it now and go back to sleep.

Suddenly, the howling wind of reality descended on the delicate country of her dreams and withered the flowers, twisted the shading trees, turned the young girl into an aging woman. Hanna jumped from her bed and ran on bare, white feet into the living room.

The door was open. It had been opened the slight distance allowed by the slack of the night chain and, through the crack of the door, a pencil was being used to lift the hasp of the chain from its socket. With the courage of the insane Hanna threw herself against the door. It slammed shut, breaking the pencil in half.

For nearly an hour Hanna lay against the door, bracing her feet on the carpet against another onslaught. None came. There was only silence outside in the hall. She did not know whether the murderer had gone away or was still waiting for her to leave the door so that it could be opened again.

As she waited there, she became angry at herself for not having realized that it would be easy to find a skeleton key to her door. She should have been prepared for such a thing. She looked down at the thin brass chain which was now the only thing between her and death. Once, she had wanted to have a bolt put on the inside and had even asked Arthur to bring a locksmith with him the next time he came; but then she had been so afraid of having two people in her rooms that she had told them both to go away, that she had changed her mind. Now, a bolt seemed the most precious thing in the world and she would have given half a million dollars for one. But how could she measure her need in money? She would give everything she had for a good, sturdy, brass bolt which only she could unlock.

But she had no bolt. And she could not stand at the door like this forever. Probably the murderer had already left and was now having breakfast or taking a bath or catching up on sleep, secure in the knowledge that Hanna was posted at the door. Later, the murderer would come back freshened, ready to try again, knowing that Hanna must leave her watch sometime and that the door could be opened. She must find a way to hold the door shut. Perhaps she could devise a warning. Yes, that would be better. If only she could know in time she would be safe.

Hanna backed away from the door and felt behind her for her little dining table. She stepped behind it and lifted it quietly. She put it in front of the door. From the far side of the room she took a large Wedgwood vase and balanced it on the corner of the table next to the handle of the door. If the door were pushed in, even slightly, it would hit the vase and knock it to the floor. The vase had been her mother's and, like her mother, it was delicate and frail and would not survive a fall even to a carpeted floor. This would be her warning. Nothing could happen to the door without her knowing, and this was more important to her in a way than having the door firmly bolted. It would almost be worse not to know that the murderer was there.

How strange it was to know the name of this person now. How unbelievable to know those features so well that they never left her for a moment. For years this killer had had no face, no voice. It had stalked by her rooms thousands of times, never revealing its identity or its plan. Now it was real and all the terrors of her life had centered at last in the body of one person whom she knew.

Dressed only in her nightgown—a figure so pitifully unarmed and helpless—she padded with bare feet across the carpet and picked up the magazine which held the picture of her enemy. Each time she looked at those familiar features it seemed that there had never been a time when she hadn't known them. The steady eyes watched her from the page and quietly promised her death. Only two nights ago they had met, and yet Hanna felt that they must have seen each other long before.

Below, in the caption of the picture, Hanna read once again the unshakable proof that this was the person who had murdered David and now was trying to kill her. She had not needed this proof, however; the eyes alone had assured her and had spoken all the truth she needed to know. Once again, looking at this face, she had the feeling she'd had last night when she had so casually turned to this page. She had felt that this picture was meant for her, that in all the other copies of this magazine in the world there was not one other which held this message. In none of the other millions of reproductions of this picture were the eyes so suffering with hate or the mouth so cruel. In no other issue of *Life* was this face so explicitly saying, "You are next."

Hanna shuddered and dropped the magazine, but the picture remained in her mind, mutely assuring her that she would die.

She went into her bathroom and automatically began to take her comb and brush and face cream from the chest. She started the water in the tub and proceeded as she had thousands of other mornings. Only by holding fast to her routine could she save herself.

After her bath, which she took with the door almost shut but open enough so that she could hear anything in the living room, she went to her bedroom and began laying out the clothes she would wear today. She chose her blue underwear, trimmed with sand-colored lace, which she had ordered from an advertisement. She laid the pants and brassière on her bed and placed a plain blue slip beside them. Then she chose a blue garter belt and her sheerest stockings. Finally she picked out navy shoes and a navy taffeta dress which she had finished making the week before.

She took off her robe and for a moment she stood, hugely naked, before the shreds of cloth and leather and elastic which would make her a civilized woman. Having no one to dress for, Hanna took particular care in choosing what she was to wear. If everything was not perfectly as she had planned it, down to her inmost garment, she would feel uncomfortable and embarrassed all day long. Other women could dress for outward appearances, but Hanna could not be so slipshod. If the color of her slip clashed with the color of her garters, or if the two were an unmatching shade of the same color, it was as embarrassing to her as a fallen stocking would be to another woman.

She ate her breakfast from her lap. The dining table had been put to a better use. Her breakfast consisted of broiled baby frankfurters, melba toast and cold, canned raspberries. Also, she had a cup of tea, brewed in a bright yellow pot.

For Hanna, the eating of food was both a duty and an exquisite pleasure. Every time she took a mouthful she could feel the strength of it flowing into her. If she concentrated very hard she could actually feel her blood bringing this reserve supply of strength to all her members. Sometimes the roots of her hair tingled with it. In this, Hanna followed the course she took in all her other actions: every time she ate a baby frankfurter she felt as if she were depositing that much strength against the time she would need it; she *saved* the food in her body. It was all to be translated into extra endurance and stamina when the time of disaster came.

Frequently she became despondent about the composition of her meals. Once, she had read an article about lettuce which said that primitive man had existed almost entirely on lettuce, not on meat as had been supposed, and that moderns suffered from a severe lettuce deficiency. (The assumption was that primitive man wouldn't have eaten anything else if he'd had a chance.) For nearly a week after that Hanna had lived on lettuce. Every time she had bitten into a crisp heart she could feel the terrible lettuce-need in her own body assuaged. Sometimes it had almost seemed as if the need had a tangible shape with little arms reaching up, begging. The arms would fall back and a sense of peace would fill her body only after she had stuffed herself with the leafy vegetable.

The lettuce period had passed (she had found a "custom canner" who had prepared fifty heads of lettuce for her at an enormous price) only to be followed by a fruit period and a protein period. During each period she had been sure that one food alone was saving her from starvation and dissolution. Finally, she had managed to achieve a synthesis, when she realized that all elements of food were necessary to build up strength. This, in turn, became as much of an obsession as the others and she would be vaguely worried all day if she hadn't had the proper proportion of carbohydrate or protein. Sometimes she would get up in the middle of the night, sick with anxiety, and eat a dish of Brussels sprouts in order properly to balance her diet.

All of this was a preparation for that inevitable day when she would be called on for all her strength and courage. That day had come and found Hanna—an accumulation of many hundreds of planned meals—sitting in a chair, munching melba toast and drinking delicately from a lightly sugared cup of tea.

After her meal she washed the dishes carefully and put them back in their proper places, but this was all the work she could get herself to do. For a while she wandered around

153

the house aimlessly. She stopped sometimes in the middle of a room and stood perfectly still for as long as half an hour. Lunchtime passed and still she couldn't shake off the lethargy which possessed her.

Spaced in between these reveries, during which she thought and felt nothing, were moments of dizzying panic. Once, she headed toward her door, determined to put an end to everything by facing the murderer. She felt that she could not go another moment without knowing what was being planned—where the next attack would be made. Then, as she had her hand on the table ready to pull it away from the door, the thought that the murderer might be waiting for her in the hall, that this very panic of hers was part of the plan, stopped her and drove her back into the lonely safety of her rooms.

Once, she was convinced that the murderer had somehow got in. She had been standing in the middle of her living room, staring at the worn spot on her carpet, when she woke to the feeling of eyes watching her. Her back was toward the bedroom and she knew, with an absolute intuitive certainty, that the killer was standing in the doorway of the bedroom, watching her. She was expected to make the first move. She would break and run and then be caught. She did not dare move from where she stood.

Then she felt the murderer creeping up behind her. She gauged the time it would take to cross the room and, in her mind, she watched the heavy club as it was raised silently in the air behind her. This, now, would be her last earthly thought. When the club struck she would fall down and down into a kind of darkness she had never seen. All of the while she imagined this she could not move. She could not face the killer and, in this reluctance to look into the eyes of the monster, there was a touch of pity. Yes, she thought, I could not bear to see those eyes again.

At another time during that afternoon she was overcome by a great rage. It was the first time she had ever

154

been really angry in her life, and the feeling was intoxicating, almost like drinking a very harsh liquor. She raised her hand and slapped the empty air, first with the palm and then with the knuckles. In her mind, these motions were given twenty times their actual power and she saw the murderer's face beneath her hand, bloody and bruised. She continued to strike out at that countenance, and the more pity and the more horror she felt at the wounds she was inflicting, the harder she struck. She wanted to hurt as she had never hurt anyone before. She wanted to make that face into a pulp.

As she stood there in the empty room, pummeling the air, her own face twisted into an angry mask which she would never have recognized as her own. She swore and spit out obscene words which she was hardly aware that she knew. Finally, on a cry from her throat, which was more like the screech of a jungle animal, this fantasy, too, left her and she sank limply into her chair, more helpless and frightened than ever.

Of all the delicate things in the world, the most susceptible to destruction is time itself. Time is time only in fiction, where the world runs according to plan and the clock is the master of the day. In the minds of lovers and murderers, beloved and murdered, a clock is pitifully inadequate to measure what it sees.

As Hanna sat quietly in her chair on this afternoon she saw more of herself and her life than she had ever seen before. A single tick of the clock in her bedroom, which had always considered itself inexorable, inelastic, was sufficient for her to travel back and forth in her life, like a passenger on a crack train. Like a passionate sightseer she sped through childhood and adolescence and middle age, not making the mistake this time of saying, "Oh, that was fine" or "That was horrible." Now she drew no conclusions, had no opinions. She merely watched, and understood.

It became clear to her why she was trapped in her room

and why she had been afraid all her life of what was now happening. It was not possible to put these things into words. It was not possible to say exactly what had happened or what would happen, but nevertheless she saw, with clarity, the whole question her life had posed, and its inevitable answer. She knew that she must fight now what she had always run away from. She could not be certain that she would lose—she did not want to lose—but then she knew that she could not entirely win this battle. Something would be lost, and that was why she had put off the fight for so long.

She remembered, now, the beginning of a poem she had found in a book Arthur had brought her.

> *I fled Him, down the nights and down the days;*
> *I fled Him, down the arches of the years;*
> *I fled Him, down the labyrinthine ways*
> *Of my own mind; and in the mist of tears. . . .*

Toward the late afternoon, while she was still trying to gather enough strength to go on with her housework, she suddenly began to smell sandalwood. At first it came in quiet little waves which broke over her rather pleasantly and disappeared. Each wave was a little stronger than the one before.

Hanna kept no perfumes and had not smelled sandalwood since she was a little girl. It was the odor of her mother. She had died when Hanna was a child, but her father had kept all his wife's clothes intact in their closets. Hanna used to play in her mother's room when her father was away, and the odor of sandalwood had remained strong in her mother's clothes all through her childhood.

Now it seemed as if her own clothes and even her hands were saturated with it. She got up from her chair and went into the kitchen. Here, it was very faint and what trace of it she smelled seemed to be that which clung to her own body. She went back through the living room. The mo-

156

ment she passed through the door of the bedroom the odor stifled her and made an acrid brown taste in her mouth.

She breathed heavily, although each breath only increased the suffocating sensation. The odor seemed to come from the closet, and she could almost see the fumes of it rising from the crack beneath the door. For a moment it occurred to her that there was someone or something in the closet which was causing the odor, and this irrational thought was superseded by the equally irrational idea that she was not in her own bedroom at all but in that old room of her mother's. The smell grew more powerful and Hanna braced herself against any such wild thoughts. Am I going insane? she thought. Have I finally begun to lose my mind and is this the way it will feel? She looked around the room, wondering if she would find any other symptoms of her madness, but her sight, at least, was not affected. She saw nothing in the bedroom that hadn't been there before, nor did she hear anything new or strange. Only her sense of smell seemed to have been affected. The odor increased with every second and seemed, by its very force and insistence, to imply something ominous.

Hanna retreated into the living room, but here too the odor had grown more intense. It hung, thickly, in the air and invisible clouds of it enveloped her head. She knew that she would have to stop it somehow. If it were a dream she must wake up, and if she were really losing her mind then she must know how far it was to go.

She turned and went back into the bedroom. The poisonous air caught in her throat. As she approached the closet she felt the odor resisting the force of her body, as if it were slowly turning the air into a kind of jelly. It was becoming a solid, something tangible which would encase her in a mold. She must stop it. She must find the source of the odor and destroy it. She threw open the door of the closet and, with one hand held tightly over her face,

157

groped among the silk and woolen dresses. The heavy, suffocating essence of that long-remembered odor descended over her head and shoulders and wrapped her in a deadly embrace. Hanna fought her way back to her bed and lost consciousness.

Chapter 14

SHE awoke suddenly and was already struggling to get off the bed before the noise penetrated her consciousness. She ran into the living room, vaguely aware that she must have been out for a long time, since it was dark outside. There, beside the little dining table which was pushed so pitifully against the door, lay the broken vase. Frantically she braced both arms against the door to hold it shut. Thank God she had heard the crash. As long as the night chain held she was safe.

Gradually she became aware that nothing was going to happen. The murderer had either been frightened away or the vase had fallen by itself. Yes, that could have happened. She had been so afraid it wouldn't fall that she had balanced it too close to the edge and it had been pushed off by some minute tremor in the building. She relaxed her arms cautiously and looked down at the shattered relic.

Could she have imagined everything? Why was she so certain that it was David's murderer who was after her? The knock on the door and the telephone call might have been Arthur. He might even have been the one who had tried to open her door. After all, she had not called him for several days and he might have thought she was sick.

With her own fear and the shock she had suffered at David's death she might easily have begun to imagine that there was some plot against her which didn't really exist at all. How typical of her this would be. How often she had done it before, though never quite so violently.

But if it had been Arthur why hadn't he identified himself? Why hadn't he left her a note on the first night when he had knocked at her door if he thought she was hiding and didn't know who he was? Why, especially, today when he was trying to raise the night chain with the pencil, didn't he call out to her when she had pushed the door shut?

The pencil! Yes, part of the pencil had broken when the door had slammed. She crouched down beside the shattered vase to look for it. It was gone.

She searched all over the floor. She crawled under the little table on her hands and knees and squinted along the baseboard to each end of the room. Her alternative now was even worse than before. If the pencil were not here it meant that it had never been here and that meant . . .

Hanna got up and went into the bedroom. She opened the closet and held one of her dresses to her face. Nothing but the cool, clean odor of cloth, and the room itself had the odor which was so familiar to her that she could call it no odor at all. Nowhere was there even the faintest trace of sandalwood. Had it all been in her mind? Had something so overpoweringly physical been entirely in her imagination? This was the only answer, and if this were true could she trust anything else which had "happened" to her?

Had she had her breakfast this morning? Perhaps she had merely lain in bed and imagined moving around to prepare it and then had imagined the taste of it. Did she have any clothes on now? She could counterfeit one sense, perhaps she had been doing the same with all the others. The touch of cloth on her back—was that real? Were her

159

eyes registering colors which weren't there? Could she now swear that she had gone to a party the other night? Was it conceivable that she had known a man named David Hammer and that he had been murdered?

Hanna rushed over to the *Life* Magazine which lay open beside her chair. Staring up at her was the face of the murderer. She read the caption beneath it again but what had once seemed to her to be absolute proof meant nothing now. Even the eyes of this person she had thought was to be her murderer looked at her impersonally, like all the other eyes in the other photographs. Perhaps she had merely seen this face and built up the rest of the story around it. Possibly, if she searched through the rest of the magazine, she would find David's picture and all the others she thought she had met. She went frantically through her magazine, and for a moment she thought she saw the woman she had noticed on the subway in a group of faces behind Marshal Tito.

Where was there an end to it? How could one tell if anything was true or false? If she had gone mad she must make absolutely certain. But how could she prove anything when she herself would have to be the judge? She would make a test. She would *try* to imagine something. She would sit down on her bed and try to imagine that she was doing a perfectly ordinary thing which she wasn't really doing at all.

She imagined that she was taking a bath. First she turned on both faucets but the water didn't come out right away and she had to imagine the turning over again. She adjusted the temperature of the water and began to brush her hair up, but before she had finished the water was already high enough in the tub. She imagined turning the faucets off but the water continued to rise. She closed her eyes tight so that the picture was very clear and turned hard at the faucets. The water rose inexorably.

Hanna began to feel a little sick. She clutched at the spread on the bed and in her mind she struggled with the

160

useless faucets. The water came over the edge of the tub and splashed onto the bathroom floor. Her feet began to get wet and still she could not turn off the mocking water. At last, she opened her eyes, grateful for the solid reality of her bedroom; but still, somewhere in the back of her mind, an uncontrollable tub sloshed its contents recklessly on a bathroom floor.

Her head ached and she felt very tired. What did it matter, really, whether this was all in her imagination or whether it was happening? Her life had become unbearable either way. What difference could it possibly make if one's life were really in danger or if one only thought it was? The result was the same—panic. The dying could be nothing compared to that.

She had to face it all now. If she started from the very beginning, when she had slipped from her rooms and had gone downstairs and out into the street, she could not absolutely swear that any of it had truly happened. Perhaps, after thirty-four years of living alone, her mind had broken loose. Perhaps it could serve her now with smells and sights and sounds which did not exist. She had often imagined things—had spent most of her life in this occupation, in fact—but she had always known she was imagining. But now, after smelling an odor which couldn't possibly be in her rooms—and smelling it so perfectly and clearly, without the slightest doubt of its character—she could not be certain any longer what was dream and what was fact.

For the first time she could envy the perfect confidence of a sane person, could be jealous of a certain lightness of fancy she had once had. A person who has begun to doubt his reason cannot afford to be childishly fanciful. Whatever is imagined might come true.

She saw now how it all might have happened. David might never have existed and all her little adventures on that night might have been nothing but a kind of advanced hallucination which had carried her out into a world she had never really dared to visit. And now, while she was waiting for a nonexistent murderer to break in on her, she was treated by her mind to a series of real shocks in which she heard telephones ring, saw her door opened by an imaginary key, and knew who the murderer of a non-existent dead man was because she had seen a picture in *Life*.

And the magazine itself—Arthur might have delivered it. Yes. Arthur might have come and gone just as he had always done. Her life may have gone on as always, with Arthur picking up the dishes of the last meal when he left while she had been buried deep in a dream of her own making. This was what it meant to be mad. And yet, if this were true, how could she tell it to herself now? Perhaps this was a moment of sanity before another attack. She buried her head in her cold hands and began to sob.

She clutched her forehead tightly at the sound of the loud banging on her door. It persisted with a kind of gleeful urgency.

Above the noise a man's voice cried: "Fire! Fire! Everybody out!"

Chapter 15

MARY hadn't liked it. There were few enough times she really came right out and asked for something he couldn't give her. Whenever his hours were irregular she always understood, but not this time.

She had wanted him to go to late Mass with her. Naturally, she could go with George and Lily but it wasn't the same. This might be the last time they could go together before the child came and she had some idea that this was already part of the little one's education. The early Masses were so crowded that they would have to wait outside for an hour before they could get a seat. She had wanted to do that, finally, but Kevin wouldn't let her. He had left, feeling about as low and worthless as he had ever felt in his life.

Accordingly, the two witnesses he was to interview dropped in his estimation. They assumed the position in his mind of "that lousy Communist" and "those rich little snobs," although Boleyn hadn't struck him as being like any Communist he had ever heard about and the Coburg-James pair hadn't been snobs in the least. These were distinctions too fine for Kevin to make on a blasted Sunday, with Mary at home—perhaps crying!

Kevin stopped at Centre Street first and was even further put out to learn that no one had succeeded in finding any kind of lead on Margot Case. The only bit of new information which had been discovered concerned David Hammer. The name was an alias. His real name had been Eddie Costello.

When Kevin arrived in Yorkville, the Communist Party, as represented by Vivian Boleyn, was easily on the top of his list of likely suspects. He found the apartment building and rang the bell downstairs ominously.

When the buzzer sounded he pushed the street door open with a bang, nearly hitting an old man who was coming out with a little camp chair to catch the morning sun. He began the long climb to the top floor. God, he thought, why did people live in a rotten place like this when for practically the same money they could live out in Queens.

A plump, youngish woman opened the door. She smiled and asked him to come in when he explained who he was. When he stepped inside he smelled Sunday morning bacon.

Kevin followed her awkwardly down the long hall from

163

which a number of boxlike rooms jutted. At the end of the hall was a cluster which was formed by a living room and a dining room and still another square which seemed to be used as a child's playroom. Altogether, with no partitions, the three rooms would hardly have made one large living room. The young woman led Kevin through a pair of French doors which took almost one whole wall of the living room and, leading him between a card table and a footstool, seated him in a large, comfortable chair.

"Vivian! That detective's here to see you," she called. From the way she said "that detective" Kevin knew he had been discussed and that she was not surprised to see him. She certainly did not seem to be upset by a detective's presence.

She turned to him and her smooth little face dimpled. "How about some coffee?"

Kevin started to frown in a manner which would suggest that a policeman on duty does not accept favors from those he is investigating, but before he could put this rather ponderous idea across she was speeding from the room.

A door banged at the end of the hall and presently a child appeared. He was about six. He stared at Kevin speculatively, not being old enough yet to know that he didn't have to wait for a parent to say "Why don't you say hello?" before he said hello.

"Hello," Kevin said, nervously.

"Hello."

The boy eyed him uncritically, turned and walked into the playroom.

What the devil was keeping Boleyn?

Mrs. Boleyn returned with a tray which held a cup of coffee and a plate of rolls.

"I made these rolls this morning," she said happily. "Eat as many as you want. There are plenty more. Heavens! I forgot the sugar." She disappeared down the hall again.

Kevin was left holding the little painted tray. The

164

fragrant steam from the coffee and the smell of the hot rolls made him realize how hungry he was. He set the tray down on the card table and guiltily picked up one of the rolls. They had been broken open and a fast-melting pat of butter nested in each.

"Here we are! Now you just go ahead and eat there before everything gets cold."

In spite of her youth, there was an overtone of confident motherliness in her voice which assured Kevin that the rolls would be excellent and that the coffee would have just the right amount of body. He mumbled his thanks and bit into a roll.

She watched him eagerly and Kevin felt his face express appreciation in spite of himself. If Inspector Dayton were to walk in now and find him having breakfast in the home of one of the chief suspects he would be fired on the spot.

"Oh, but you must try some of the jam. It's not store jam. I made it from some real blackberries we picked at Mohegan Lake."

He tried the jam, which was wonderful, and tasted the coffee, the best he'd had in years—though he didn't consciously compare it to Mary's.

Mrs. Boleyn took all of this in and, seeing that she had scored again, leaned back contentedly in her straight-backed chair.

Kevin was confused. Not only by Mrs. Boleyn but by this curious little room which was filled with bric-à-brac and old souvenirs of a seaman's travels. There was an air of aggressive domesticity here. Kevin felt that the home of a Communist ought decently to be barer and more utilitarian. And Mrs. Boleyn should have been a large-boned, plain-faced, efficient woman, instead of this excitable little creature with crisp, newly made, blond curls on her head. Also, he had rather expected a large picture of Stalin or Molotov. Instead there was a print of Van Gogh's "Sunflowers."

Kevin picked up another roll and spread it thickly with

165

jam. He felt rather like a greedy little boy. As long as he was hungry he might as well eat, he reasoned, since he had made the mistake of taking the food in the first place.

He looked up again at Mrs. Boleyn and realized that she was positively rejoicing in his appetite. Did she really suppose that she could protect her husband this way? No, he decided. That wasn't it at all. This was merely what she did for anyone who came into the house, male or female, whether they came early in the morning or late at night. She didn't really think of him as a policeman. She was one of those people who see others only as mouths and taste buds and stomachs. Her mission in the world was to feed. This was her politics. She would approve of her husband's activities if only because they brought so many hungry people to the house.

Vivian Boleyn entered. He was wearing slippers, old tweed trousers and an open-necked shirt which was far too white to have been washed anywhere but at home. He stood in the doorway, very straight and slight, and there was something about him which reminded Kevin of the child who had just passed through the room.

"Good morning, Lieutenant." He did not seem to think it strange to find the policeman eating breakfast.

"G'morning Boleyn," Kevin said, swallowing whole the rest of his roll.

Boleyn's face looked newly scrubbed and there was a tight glaze on his jaw which indicated that he had just shaved. He seemed in excellent spirits and a spit of damp hair curled up exuberantly from the side of his head. For a moment Kevin was jealous. Here was a man spending a comfortable Sunday at home, while he had to tramp around the city, far from his own home, to solve a mystery which was none of his making.

Mrs. Boleyn stood up. "Now, if you'll both excuse me I've got some work to do."

She beamed at Kevin and as she passed Vivian she stopped long enough to straighten the back of his shirt collar. At that moment Kevin found it difficult to believe that this was the man who had been described as a ruthless official of the seaman's union. However, as Boleyn moved to sit down, Kevin recognized the lithe movement of a professional fighter. In spite of his small body and rather childlike face, the man immediately commanded a certain amount of physical respect.

From the playroom came the sound of a playing chant, the kind children sing to themselves when they think no one is listening.

"That's your kid, isn't it?"

"Yes, has he been bothering you?"

There was in this remark, Kevin saw, a kind of casual lack of interest in the child which unsuccessfully attempted to cover the really towering pride the father felt in his son.

The boy could be seen through the door of the little room next to theirs, pushing a toy fire engine.

"Clang dang! Clang dang! Save all the people or they'll burn away! Up that ladder way high. Save that madam! Clang dang. Send more cars!"

"Nice kid. Does he go to school around here?"

"Just up the street. Highest marks in his class."

The attempt at modesty was abandoned and Vivian Boleyn watched the young man with the fire engine as if he were certainly the most miraculous creation on earth.

Kevin wondered if he would ever get to feel this way about his own child. Probably would. Probably human nature. Suddenly he wondered how he would feel if Boleyn turned out to be the murderer. What if he had to arrest the boy's father? Damn it! It was none of his business thinking about things like this. He had a job to do and he was going to do it. All at once he was blaming the whole thing on Boleyn. What right had this fellow to go around getting himself mixed up with Communists and unions and all those other things when he had a family to take care of? If he were alone, well that was his own business, but with a wife and a kid . . .

167

"How long have you known Eddie Costello?"

"So you found out."

"Yes, 'so I found out,'" Kevin mocked. "Just answer my questions. How long did you know him and why didn't you tell me his right name?"

"I didn't think it made much difference—telling you his right name, I mean," Vivian said, mildly. "I knew him when I was a kid, but only to say hello to."

"How did you first get to know him?" Kevin quieted down. He was here for information. No use trying to pick a fight.

"We both grew up on the upper West Side and we both went to the same parochial school. You know how it is. You get to know quite a bit about a fellow without ever actually being friends with him."

"What was he like?"

"He was the kind of guy who would do anything on a dare. Kid stuff, you know—like climbing the suspension cable on the George Washington Bridge, or jumping from a second-story apartment window onto a mattress. He used to break into stores at night and steal little things, not for himself so much but just to show off."

"Anything serious?"

"Well, you never knew about him. He used to get into lots of fights. Not the kind of fights young kids have, either. I saw him face five fellows once, over in Highbridge, with nothing but a broken bottle in his hand. Not one of them would go near him. They probably wouldn't have minded being cut up a bit if they could have got in a couple of licks of their own, but David was the kind who went for the eyes."

"Did you ever tangle with him?"

"Not when I was a kid, I didn't. Only later on. I suppose you know all about that."

There was a question in Boleyn's voice, and Kevin could see that he was trying to decide just how much he should tell.

168

"I know most of Hammer's activities since he joined the Communist Party in 1937," Kevin said, truthfully, "but I'd rather have the story in your own words."

For a moment Vivian hesitated. He was obviously reluctant to bring the Communist Party into the story at all. Then he smiled and showed his perfect readiness to talk. There was something so open and honest about Vivian's face that Kevin had to remind himself that he was not dealing with a child but with a man whose cleverness and cunning were respected by people much more acute than himself. Boleyn had obviously decided that there was no point in withholding a story which was already known and, going even further, had decided to tell it with the greatest show of co-operation possible.

"When I met him the second time he had just come into the seaman's union. He had got a hell of a lot smoother. First of all, he seemed to have discovered that he couldn't fight everyone so he worked just as hard in the opposite direction."

Vivian stood up and began to walk back and forth, not nervously but because he didn't seem to be used to talking while sitting down. He passed in front of a Malay mask and Kevin suddenly had a picture of this wiry, well-scrubbed little man in Malaya, talking to a group of natives in the same earnest manner. Without knowing why, it seemed a little funny.

"You never saw a man work so hard at making friends. He seemed to have a knack for it too. If one of his shipmates was feeling sorry for himself, David would be around to listen and sympathize. If the guy wanted to go out and get drunk, David would go along with him and bring him home at the end of the night and put him to bed. It wasn't so much what he did as the way he did it. He could make you think he was the only one in the world who felt just the way you did about things. He even fooled me a couple of times."

Vivian took a wicker basket of apples from a table and

offered one to Kevin. He rolled one into the playroom for his son and picked out one for himself. He stood beneath a machete, which hung from the side wall, and bit out a great chunk which he proceeded to chew enthusiastically. Once again Kevin marveled that this man was not only to be considered a potential murderer but a dangerous radical. He looked more like Tom Sawyer at that moment.

"I've worked with those fellows a long time and I know pretty much how they react. Some guy listens to their troubles for half an hour and if he's smart he can get them to pay him back five times what the listening was worth. It works out all right most of the time because if a guy is friendly it's because he really feels that way; but David expected to be paid back every last cent on his investment, with compound interest.

"In a little while David had built up quite a back-log of popularity and he began to look around for a place to use it. He decided on the Communist Party. That may seem peculiar to you in these days, but then we were in the middle of the depression and a lot of people saw the revolution coming in a few months, or years at the most. David wanted to get in on the ground floor."

Kevin remembered David's face as he had seen it for the first time. He remembered that he had thought it a likable face, even marred as it was by the awful wound. Every one of these people, for their own reasons, had grown to despise David—they did not even try to hide it —and yet, wasn't it after all their own fault? They all took what they wanted from him when he offered it. It was only when he began to demand repayment that they found they hated him. Zimmer had asked for help with the Communists, Theodora Dennis had asked for marriage, Boleyn and his Party—they had probably asked for something too.

"There's no point in going into this thing deeply," Vivian continued in a rather professorial tone, "but I suspect that the old Party members' hopes were a good

170

deal less sanguine than David's. Their immediate objective was not so much Communism in America as Communists in America. David had a big following in the union and we wanted him with us. Even then I felt there was something fishy about him but the only way you can find these things out is to try. In the meantime the other members felt he could do some good recruiting for us."

"Had you been a member of the Communist Party very long at this time?"

"Not long."

"And did you, also, think the revolution was about to come?"

Vivian smiled and Kevin knew that this was a question he would not answer. The subject was a strange one to Kevin in the first place, and he felt a little uncomfortable in it. Sometimes he and George had talked about Communism and they had repeated to each other some things they had read in the newspapers, but neither one had been very much interested. George had once done some work for the Democratic Party in Queens, but that was about as close as either one of them had got to politics.

Since he had entered this case Kevin had tried particularly hard not to let political opinions influence his judgments. He was after the man or the woman who had smashed David Hammer's head with his own statue. If he allowed his attention to veer off into politics he knew that he would never get anywhere.

"Why did Costello change his name?"

"Hammer was the name he used in the Party. He was still known as Costello in the union."

"You said you tangled with Hammer. How did that happen?"

"We were both running for a small office in the local. The Party ordered David to quit and back me so that we wouldn't split our votes. It wasn't an important office— just an honor, really—but David wouldn't stand for it."

"Would you have quit and supported him?"

171

"I would."

"Then why didn't the Party switch from you and back him?"

"That's just what David hoped would happen. He knew we wanted the post for someone in the Party, and he reasoned that if he held out a little while he'd come out on top. That's not the way we work. Blackmail doesn't pay anyone. It was worth losing the election to find out about David before he got where he could really do some damage."

"You lost the election then?"

"Yes. I lost and David lost. He never forgave that. He thought I had cheated him out of what was rightfully his. A few months later he disappeared—quit the union. The next we heard of him he was a 'newspaperman.' "

Kevin swore to himself. Every time he tried to get this story on a personal level, Boleyn dragged it back into the land of politics—a land where everything was right if you believed and everything wrong if you didn't. To a Communist Boleyn's story would probably sound perfectly reasonable and right, but how would it sound to a man like Barton Zimmer?

"David became a professional anti-Communist."

Vivian spoke these words with a boundless contempt as if this were the lowest thing in the world. It is to him, of course, Kevin thought, but there are others who would say that a Communist was the lowest thing. It all depends where you're standing. At this moment Kevin wasn't exactly sure where he stood.

"Hammer's column bore down pretty heavily on you personally, didn't it?" Kevin said.

"Yes."

"And that made a lot of trouble for you."

"In the union, it didn't. All the men know I'm a Communist. They're only interested in how I do my work. That's what I'm being paid for."

172

"Still, you would have liked to have him out of the way."

"And this is my motive for killing him? I'm afraid you'll have to prove that."

"Oh no. I have a much more direct reason for your killing him. He was trying to blackmail you."

Vivian returned to his chair. His face was impassive but his body was suddenly tight.

"I found this information in the papers you were looking for when you came back to Hammer's apartment after everyone had left on the night of the murder." Kevin was not absolutely sure that Vivian had come back, but it was worth assuming.

In Vivian's silence his guess was confirmed. The boyish affability in his host's face had gone and in its place was a look of tired caution. For the first time Boleyn looked his age and Kevin could now believe that this man sitting before him was the trained revolutionary he had expected to find.

"This, of course, explains why you didn't inform the police of the murder immediately. After you didn't find what you were looking for you had no other choice but to call."

Vivian remained silent. The cozy domesticity of the room, with its implication of a happy young family enjoying a Sunday at home, seemed to have dissolved away like a good dream. Kevin realized now that it was the conscious expression, by a fatigued, aging, determined little man, of a kind of life he could never really have or enjoy.

"Hammer's data contained a great deal of information about you and the activities of the Communist Party in the seaman's union. I don't know how much is true or how much is false. What interests me most is a series of letters he had written you—and several replies of your own—in which he is shown to have been trying to blackmail you.

173

"For a large amount of money—he suggested that you could lay your hands on this money very easily as treasurer of the seaman's union—he promised to let up his attacks on you and to destroy a piece of paper he had. This paper, an affidavit signed by a woman who claimed to be your mother and verified by several witnesses, states that you were born in Australia."

"There is no proof of any of this!" Vivian's voice was low but it had a stinging quality which made it sharply audible.

"I'm not concerned with proving it," Kevin said. "I merely know that your replies to his letters showed that you were disturbed at his possession of such information."

"Of course I was disturbed. That doesn't necessarily prove the information was true!"

"At any rate, the document states that you were taken to this country when you were a child, that you were brought in illegally from Mexico, and that you were given to a young couple by the name of Boleyn who raised you as their own son. Your real mother, according to this, seems to have felt that you were too much of a burden."

"I think you must know enough about Hammer now, Lieutenant, to realize that this was just his kind of trick; that he would take great pains to have a document like this forged so that he could have a hold on his victim. David couldn't bear to have relations with anyone without having some trump card like this tucked away. The paper is false and you know it."

"I don't know it and by the tone of your letters I think even you weren't so sure it was not the truth. The point is, as Hammer made clear, that this information, together with corroborative evidence which he was willing to furnish, would have interested the FBI. He said—and you seemed to be worried that he was right—that they could have had you deported as an illegal alien."

"That's not as easy as it sounds."

Kevin leaned forward. Now, he felt, was the time to

174

press him. "I didn't come here to talk about this. Maybe they can deport you and maybe they can't. That's not my business. Please tell me, now, exactly what happened when you went to Hammer's study during the party."

Vivian hesitated a minute. Suddenly his whole manner changed. His face once again assumed an air of boyish frankness and his voice seemed to promise great intimacy. Only his eyes remained cold and searching.

"Frankly, I *was* worried about the paper David had forged. You see, I was unfortunate enough to have been born in a town which, up to twenty-five years ago, didn't issue birth certificates; and any lie like this, backed up by the kind of false witnesses I knew David would produce, would be likely to give me a lot of trouble. When he asked me to come to his house I knew that it was to discuss this, and I went into his study hoping to find out from him exactly what kind of a case he had built up against me.

"I spoke to him for a while and told him that of course I would not be blackmailed by him. He threatened to take the information to the FBI and I told him to go ahead. There was nothing else I could do. Then I left. That was the last time I saw him alive."

"You left him how? Dead?"

"I did not kill him. I can't say I'm sorry that someone else killed him, but I didn't do it."

"You said you were the first one to leave the room to visit Hammer?"

"I don't know if I was the first but I know that I went very shortly after David left the room and I remember that Barton Zimmer went after me, not before."

"At what time did you come back to the apartment after the party was over?"

"About two o'clock. You are quite right, I did return. In the same position I don't believe you would have acted differently. I wanted that paper if it was there. With David dead it was not as dangerous to me as it would have been otherwise, but it was worth taking the chance to get

175

it back. Naturally, I didn't want myself or the Party involved in this cheap murder at all. I assure you, we have enough to worry about."

"Did you know that he was still alive when you came back?"

Vivian was startled. "No—I didn't. My God!"

"He didn't die until five the next morning. You were very fortunate that he was killed, weren't you? In fact, it looks as if you gave fortune a little help."

Vivian looked up angrily. "Well—what's keeping you?"

"Keeping me from what?"

"From arresting me and announcing to the newspapers that the Red Killer of a distinguished newspaperman has been captured after a furious hand-to-hand struggle. You've seen the newspapers this morning. They're already full of David's murder. His own paper has probably got every one of its reporters out on the streets looking for a Communist to pin it on. You wouldn't have to do a thing. Arrest me and the newspapers would have me tried and hung in three days."

Kevin floundered upright in the awkward, overstuffed chair. His huge, healthy body, which would have counted for so much in a free-for-all fight or in some other appropriate police activity, made him look clumsy in this tiny, cluttered room.

"God damn it!" he shouted. "Any more of that kind of talk from you and I will arrest you. I work like hell to keep politics out of this thing and you come along with your lousy insinuations! Is it my fault you're a Communist? I didn't ask you to get mixed up in this, did I? I'm trying to find the murderer of David Hammer and none of your complaints about persecution are going to help you a bit if I find you killed him!

"I deliberately kept the names of all the suspects out of the papers and I would have withheld the fact that there was a murder at all if I could. I want you to understand that I'm not explaining anything to you. I don't

176

have to explain a damn thing—especially to you. If I come here with an order for your arrest you'll know it's because I have positive evidence that you are a murderer. Personally, I think you are!"

Kevin stood up and his thigh bumped against the tray which still held the empty coffee cup and the empty plate. He caught it before it fell, making a great deal of clatter.

"Where's my hat!" he said, already finding his anger beginning to vanish and feeling awkward in this ridiculously small room.

Vivian rose and held out his hand. "Good-by, Lieutenant. Your hat's in the hall. I'll get it."

Kevin followed him down the hall, and as they passed the kitchen Mrs. Boleyn poked her doll-like head out and smiled hospitably at Kevin.

"Oh, dear! Are you going so soon? Sure you won't have another cup of coffee? I can fix it in a second."

"No, thank you," Kevin muttered.

"Well, come back again. Don't stand on ceremony. Good-by!"

Kevin took his hat from the slim little man in the white shirt and left without answering the good woman.

Chapter 16

KEVIN stopped before the small, private house on East Sixty-seventh Street. The surface it presented to the street was perfectly square. One entire side of the square was composed of opaque, bluish glass brick. It didn't really look like much in the way of a house but Kevin recognized it as "modern"—Mary had shown him one like it in *House Beautiful*—and he knew immediately that it had cost as much to build as five ordinary homes. It was sandwiched in between two heavy-doored mansions, the kind that look more like gentlemen's clubs than houses, and seemed somehow defiant and out of place.

The door was almost flush with the street and it gave him the odd feeling that the house after it had been built had settled into the ground about three feet. Compared to his own house—or half a house—it was extremely uninviting. He rang the bell beside a small plaque which said "Coburg-James."

As he waited he found it difficult to remember what either of them looked like. He knew that they were both good-looking and athletic with fair complexions, but he only remembered himself using these words about them when they had been in his office; he didn't remember *them* at all. Each member of this strange couple had tried so hard to efface himself and be like the other that they had succeeded merely in leaving no definite impression of themselves at all.

The door opened and an old woman in black faced him. She listened grimly to his request, asked his name, and closed the door in his face. A few moments later Sandy Coburg-James greeted him.

"Come in, Lieutenant. We've been expecting you. Have you any news?"

He had forgotten, entirely forgotten, how beautiful she was. Kevin wasn't more than usually flirtatious but now he found himself stepping through the door with a kind of extra swagger. He was conscious of smiling too broadly and when he took off his hat he could hardly keep his hand from straightening his tie or from smoothing down his hair.

She took his hat and hung it in the closet. Every movement she made had a physical grace compared to which the sluggish maneuvers of other people to get from place to place were merely pathetic. Kevin remembered now that her husband had the same fluid way of moving.

"I'm sorry Maggie kept you waiting outside. She thinks it's her job to defend us from everyone."

They were standing in a foyer and Kevin suddenly found himself staring at a bristling metallic object which hung from the ceiling. It seemed to be some kind of fish or bird with many fins mounted at the end of long wires and with three or four oddly placed wings. Slightly above the mass, suspended from a piece of wire by a thread, was something which looked like an eye. All of the parts were balanced in relation to each other and swung around crazily, a wing or a fin sometimes rising above the eye.

"Like it?"

"MMMmmmmmmm," said Kevin.

"You know what it is, don't you?"

"Not exactly," he said, feeling that it was best to confess his ignorance now in case she had still more of them.

"It's a mobile. You see how it moves on its own weight. We were very lucky to get it. We can look at it later if you like," she said, leading him into the room off the foyer.

Kevin was more than grateful to be taken away from the object but he was a little depressed to find Peter Coburg-James in the next room. He might, after all, have been out of the house, in which case Kevin would have had to postpone this disagreeable interview with the two of them.

Peter was out of his chair and across the room, holding out his smooth brown hand, before Kevin could say hello. His grip was neither too strong nor weak and, in spite of his friendly manner, he seemed to retain an air of aloofness which was as invulnerable as it was unconscious.

Like its inhabitants, the room was graceful, light and removed, somehow, from any kind of life Kevin had ever known. A soft, faintly blue light illuminated the room through the glass brick front, and high above—the walls of the room rose uninterrupted for two stories—a partly

179

shuttered skylight filtered the sun for the benefit of those below.

The furniture contained none of the intimate frills and curlicues that Kevin was used to. All of the table legs dived straight into the pile of the carpet without so much as a hint of a lathe-turned knob or ridge. Some of the chairs couldn't even be said to have legs, being perched instead on top of X-shaped boards. Knowing the tremendous wealth of these two, Kevin was also surprised to see that so much of the furniture was constructed of plywood and canvas. On one wall was a huge mural depicting men engaged in a titanic struggle against some force which didn't seem to be pictured but had something to do with wheels and ratchets and pistons. The ponderousness of this painting didn't destroy the general air of delicacy. In fact its somber grays and blues added a kind of restfulness and peace to the room which might otherwise have been too insubstantial.

"Do you mind the music?" said Sandy, as she indicated that he should sit on a couch which was only a foot above the floor.

"No. No, this will be fine, thank you," he said, apprehensively gauging the distance down.

He squatted as far as he could and let himself drop the rest of the way. The couch was made of some springy substance stretched tightly over the low frame, and his two hundred and ten pounds bounced several times before he was settled. From somewhere in the far corner of the great room came the sound of music. Kevin's knowledge of music was limited but he could recognize Tchaikowsky's Sixth Symphony, Beethoven's Fifth and one or two things of Bach. He decided to take a chance.

"Bach, isn't it?"

Peter looked at Kevin good-naturedly. "I know," he said, "lots of people make jokes about it but even if he doesn't follow the score exactly I think it's a much better recording than Koussevitzky's."

Sandy laughed. "No, silly. He really meant 'Bach, isn't it?' He wasn't being sarcastic." She turned to Kevin. "You'll have to forgive him. I just gave him these records and he thinks everyone is trying to make fun of them."

Kevin was deflated. He had made a prodigious guess and would have been happy enough to know that he had come anywhere near the mark. These people couldn't even conceive of anyone not knowing the composer of a piece. They had shifted their attention to the more abstruse question of what *conductor* was playing. He still didn't know if he had guessed right or not and he decided not to press the point.

Seeing himself here in this room, with his knees jutting up almost to his chin, he realized that he had been at a horrible disadvantage ever since this case began. None of the people he was involved with were playing this thing fair. Oh, he expected lying and deceit and even—he was almost wishing for it now—a certain amount of violence. He had risen to his position because he had a good mind, a pleasing personality, and a strong body. That was enough to handle most sane criminals, but these people were all loonies. What he knew about this couple made them probably the worst of the lot.

Here they were, treating him as if he were paying them a social call when they knew perfectly well that both of them were seriously suspected of committing a brutal murder. As he looked at them now he could not imagine either of them in a jail or being strapped into an electric chair. That was the whole trouble. They couldn't imagine it either. They had lived above the law all their lives and could not imagine anything so sordid as the consequences of a murder penetrating their world, even if they had committed that murder.

Kevin shifted on his couch and found himself staring at Sandy's body as she stretched back comfortably, and with perfect poise, in a plywood chair.

"You should know," he said, "that I have discovered

181

that David Hammer was blackmailing you and that I know why he was."

The lilting string music seemed to grow louder in the silence of the room. The old woman who had kept him at the door came in with a thermador and a pitcher of water. She put them on the kidney-shaped coffee table, glaring at Kevin as she did so, then went to a little cabinet and took out a bottle of whisky and three glasses. She placed these on the table also and left the room.

"What is your relation to each other? I mean your blood relation."

Peter got up and went to the coffee table. He picked up the bottle of whisky and said calmly, "We're cousins."

"None for me, thanks—Hammer claimed you were brother and sister."

Peter filled two glasses, put some ice and a little water in each and handed one to Sandy. He remained standing next to her and Kevin was struck by their really great similarity. It was almost impossible not to believe they were brother and sister, seeing them together like this.

"He would claim anything in the world in order to get money," Sandy said.

"He had photostats of birth certificates, showing that you were both children of the same parents."

"They were forgeries, of course," said Peter. "My mother and father died in an auto accident when I was a child. I was raised by Sandy's parents. That's all there is to it."

"David was in Poland before the war," added Sandy. "He bribed the magistrate in the town I was born in to issue a false birth certificate for Peter in an attempt to prove he was my brother. Before he left America he had met Peter and me at a party. We had just been married and . . ."

"It isn't necessary for us to explain anything. The story is untrue. We don't care to discuss it."

"You don't seem to understand," said Kevin. "I don't

182

happen to be concerned with the legality of your marriage. What interests me much more is the fact that Hammer's records show that one hundred thousand dollars was paid by you to him several years ago and that he recently asked you for another hundred thousand. I would like to know why you went to his party the other evening."

"To pay him another hundred thousand dollars," said Peter, quietly. It seemed to be a physical effort for him to speak of David. Beneath his casually spoken words Kevin could feel a loathing which seemed all out of place in this pleasant young man's character.

"Did you pay it to him?"

"No. When I saw him gloating over his easy victory I just couldn't do it. It wasn't the money at all, but I suddenly knew that he would never stop. I told him he could go to hell."

"What happened then?"

"Nothing happened then!" interrupted Sandy.

"That's quite right. Nothing happened. David laughed and told me he'd let me think it over and then I left."

"You know, of course," said Kevin, "that it's quite natural for me to put another end to that story."

"I've already told you," said Sandy, "that I heard David whistling when I passed his study, and that was long after Peter had gone to see him and had come back into the living room."

"You are just as much of a suspect as your—husband. Perhaps you didn't just pass his study. Perhaps you went in and spoke to him awhile. Perhaps you killed him."

Peter spoke. He made his voice particularly clear as if he were trying to explain a problem to a child and wished to make certain there would be no misunderstanding. "I don't believe you have any proof that either of us was involved in this and if you would look at it sensibly you would see immediately that neither of us would think of doing such a thing, no matter how much we disliked the man."

"Why wouldn't you think of it? I probably would have."

"We aren't as used to crime and violence as you are," said Sandy. "At the very least we could have paid him the money. It would have been more sensible to do that than to expose ourselves to the charge of murder."

Kevin noticed that both of them had the habit of using the word "we" as someone else would use the word "I." It seemed to be difficult for them to think of themselves separately.

Kevin looked at Peter. "But you just told me that when you last saw David you knew that he would never stop blackmailing you. This meant, of course, that merely paying him money was no longer a solution. What was your solution?"

"It was simply to let him go ahead and make whatever trouble he thought he could."

"Why didn't you do that before? One hundred thousand dollars seems a pretty high price to pay merely to avoid a little trouble."

"Things were different five years ago. The war was going on then and we had no idea what was happening in Poland. After the war we learned that David's sources of —misinformation had been destroyed. The false records which he had rigged up had been burned along with all the other records in the town. All David had to show for his research and his careful planting of false records were two photostats with no one to back them up but himself. The most trouble he could have caused was—possibly some disagreeable gossip."

"You are trying to say that you wouldn't have killed Hammer because he could no longer do you any real harm?"

"Exactly."

"Of course, if he were dead he could do you even less harm, aside from the probable pleasure his death would have given you. Also, if he were dead, you would have the opportunity to search his belongings for the last bit of

184

evidence against you—this is what I am certain you did after everyone had left the party. If you had succeeded in getting the photostats and your mutual correspondence you would have destroyed not only the information itself but also your own motive for the murder."

"But since we didn't have anything to do with his death, what's the use of discussing it?" said Sandy.

There was a quality of pleading in Sandy's voice which was a genuine appeal to Kevin to stop talking about this silly business, to have a drink and forget it, perhaps to go out and see the mobile.

Both of them seemed entirely unsuited for this kind of conversation. Somehow the seriousness of his interview had failed to impress them. It was inconceivable to them that this pleasant young detective should really mean them any harm. Peter, at least, would have been perfectly capable of killing David Hammer but he would never for a moment consider it a case of one man killing another. Kevin imagined that, for Peter, it would be rather like killing some troublesome form of lower animal. He wouldn't even consider David as being of the same species as himself.

Seeing them now, so handsome and self-assured, so perfectly formed physically and mentally, they actually did seem to be the vanguard of a new race of men, a race as yet so exclusive that they had been able to choose only themselves as mates.

Peter poured more drinks. The music had changed and now a man was singing something in Italian. The machine which was playing the records seemed to be hidden behind the partition of the far wall.

"I'm afraid we'll have to discuss it," said Kevin. "You seem to forget that's why I'm here."

"Of course I haven't forgotten. It's your job, I know." Sandy spoke the word "job" with emphasis as if she wanted him to understand that she didn't underestimate the importance of "jobs" in other people's lives, although

185

she and Peter, privately, felt such things were a bit over-stressed. "And when you have a job you must do it as well as you can, but we've told you everything we know and I hope we don't have to go over it again."

"What would have happened if David had been able to prove his charges against you?" Kevin said.

"I told you before," said Peter, coldly, "that the charges were false and that he could prove nothing."

"There is a law against—incest." At his use of the word the couple looked at him in a shocked manner which was a comment on his taste. "And I suppose your marriage would have been set aside and you would find yourselves liable to prosecution."

"I believe *he* imagined some such thing." Peter's manner implied that even to be able to imagine it, as Kevin had just done, was to set oneself outside the range of human sympathy.

"From seeing you I can guess that either one of you would commit murder to avoid this."

"Look here!" said Peter, angrily. "There isn't a single statement you have made which you can prove and we would prefer to drop the whole subject. If you can't speak decently I'm afraid you'll have to leave."

"I haven't charged either of you with anything yet, and I'm afraid I'll have to go on speaking, decently or not. Perhaps you don't realize it but if the tabloids were to get hold of this story it would be just about as bad for you as if David Hammer had actually done what he threatened to do. I don't have any desire to persecute innocent people, or for that matter, even guilty people, as long as they're not guilty of the crime I'm interested in. That's why your story hasn't got into the tabloids and that's why it won't as long as I'm in charge of the case. In exchange for this I'm merely asking for information—an easy thing to give if you're innocent of this murder."

As he spoke of tabloids the handsome couple showed more fright than they had at any other time. Here was one

186

terror that never ceased to stalk their perfect world. If they could be considered the advance guard of a new race then this "tabloid" must have held the same peril for them as the mastodon held for primitive man.

"After all, Peter," Sandy interrupted, "this is his job."

"I suppose that's true," said Peter. "Please forgive me. We have been under such a strain with this whole thing. Not only since Hammer's death but long before."

"I understand. I particularly want to know if you can tell me anything about Margot Case."

"We'd never met her before," said Sandy. "I'm afraid we know nothing more about her than what we've already told you."

"You mentioned that she said, just before she left the party, that she knew who the murderer was."

"Well, yes. But I really think she was just hysterical because when we asked her about it she said that she really didn't know and then she ran out."

"Can you describe her to me again?"

"She's very difficult to describe. She was a large woman and looked like any other middle-aged woman except that sometimes there seemed to be something wrong with her—physically, I mean—as if she'd been sick for a long time or as if she weren't used to moving around much. She almost hobbled when she walked. Of course, the only time I saw her walk was when she was really sick, but even when she was sitting down she reminded me of an invalid."

"Can you describe her clothes?"

"Well, she was wearing a brown satin dress, I believe—yes, and I noticed her shoes particularly. They were the old-fashioned button shoes and I remember being surprised that she had such small feet."

"You speak of her now as though she were sick and yet you said before that you thought she would have been capable of picking up a sixty-pound statue.

"Well, she was a big woman, and I don't believe there was anything really wrong with her."

Peter nodded his head to confirm Sandy. "Yes, she would have been able to do it."

"Have you found any trace of her?"

"No," said Kevin, "we haven't. She's disappeared completely."

"Then she must be the one who killed him," said Sandy.

"I'll know when I find her."

"You really believe she did it, don't you?"

"No, I don't believe she did it. She's the only one of all of you who acted normally after the murder was discovered and, more important, she's the only one who didn't have a strong reason for killing Hammer. The only thing I'm worried about is not finding her quickly enough. If she was telling the truth when she said she knew who the murderer was she's in as much danger as Hammer was. Perhaps one of you has found her already."

"One of us!"

"Now really, Lieutenant. I think we've made it perfectly clear that we had nothing to do with this." He stopped. "Listen to that! Magnificent! That's the Bruno Walter version with Pinza. Nothing like it in the whole opera. 'Se—vuol—ball—arrr—eee.'" He followed the singer, beating time to the music with his tinkling glass.

"Maybe we could play something Lieutenant Corelli would like," Sandy said. "Perhaps something by his namesake?" She smiled beautifully at Kevin.

Kevin was suddenly depressed. He thought of Mary waiting for him at home and of the fine trees and occasional patches of lawn before the houses on his street, and he wished that he could be there without having to ride the long distance in a screeching subway car.

Somehow, the sight of this handsome young couple added to his homesickness and he was aware of almost actively disliking them, not because of anything they had done to him but because they seemed so cold toward everything he cared for. They were like two beautiful snakes, sunning themselves in a fine cage. Perhaps they had their

188

own quarrels and snakelike emotions but they felt nothing like what he felt for anyone and nothing like what he would ever feel.

Kevin stood up, a movement which was in this house almost an athletic feat. "I have to go."

"Oh, that's too bad. Sure you won't have a drink before you leave?"

"No, thanks."

"We'll hear from you again, of course."

"Yes."

Sandy preceded him, by her grace making him appear to himself as some sort of lumbering caveman.

As the door closed on him Kevin saw the happy couple standing together under the metal bird-fish. They had begun to speak and Kevin could tell that he was already dismissed from their minds. The monster had been set to jigging in the draft; a fin clattered on a wing and its bottle-glass, blue eye winked merrily in the light.

It was typical of his agitated state of mind that, as he walked briskly up the street to the subway, he should be thinking more of a metallic creature which had seemed to wink at him than about a murder which the State was trusting him to solve. Inspector Dayton would not have approved.

BOOK THREE

Chapter 17

SHE could hear the banging on other doors down the hall. The man's voice shouted the dreadful words over and over.

"Fire! Fire! The building's on fire! Everyone out. Follow me!"

At first there was no response to his ecstatic cry, and for a moment Hanna clung to the hope that he was lying or that he had merely gone out of his mind and would be quieted soon. In that moment the alarmist himself seemed to share her doubts and his repeated warnings began to lose their fanatic conviction. But as soon as the doors began to open and he found himself with the proper kind of audience his voice rose again in dramatic appeal.

"Everybody out! Follow me!"

Now, all of the doors in the hallway except her own seemed to have opened and her neighbors were rushing out. Hanna had always been aware that she had neighbors but she had preferred not to think of it. It was terrifying now to realize that there were so many of them and that they were milling around outside her door.

"For God's sake hurry! This way."

The man who had given the warning was trying to make his voice heard above the screams of the women and the anxious questions of the men. The hysterical note of danger was no longer in his voice. There was, instead, the calm note of authority. Several of the men asked where the fire was. The leader did not seem to hear them.

"Get everyone into line there! For God's sake, shut that woman up! Follow me. There's no danger if we don't get hysterical!"

Hanna lay up against her own door. She could not force herself to open it and join the others. She could not relinquish the idea that her only safety lay in her own rooms and that these frightened people outside were a greater danger to her than even a fire.

The crowd outside seemed to be moving now, toward the stairway.

"Stay in line there! Two of you men bring up the rear. Make sure there are no stragglers."

They were going. They would leave her now, alone. Suddenly she smelled smoke and for the first time she could conceive what a fire would mean to her. She imagined it eating through the walls of her rooms and crawling in a bright ridge across the carpet toward her. Once, she had spilt hot soup on her leg. It had hurt so much— almost more than anything had ever hurt before. She wouldn't be able to bear it. She must leave with the others.

She began to pull at the night chain on her door. Already the others were at the end of the hall. Perhaps they would leave her. It was as important for her now that she didn't lose these people as it had been important that she hide from them before. She would call to them. Perhaps the men who were assigned to see that there were no stragglers would take care of her and help her down.

There was a warning shout from the end of the hall. "Turn back! Turn back! The fire's in the stair well. Down the fire escapes! You there! Keep that line. Follow me!" There was a note of anger and see-it-through determination in the leader's voice as if the idea of going down the stairway had been someone else's.

Hanna slammed her door shut and fastened the night chain. She heard the frightened, disciplined column of her neighbors pass her door again. No one seemed to have noticed her frustrated attempt to join them. Their clamor

191

died out as they were marched into a room at the other end of the hall.

The leader stood in the hallway and shouted to the last of the squad. "In here! Take the fire escape one at a time. Two of you men stand at the window and see that the women get out first." (That would have meant me, Hanna thought.) "Take it easy now!"

Outside her shutter Hanna heard footsteps on her own fire escape. Some leader from another floor was marshaling his charges down to the safety of the courtyard. Everyone was leaving the building, leaving her. Soon there would be no one else in this big, hollow place, and she began to realize how much she had depended on the presence of other people over her and under her and all around. They had kept her from being entirely alone and their impersonal presence had been a kind of comfort.

A joyous fire siren sounded from the street. As the first group of people reached the court they began to shout their encouragement to their companions above. Hanna stood rigidly in the middle of her living room. Her little lamp with the parchment shade lit the scene peacefully. The thought of the thousands of evenings she had spent here made her want to cry. Could she leave anything which was so precious to her? What about her little white cups and all her clothing? How could she leave them to die in the fire? Even if she were to join the others and save herself, every part of her life that meant anything to her would be destroyed. Perhaps it was not a bad fire. It would have to cut through so many solid walls and heavy floors before it could find her. No. She still had a little time. If she had to leave, she could not leave so quickly.

As the odor of smoke grew heavier she wandered aimlessly about her dimly lit rooms. She took out all her dresses and laid them on the bed, even the ones she had not finished—feeling, in fact, especially tender about them. In her kitchen she opened the storage cupboard and smiled at all the cans of food she had saved against some

192

disaster. She opened the icebox and ate a sliver of roast duck. Then, for a while, she returned to her old chair in the living room and sat in it, holding her book of Emily Dickinson poems on her lap.

Gradually the noises on the fire escape began to die down. Through her shutter she could see the glare of flashlights. The last fleeing tenant was cheered as he reached the bottom rung of the escape. Immediately, with the threat of death and disaster withdrawn, the tone of the crowd changed from delicious terror to disgruntled worry about the fate of its belongings if the fire weren't checked.

Finally, the sound of the crowd disappeared entirely as the group trailed out through an alleyway to the front of the building to check on the work of the Fire Department. Hanna got up and went to the shutter. At first she thought that she would try to take some of the things she loved most, but now she knew it was better if she left everything behind. That way she would have less to remind her of what she had lost.

She was not afraid now. Perhaps she would be later, but now she felt herself to be very strong. Perhaps it was the nature of the disaster which gave her so much courage. No matter how terrible it was, a fire was a dumb thing and did not really mean to hurt her. A fire was big and fierce and terrible, but it didn't hate her. It didn't really wish to kill her.

She opened the metal shutter and put one foot on the sill of the window. In the moment before the hot flash of light blinded her completely, she saw only a pair of man's legs bracing themselves against the outer railing of the fire escape. Hanna threw her arm over her eyes and lurched back into her room. She felt for the fastenings of the shutter and managed to lock it before she fainted.

Chapter 18

APPLE TERRACE was one of those suburban streets on the verge of being engulfed by the city. The stubborn trees along its cracked walks had absorbed almost their limit of smoke and grime, and there was hardly a time of day when one of the huge community apartment houses near by didn't cast its ominous shadow over the little street.

Most of the people who lived on the Terrace didn't own their own homes, and the little frame structures, consequently, were almost always in need of repair or paint; thus, in their senility as when they were first built, these houses managed to look identical. Only a few of the buildings were in good repair. One of these was Kevin's. He and George were very proud of owning their own home. Someday, when the housing shortage was eased, they hoped to move out further on the Island where there was still some open land. It did not occur to them that if many other men were planning the same thing, the open land wouldn't last very long.

As Kevin came striding down the street, breathing deeply and planning some fine, future vacation trip with his son, he saw George on the front porch of their house sandpapering an old armchair. He was always grateful to see George. After an exasperating day like today George always made him feel that a good talk was all that was necessary to straighten everything out. The afternoon sun planted the monstrous shadow of the Gloucester Arms firmly across his lawn, but even in that unnatural twilight Kevin's morning-glories seemed to be nodding a warm greeting to him and he quickened his steps.

George stood up and stretched his back.

"Don't ask me why," he said, looking at the ancient armchair. "I just got started and I wanted to finish."

That was just like George, Kevin thought. He had to

finish anything he started. It didn't make any difference if he had no use for what he was working on after he finished, he just liked to see that a job got done. He would probably paint this chair after he had sandpapered it and then put it down in the basement or off in a corner somewhere and never use it.

George's place was full of the useless fruits of his energy: pipe racks, kits for shoe polish, and a series of elaborate pot-holder and dish-towel racks and foot-powered cream whippers and potato mashers. All of these latter things worked perfectly but with such complicated mechanism that Lily had to duplicate them in the five-and-ten in order to get her work done. Lily made fun of George for all of these things but she was, as usual, a little awed by his prowess if not by his usefulness.

"Is Mary in?"

"She's inside with Lily going over a list of supplies for the baby. Good God, Kevin, if that kid of yours could be born full-grown he'd have enough clothes to last him for the next thirty years."

Kevin nodded. "I guess Mary is getting pretty jumpy."

"Lily too. You'd think she was going to have the baby herself."

Kevin drew up an old, straight-backed chair which was kept on the porch and George sat down in his newly sanded rocker.

"How's your case coming?" George said.

"Rotten. Screwiest bunch of suspects I ever saw, and the only person who might give me any real evidence is missing."

"That's this old woman you were talking about?"

"Yes. Not a sign of her and we've had an alarm out in every surrounding state since the day after the murder was committed."

"You think she left the city?"

"She could have gone in and out of the city a dozen times for all the description I have of her."

195

"No one knew her at all?"

"Everyone at this party that night claims that it was the first time he saw her."

"How far have you got with the others?"

"Too far. It sounds funny but that's the way I feel. You know I told you that they all looked as if they were covering something? Well, they were each covering a perfect motive for the murder. Every one of them was being blackmailed by this fellow, Hammer. All of them except one woman, and she was put through the wringer another way. On the surface of it that looks just fine for me but actually it puts me right back where I started. They couldn't all have done it."

"Did you see the papers this morning?"

"Sure. Just what I said, isn't it? They're already beginning to smell politics. Who would want to kill an anti-Communist except a Communist, they figure. Boy, I'd like to tell them. The kind of stuff this fellow had locked away in his safe-deposit box would curl your hair. There are about twenty people in New York City who have probably been worrying themselves sick all weekend."

"Is it possible that any one of them killed him?"

"No. It had to be someone who was there that night."

"And you're not going to tell the papers who your suspects are?"

"Not unless I have to, George. Funny thing, I think they all know this—the suspects, I mean. That's why they're so glad to have me handle the case. You know me pretty well, George, and you know I wouldn't be trying to protect anyone I thought was guilty. Well, one of these five suspects of mine I'm sure is guilty and yet I'm protecting that one along with the others. I'm not doing that because I want to, I'm doing that for just two reasons. . . ."

"I think I know the reasons."

"Then you tell me, George. It would help a lot."

"Well, first of all because you want to clear this case up as soon as you can and you think a lot of publicity is going

196

to kill your chances of solving it. Second, Kevin, I think it's because you take pride in your work. Like me now, with this chair. I could just as well have put a coat of paint over the old coat. No one would have known the difference and for all I'll use it again it's just plain silly. But it's not only how this chair will look that's important, there's something else even more important. It's how it *is*.

"You could probably make this case look pretty good to the newspapers if you handled it right. From what you say you could probably railroad one of these people into an arrest. From here it looks like your best bet would be the Communist, but perhaps you could even work a better angle. The only thing is that your case would look pretty good but it wouldn't *be* very good. You wouldn't be proud of it."

George began to color up. It was the longest speech Kevin had ever heard him make. Even George was a little amazed at his own loquaciousness, and to cover this obvious fault he began to scrub the arm of the chair with a piece of sandpaper.

Kevin tried to steer the subject onto less personal ground. "Well, I don't suppose any of my ideas are going to make much difference from here on. I'm sure Dayton will take this out of my hands tomorrow. It's getting just a little too hot. I'll be just a high-paid errand boy and maybe that's just as well."

"How's the grass?" George said, suddenly. "Do you think it needs cutting?"

"Might be able to stand a little trimming," said Kevin, looking down critically at their tiny lawn.

"I'll go get the lawn-mower." George stood up quickly.

A lawn-mower had been one of their extravagances. They had hardly enough grass to cut with a sickle but they planned to keep the machine for the bigger house they would purchase someday, further out on the Island.

"Be out in a little while," said Kevin. "I think the vines

197

need spading too. I want to go in and see Mary first."

George didn't answer. He was already on his way to the back of the house to get the lawn-mower.

Chapter 19

READING his paper on the subway Monday morning, Kevin was discouraged to see that the subject of David Hammer's death was given even more prominence than it had been given on Sunday. There was a good deal of comment on the "mysterious" attitude of the police in their attempt to keep the facts of the case out of the papers. Some reporter had already interviewed the Bienholtz family, who lived in the apartment below David's, and had learned that a party had been given on the top floor on the night of Hammer's death. Mr. Bienholtz commented on a loud thump which he and his wife had heard through their bedroom ceiling some time after midnight. There was a description of David Hammer's activities as a columnist and it was pointed out that, since the murdered man was known as an "implacable foe" of Communism, there was some consideration bound to be given to the statements of "usually well-informed sources" that the Communists had carried an assassination. "At least," continued the article—the paper Kevin was reading was noted for its conservatism—"this is an inference which must be drawn in the absence of more exact information from the police."

The man sitting beside Kevin was reading the paper for which David Hammer had written. Its tone was not so reticent. A banner head in blood-red ink shot across the top of the first page: "REDS BLAST ANTI-RED WRITER." Kevin read as much of the article as he could see over his neighbor's shoulder but could find no other intimation of David Hammer's having been shot to death. The article did not seem to be inhibited by the fact that practically no information beside the mere fact of David's death was available. It reported—with so much color and energy that Kevin found himself strangely excited by the story—dark doings on the waterfront where Hammer's bitterest enemies were known to be hiding out. It stated, incontestably, that the entire Communist Party was preparing to go underground.

A reporter had crawled to the roof of the apartment house of a Communist leader named Vivian Boleyn, who had been heard threatening to "get" Hammer at a recent union meeting, and smelled smoke from the chimney. He had crawled down the fire escape and had seen a "beautiful blond woman" burning papers in the fireplace. The article also had a number of uncomplimentary remarks to make about the police, implying that "pressure" might well have been exerted from a source high in the national administration to play down this "monstrous political murder."

Kevin had been in his office only a few minutes when Inspector Dayton called for him. He wearily gathered together his file on the case and trudged down the hall to his superior's office. At least, he thought, the responsibility will be off me. Let them all kick it around for a while. I'll just take the orders.

Kevin liked Dayton and he had been aware for some time that he was one of the Inspector's favorites in the Department. The Inspector's way of showing a man that he was a favorite was to keep him working hard. He had an idea that this was the only way a man could learn a job and in this, as in nearly everything else, he was right.

When Kevin walked into Inspector Dayton's office he noticed that, as usual, his superior didn't seem to be doing

199

anything. It used to make Kevin angry that this gaunt man never seemed to have a bit of work to do himself, although he worked everyone else unmercifully. Sometimes, when Kevin would be buried under a pile of work, the Inspector would drop by his office with a bag of golf clubs hanging from his great, bony shoulder and tell him, with sadistic glee, that it was such a beautiful day he had decided to take the day off. Before he would leave, the old man would pointedly tell Kevin that he wanted his work done in some impossibly short time.

It was only after he had worked almost a year under Dayton that Kevin discovered that the Inspector carried the load of the Homicide Bureau almost single-handed and that he was known as an absolutely tireless worker. The fact that he never seemed to be busy did not alter the other fact that he accomplished enormous tasks. Perhaps, Kevin had decided, the clue to this paradox lay in the Inspector's many happy years working as a policeman on a beat. The old man hated working indoors and he hated particularly the degradation of having to work with pieces of paper instead of with people. If there was anything Inspector Dayton disliked more than a piece of paper, it was a piece of paper with writing on it. Consequently, when a report came to his desk he would tear through it like a man obsessed, anxious to finish it and throw it at someone else before he was trapped forever in its skein of words. Added to this fear of the written word was a passion for accuracy and a prodigious memory. The Department had found in Inspector Dayton the ideal man to do its paper work.

The old man looked up. The skin on his face was about the texture of the uppers on a pair of well-worn police shoes. His face was creased with wrinkles but, as is often the case with solid older men, the wrinkles themselves had grown firm and indestructible. They gave him a grotesque and rather haughtily offended look.

"Well, Corelli, I hear your wife's going to have a baby."

"Yes, sir, in less than a week, we think."

"I suppose you'll want some time off to stay with her?"

"Yes. Yes, I would like it very much."

"Well, you can have it!"

Kevin relaxed. Then all his worries had been for nothing. Good old Dayton.

". . . If . . ."

The old man seemed to take a huge delight in the effect of his word on Kevin.

"If you clear up this case of yours by the end of the week."

"Well—I don't . . ."

"Good God, man! Don't mumble! Can you do it?"

"Yes."

Now what had he said? It was all right to promise himself to do it in a week but to promise Dayton was a different matter. The Inspector didn't like anyone to break his promise. In fact, he wouldn't even consider it possible that anyone would dare break a promise to him. You either made a promise and kept it or you didn't make it.

"Well now, that's fine! That's a big load off my chest. I'll just tell the District Attorney that we'll have this thing all straight in a week." He leaned back in his chair and appeared to be about to dismiss the subject from his mind.

Just as if it were all solved, thought Kevin. And now *he'll* promise the D. A. The consequences of this almost made him sick. He opened his file so that he could explain the case, hoping to get some help at least.

"Now don't go showing me any of those damn papers of yours! Hell's bells, what would you do if the world's paper supply was suddenly exhausted? You'd freeze in your tracks! You young idiots can't even talk unless you read what you're supposed to say on a piece of paper. You wouldn't know what to eat without reading a menu. You don't know where you're going without reading it first on a sign. We don't have men on the force any more. We've got librarians!"

Kevin slapped his file shut angrily.

"And don't you go telling me about this case of yours, either. I've got enough to worry about. A man was killed, I understand. Well then, if a man was killed someone must have killed him. Find him! Now get out of here. I'm planning my vacation."

"But the papers . . ."

"Papers! Lord God, man. Can't you get papers out of your mind?"

"Newspapers, I mean."

"Never read 'em!"

Kevin stood up, miserable and angry.

"I'll do my best."

The Inspector looked up kindly. "Oh, you don't have to rush it too much. You've got a whole week. Give me a ring when you've finished and then take two weeks off."

As Kevin was leaving, Inspector Dayton picked up the phone and said to the operator, "Hello—connect me with the District Attorney and then get me the WashuWashu Travel Bureau. Hmmmm? Well, how the hell do I know? Look it up in the book!"

By the end of the week Kevin had done nothing in particular to merit the Inspector's confidence. He had no positive proof of the murderer's identity and he had made no progress in finding Margot Case. He was quite certain he knew who the killer was, but this information was useless to him without objective evidence. Instinctively he felt that only one person could have committed the crime, but though he subjected this person's story to the most careful scrutiny and placed the supposed killer under a twenty-four-hour watch, he could prove nothing.

Late Friday evening, just before he got on the subway train which would take him home, he bought a copy of *Life*. He was thinking that this would probably be the last evening he would be going home as an employed man. When he told Inspector Dayton tomorrow that he had failed to break the case, he knew the old man would not forgive him for breaking his promise. Kevin hung to the strap with one hand and opened his magazine.

Several stations later, pushed and battered by the early evening crowds, he managed to finish the article on hush-hush plans for space craft to be used in the next war. At this rate, he thought, the magazine would last almost all the way to Jamaica and he wouldn't have to think of his dreadful predicament. He turned the page and came upon an extremely funny-looking picture of a woman with one foot on a windowsill. She was obviously surprised at having her picture taken. There was a suggestion of terror in her eyes also, but this only made the photograph laughable since the reader was immediately assured that the woman had no real cause for fear.

"PICTURE OF THE WEEK—Recluse . . . Miss Hanna Carpenter, caught by *Life* Photographer Hugh Jennings taking French leave from her own rooms. Jennings, sent to cover last weekend's fire at rundown Hotel '38' in Manhattan, climbed the old-fashioned fire escape in rear of building (see following page for other pictures) and snapped the aging recluse in her first venture outside in over thirty years. A moment after the picture was taken Miss Carpenter slammed an ancient steel shutter in Jennings' face. Hanna Carpenter is the sole heir to the fabulous 'Bertie' Carpenter's mining fortune."

One thing in the picture attracted Kevin's attention. The foot, balanced so awkwardly on the windowsill, was encased in a tiny, buttoned shoe. Kevin began to edge through the crowds to the door of the train. At the Fifth Avenue station he jumped out and sprinted up the steps, bucking a crowd coming down.

In the meantime, other people had seen the picture and were in even less doubt than Kevin about the identity of the recluse. Mr. Barton Zimmer saw the picture over his secretary's shoulder and immediately phoned the Hotel "38." Peter and Sandy Coburg-James, who were inveterate readers of the magazine, recognized Margot immediately. Theodora Dennis had been having her hair done when she saw the picture. (It was typical of her that, although her hair always looked as if it hadn't seen a comb for weeks, she visited the shabby beauty parlor near her studio incessantly.) She telephoned immediately. Even Vivian Boleyn, who detested the magazine, found himself reading a copy in the union hall that day. He muttered continuously to himself as he read it, as if this would partially excuse his transgression. When he saw Margot's picture he called her and, explaining that he had read the article about her in *Life*, asked to see her.

They were all, naturally, a little surprised to find themselves greeted so warmly and invited to her rooms at five o'clock that afternoon.

Chapter 20

FRIDAY afternoon Hanna dashed around her apartment trying to get it into shape for her expected guests. Everything seemed suddenly very dingy and untidy. She had never noticed before how terribly chipped her walls were. The varnished door of the kitchen was disfigured by great splotches which revealed the bare wood. The sills of her windows were marked by deep cracks which held deposits of ancient dust. She had always tried to keep her house clean, but somehow a heavy film of age had covered everything in spite of her efforts. She was really surprised to notice that one whole section of a wall had lost all of its paint. She had seen it many times before but it had always been a part of the whole picture and it had always seemed perfectly natural to her that this particular section of wall should have no paint. Now, for the first time, she was seeing her rooms through other people's eyes and she found herself shocked at the scene.

She was busy cleaning the dust out of the cracks on the windowsills with a hairpin when she heard three long and three short knocks on her door. This was the secret signal she and Mr. Howard had agreed upon. She held the door open on the night chain until she could make sure it was he.

"Good afternoon, Miss Carpenter. Fine day, isn't it? Bit chilly, but fine."

A remark about the weather was Mr. Howard's traditional way of greeting her. He seemed to prefer to ignore the fact that his client never went outside and didn't care if it was a fine day or not. To have shown any recognition of her situation would have meant that their relationship was more personal than that of banker and client.

Hanna greeted him in the businesslike manner she knew pleased him so much. Mr. Howard was burdened by his usual brief case and by a large paper bag and a copy of *Life*. She could see that the bag was embarrassing him. It was not the sort of thing he would have chosen to carry during business hours. It had been a measure of his respect for her that he had merely said "Of course" when she had called him and asked him to make the purchases for her. She took the bag and the magazine from him, resisting the temptation to open the latter immediately.

"May I have your coat?"

"Yes, thank you."

"I'm really very grateful for your going out of your way to get these things for me."

"Oh, please. Don't give it a second thought."

This had, of course, been her second thought and Hanna knew that he had expected her to give it. There was something pleasurable in her relation with Mr. Howard. An air

205

of courtly formality was understood to be necessary in all their dealings. They had, these two, everything in common in their business interests and nothing in common in any other. To ask Mr. Howard to do an errand for her which had to do with anything else but business was a small violation of their pact and it was very necessary for her to assure him that she was extremely grateful for his "going out of his way."

"I think you'll find the—the ingredients acceptable. The olives are there also."

"I've never had a martini before, Mr. Howard. Do you suppose . . . ?"

"Certainly. There are different formulae. Some use one part vermouth, two parts gin; others use one part vermouth and three parts gin, and still others use four parts gin." His face made a slight grimace of conservative distaste at the last formula.

"I think I'd prefer three parts gin."

"That's what we use."

The thought that Mr. Howard drank martini cocktails at his home was somewhat shocking to Hanna. Perhaps he had parties which other bankers came to. Wasn't he just as shocked at the thought of her having a party? What kind of people did he think she would invite? Maybe he hadn't thought she was going to have a party. Maybe he thought . . .

"I'm going to have a little group of people here at five."

"Of course."

"And when I make the mixture," she said, "do I put ice in it?"

"You pour the vermouth and the gin over some ice cubes and stir quickly. Then you pour it out into the glasses before too much of the ice melts."

"And the olive?"

"You put that in the bottom of the glass."

"I can't really thank you enough."

"Don't mention it."

206

Mr. Howard laid his brief case on the table. It was fastened to his wrist by a stout chain which ran from the bag to a single handcuff. He took a small key from his vest pocket and unlocked the bracelet from his wrist.

"I had a guard bring me to the hotel," he said. "I don't like carrying such large amounts through the streets."

This was not a reproach to her, Hanna knew; it was the voicing of a principle. Mr. Howard looked on all money which wasn't safely locked up in a bank as being an unnecessary provocation to lawlessness. Also, he felt that the use of large amounts of money for anything but investment was unnatural and, in a way, immoral. Naturally, a certain amount of change had to be spent for food and clothing and living quarters. If he hadn't admired Hanna's business sense a great deal, Mr. Howard might have advised her strongly against any project which would require a quarter of a million dollars in large bills. When they had spoken on the phone this afternoon he had advised her to carry out her transaction by check, which could be properly endorsed and stamped, but she had insisted on having the money in bills.

He opened the case now and took out all the packets. Hanna could see that he was uncomfortably aware that no metal cages or burglar alarms or armed guards now stood between this treasure and the coarse, material world outside. She had always thought of her place as a fortress; but to Mr. Howard, who operated a far more efficient shelter, her rooms seemed dangerously public.

"Do you want a check for this amount?"

"Well, yes. I should like to take it back with me."

Hanna went to her little desk and took up her pen and checkbook. "If you didn't take the check with you and something were to happen to me . . ."

"We'd just be out of luck!" Mr. Howard laughed heartily, as if this would be a good joke on the bank.

When she had written the check he carefully dried it with a blotter which he kept conveniently in one pocket of the case. He put the check, with the blotter, back into the case and locked it. Then he fastened the handcuff to his wrist.

"I hope," he said, indicating the money which still lay neglected on the table, "that you're not going to leave that around for very long. I imagine that it would be relatively easy for someone to break in here."

Hanna looked up, startled. If Mr. Howard had thought about it perhaps he would have realized that this was the wrong thing to say, but the sight of this money being treated as so many worthless bits of paper had made him less cautious. They were both almost equally concerned with the idea of someone breaking in; it was merely the motive for their concern which differed.

"I won't have to worry any more in another hour," she said, calmly.

"I'm glad of that. Can't be too careful, you know."

"I know."

"I believe our regular visit is due next month."

"Next month? Oh yes, I'll call you."

"I don't think it will be necessary to make any major readjustments. Your securities are doing exceptionally well, as usual."

"Thank you again, Mr. Howard, for everything."

As she crossed to the door she looked down and saw the shattered end of a pencil sticking out from under the rug. Hanna started to pick it up, then, remembering she had a guest, she left it where it was. What did it matter anyway? When it had meant something to her, when it would have been a welcome proof that she had not imagined the incident at the door, she couldn't find it. Now, when it made no difference whether she had proof or not, she had nearly stumbled over it.

"It's been a pleasure, Miss Carpenter. Always a pleasure."

Hanna opened the door and they both peered into the hall cautiously. As the door closed, Hanna saw Mr.

Howard look past her shoulder and she knew that he was saying farewell to the defenseless money. There was a look of fear in his eyes—perhaps not exactly fear, she thought, but some rather nervous emotion which would have subsided if she had told him that she had changed her mind and wanted him to take the money back to the bank where it belonged. Oh, if only she could be so well looked after as that!

When he had gone Hanna rushed over to the table and picked up the new copy of *Life* which he had brought. She ruffled through the magazine and found nothing—but Mr. Boleyn said he'd seen her picture. Could it have been this magazine? How was it possible? And yet he'd said . . .

She went through the magazine again, slowly, taking one page at a time. In spite of herself she paused to look at the full-color picture of the dissection of a rat. The rat's brain was laid out separately on a piece of paper. All of the little creature's organs were catalogued and pointed out with black lines. What was the use of that, now? The rat was dead and these little bits of flesh which were its organs had no use, no function at all. How was it possible that she, who would someday be no more than this creature who was all spread out and pinned down—how was it possible that she could feel and understand all of this when, possibly in a short time, she herself would be no more than an ugly piece of flesh? No—not even that, finally.

She turned the pages. Here was a section of new bathing suit styles, there an article about deep-sea diving. Then she came to "PICTURE OF THE WEEK" (she always read the captions before looking at the picture): "Recluse . . . Miss Hanna Carpenter, caught by . . ." She looked up at the picture and found herself staring straight into her own horror-stricken eyes.

Though she recognized herself, there was a moment of doubt. Could that be all? Could all of these past days and years of fear and anguish be summed up so easily in this

209

foolish face? Oh, there was fear there, but only a cheap imitation of the fear she remembered. Those were her own eyes, wide with terror, but at most it was a reasonable terror, something which could be explained in a moment. There was no suggestion in these eyes of the dreadful, unreasoning panic of that moment.

This picture was a lie. It might just as well have been a picture of a girl on an aquaplane or a young man demonstrating a new automobile, for all it told anyone what she had felt at the moment it was taken.

Mixed with her disappointment at the falseness of the picture, there was also a great feeling of relief. At least no one had seen her as she actually was, ugly and naked and pitiful; she could not have borne that. Perhaps others who had their pictures taken were just as grateful, she thought.

Strangely, Hanna was not so surprised that a picture of herself *had* been taken. On that night, when she had awakened on the floor beneath the closed shutter, she had known, dimly, that some such thing had happened. She had once posed for a photograph taken with flash powder and remembered the sudden white light and the hot feeling on her skin. Also, thinking of it now, she was not dumfounded at the thought that this picture had appeared in "her" magazine. Her world was too small to admit coincidences.

Seeing the picture now, grossly inaccurate as it had proved to be, brought back those moments to her with a new clarity. When she had come to on the floor, and had tried to convince herself that she was all right, that she hadn't really been harmed, she'd found that the minor distinction she could make between being harmed and unharmed no longer seemed to make any difference. The shock of the incident had broken all her resistance.

Then all her doubts of her own sanity had disappeared. The possibility that she had only imagined her danger and that the death of David was only a dream of her own making was completely dismissed. There *was* something outside that wanted to get her. It was a thing which had no form, no color and no substance and it hovered over the world outside, waiting for her. Sometimes this thing took the form of other people, like David's murderer, and sometimes it caused seeming accidents, like the man who had photographed her. But they were not accidents. They were all part of a carefully designed major plan to annihilate her. It had been no accident that she had gone to David's party. Even David's death was part of the plan. And now she knew, because she was meant to know, who the murderer was.

She remembered how she'd dragged herself from the floor to her chair and had begun to cry hysterically. Great, tearing sobs had shaken her body. It was as if she had become an instrument merely to express an agony and pain which was beyond her own feeling. As the sobs had wrung her she'd become convinced that there was another person inside of her, stronger and more agonized than herself, who was using her to cry out some pain which was beyond her feeling.

Hour after hour it had continued and she had become frightened as she realized that her body could not bear the sobbing much longer. The blood vessels over her eyes had broken and the inside of her throat was raw flesh which burned at the touch of her own saliva. Toward the next morning she had fallen into a stupor beneath which she could still hear her own cries. At last, she had stumbled into her bedroom and had fallen on her bed. Slowly and gratefully she had lost awareness of the shooting pains in her head and the soreness of her twisted organs.

She had awakened the following evening, hobbled into the kitchen to make herself some soup, and had gone back to her bed. The next morning she had got up again feeling incredibly sore, but feeling nothing else. She had known that she could not survive longer unless she could face this thing and rid herself of her own fears, even if it meant risking her life.

211

The fire had been the work of the murderer. She was sure of this. The enormity of such a crime, in endangering so many other lives beside her own, did not particularly impress her. There was nothing this thing outside, whether in the body of the murderer or in some other form, would not do to destroy her.

The remaining days of the week she had waited for the murderer's next attack. When it came, she would not resist. She would open the door or unbar the window and let the killer in. Throughout the week she had waited, thinking each day that she had only a few more hours to live. And then, Friday morning, the murderer had called and asked to see her. She had arranged a meeting at five o'clock. Shortly after, the telephone had rung again. Only then had she made some move to save herself. Within a few hours, as the others called, she had arranged to have all five come to her rooms at the same time. Her only hope would be to plead with the murderer while the others were here and could protect her.

Chapter 21

BY FOUR-THIRTY Hanna had got herself dressed. She had finished what cleaning she could reasonably do in the apartment with a feverish efficiency which left her, exhausted and trembling, with plenty of time to spare before she could expect her guests.

She sat down and tried to read but every sound in the hall made her throw down her book and run to the door. Once she heard voices at the far end of the hall and she hurried into her kitchen to see if she had everything laid out for the drinks. The voices died down and she went back to her book.

Her stomach began to growl and she read the same paragraph in her book three times without knowing what it said. Then the door of the elevator banged and she heard steps coming down the hall. This was for her. She knew it. She could see the person outside stop before her door. Still, when the knock came it struck her senses as hard as if it had been a complete surprise. Suddenly she found herself begging for just one more moment alone. She understood, now, how much these last thirty-four years had meant to her. She had always thought of it as a terrible, fearful time, but now that it was going, perhaps forever, she wanted only to think of the nice things about it. The knock came again and Hanna rose calmly and opened the door.

"Oh, please, won't you come in. The others will be here in a few minutes. Let me take your coat."

"Others?"

"Yes, I didn't tell you. It's—well, it's a sort of little party."

Theodora walked across the room and sat down. She said nothing else but Hanna did not feel that she was deliberately rude. Hanna took her coat to the bedroom and returned to her guest.

"Won't you have a drink?"

"Yes, thanks."

"I have martinis."

"I'd rather have plain rye with ice, if you have it."

"Oh, I'm afraid I don't. You see, I asked Mr. Howard what was a nice drink and he said martinis and I got them for everybody. I'm dreadfully sorry—I . . ."

"It's quite all right. I'll have that."

Hanna went into her kitchen. She looked at the table with everything laid out on it and she realized, suddenly, that she couldn't make a martini. It had sounded so simple when Mr. Howard had told her, but now she couldn't even remember what you were supposed to have one part of and what three.

A voice from behind her said, "May I help?"

"I'm afraid I've never made anything like this before."

"That's all right. I'll do it."

Theodora put some ice cubes in a large drinking glass.

"Four or five to one?"

"Four or five what?"

"Four parts or five parts of gin to one vermouth. Which do you prefer?"

"Oh. I thought—would four be all right?"

There was a knock on the door and Hanna ran out of the kitchen.

They were all seated in the living room now, all of these people whose lives had got mixed up with hers through a terrible accident. Long ago, Hanna had thought that a friend might someday come to visit her here. It was to have been a very casual visit, during which she and her friend would talk quietly for a while about books and the distant struggles of the world. Only with the greatest courage had she been able to imagine this friendly intrusion. It would have marked one of the most terrifying moments in her life if she had been able to imagine then what had now become a reality: that five hostile people would one day enter her rooms at her invitation and that one of them should wish to kill her. How had she been able to do this? From what deep well in herself had she drawn the fortitude to face these people?

In the midst of these thoughts, while Theodora was pouring the drinks, Hanna was aware of one consolation. She was not mad. She had not imagined that these people existed. She had not imagined that there was a murderer. These people were real. She had shaken hands with them and taken their coats and hats to the bedroom. This alone proved nothing—hadn't she smelled sandalwood in her

214

bedroom as clearly as if it had been real?—but there was something else, a dullness, a lack of significance in the actions of these people which certified their complete reality.

For a moment Hanna was tempted to tell them all to leave, that she had made a mistake, that she hadn't meant to invite them here after all. In a way, now that they were here, she was no longer afraid of them. She merely hated them. When Barton Zimmer had sat down in one of her sweet, patient little chairs she had almost screamed. The chair had creaked so pitifully that Hanna had forgotten all her own fear of the man in her desire to defend it from his awful weight.

Sandy had just come back from the bathroom and Hanna could hardly restrain herself from rushing in to see if the tap was still dripping or if the basin had got dirty or if the soap was melting away in a pool of water. Even the eyes of these people, traveling casually and uncomprehendingly over her shabby possessions, seemed to her to be committing a great affront to her own person.

Barton Zimmer leaned over and placed his sweating glass on the bare table. As he moved, the chair moaned and dug its sharp little feet into the threadbare carpet.

"Now, Miss—ah—Carpenter. I think you might explain why you asked us here. I had no idea that you were going to ask any other people."

Theodora finished pouring Peter's drink. She took her own and sat down in Hanna's ancient overstuffed chair. The tortured springs gave completely to her weight.

Sandy spoke. "We didn't know anyone else was to be here either. We hardly thought—we thought that you wouldn't want to have a lot of people here after what we read about you in *Life*."

"I'm sorry," said Hanna, "that I didn't tell you all I had invited the others. At first, I didn't know there would be anyone else, but when each of you called I decided that I would have a little party."

215

"I think," said Vivian Boleyn, "that it would be to the point to tell Miss Carpenter why we all wanted to see her. I'm quite sure the rest of you came for the same reason I did. I want to know if you know the identity of David Hammer's murderer."

Vivian was standing. He leaned slightly against a wall as he spoke and his shoulder brushed off a tiny chip of paint. Hanna clenched her hands around her cold glass and took a deep drink to cover her agitation. How she hated him!

"Yes," she said quietly, "I do."

"I think you'd better tell us who it is," said Theodora. "You see, all of us are under suspicion and the newspapers have been raising so much of a fuss about the murder that it would put us all in an embarrassing position if our names were to come out."

"Naturally," said Sandy, "we don't want our names bandied about in the tabloids."

"Also," said Barton Zimmer, "you are one of the suspects, and though you may be perfectly innocent of the crime, it would save you a great deal of trouble with the police if you were to name the person responsible for this act of violence."

Barton looked at Vivian Boleyn as he spoke, so as to make his suspicion of the identity of the murderer perfectly clear.

Hanna was quiet for a moment. I'm being tested, she thought.

"No," she said, at last. "I don't intend to tell any of you."

As she spoke she felt the murderer's eyes on her. Now the time had come. She must convince one person that she was not lying.

"One of you here killed David Hammer. I know that because of something David told me. It doesn't really matter what he told me. All that matters is that I know who killed him."

216

She took another sip of her drink and felt the effect of it almost immediately. Oh, how could she ever really explain how she felt?

"All of my life I've been afraid, terribly afraid that something would happen to me. I don't know what it is that I've been afraid of, but I suppose mostly I've been terrified of people. Long ago, when I was still trying to live with other people, I realized that even the most perfect stranger was either deliberately cruel or unbearably kind and that if you were to dare to love someone, even just a little bit, the whole universe would go out of its way to destroy that love—please, I'm not being irrelevant. I'll get to the point in just a moment. I've often thought the whole world was run on some terrible principle of supply and demand so that when there was a plentiful supply of something it was because no one wanted it and when there was a great demand for something it was because no one had it. The only way you could have something that you wanted was to pretend not to want it, and it wasn't even enough to pretend not to want it, you had really not to want it—then, of course, it would be given to you freely.

"Once, I wanted a dress for a party and my father wouldn't give it to me—he was afraid I would grow too extravagant, although he could easily have afforded all my petty extravagances. It was only after that party was over, during which I had hidden in the bathroom because I thought I was ugly, that he relented and bought me the dress which I could not use again and did not want."

Hanna finished her drink and continued speaking. It seemed to her that she was not the person speaking at all. It was Margot Case who was talking to these people. Suddenly Hanna felt at peace. Margot would explain everything. *She* would be able to make everything clear to them.

"I suppose that most people find this out sooner or later and learn not to want things any more, at least not to want them so strongly that they can't do without them. I don't

217

know how this is done but I think it must be like committing suicide in a way. You take the part of yourself that wants too much and you kill it. Then you're all right. Then you're grown-up and you can have some of the things you wanted even though you don't really want them any longer. The terrible thing about it is that these people then begin to hate those who still want things. They think: Why should she have what she wants when I could never have what I wanted? They think it's their duty to destroy you, even if they've never met you before, and they promise you all kinds of happiness if you'll only be like them, if you'll only submit to having part of yourself murdered.

"I can't explain it to you any more except to tell you that this is why I never leave these rooms. I haven't left them for thirty-four years except once, and that time you know about."

All five of her guests were looking at her with pained expressions, and Hanna suddenly realized that they were embarrassed. Her mind was whirling slightly now and she knew that she must hurry before she became too drunk to talk.

"I don't know how to prove it but I think that you're all a little like me. All of you *want* something. I think each of you even wants something so much that you almost couldn't live without having it. I'm sure you all know what I mean when I say that everyone in the world, even people who should not care one way or the other, goes out of their way to kill that thing that you want. They resent you, not because you are better or worse than they are, but because you haven't given up that one thing which is still important to you. Their resentment is very understandable, I suppose, and they will very kindly give you what you want after you have ceased to care—but not until then.

"The reason I have spoken about this is to explain to one of you that I don't care whether you are punished or

218

not for killing David. I don't even dislike you for wanting to kill me, since I know that you don't really hate me, you are just afraid that I will tell what I know—that I will be like all the other people in the world who want to hurt you.

"I have given one of you a gift of money. You probably have no use for the money at all, since that's the way things usually work out, but I have merely wished to show you that I want you to be happy. All I ask is that you leave me alone and I promise I will tell no one. If you like, I can double or triple the amount of money. I'm sorry but it is all I have to give. I would give something more valuable if I could."

"Are you sure you feel quite well, Miss Carpenter?" said Peter. He leaned forward and looked at her anxiously.

"I don't think she'd better have anything more to drink," said Theodora.

Hanna felt herself slipping away from the firm ground of reason. How stupid she had been to take the drink. Now, of all moments, when it was so important that she retain control of herself she had deliberately made herself drunk. She tried to remember what she had just said. Had the murderer understood her? Idly, she found herself thinking that she had not watered her philodendrons for a week. Poor, parched leaves, she thought. What a horrible thing to do. She could feel their terrible thirst in her own throat.

Vivian Boleyn spoke. "I understood you to say, Miss Carpenter, that you have given one of us in the room here a quantity of money. I don't know whether to believe you or not, but I assume that you have given the money to the person you believe to be the murderer of David Hammer."

"Yes," said Hanna, "I didn't know what else I could give to show . . ."

"Does the person to whom you gave it know that he

219

has it?" said Barton Zimmer. "I mean, did this person accept the money from you?"

"No, I just gave it," said Hanna, thinking of the heavy envelope she had fastened with a safety pin on the inside of one of the coats in the bedroom. "Please, let's don't speak about the money. I only meant it as a way of saying . . ."

"I believe I understand what she has been trying to say," said Theodora. There was something calm and comforting in her voice. "First, she believes that she knows who killed David. Second, because of what she knows, she thinks that one of us will now wish to harm her and she's trying to tell one of us that she won't inform the police. Then, of course, there's the matter of the money which she may have sent to one of us or hidden in our belongings somewhere."

"How much money was it?" said Barton Zimmer, efficiently. Here was a subject which he felt thoroughly competent to handle.

"A quarter of a million dollars," said Hanna, weakly. She had decided that she would water the plants as soon as her guests left. Then she would have time to think about what she had done.

"My God!" said Vivian, half impressed and half amused. "Murder has certainly become profitable."

"Just one minute," said Peter, "this is all too confusing for me. Assuming you are right, and that you know who the murderer is, why did you then invite that person here and confess to us all that you knew who it was, and then, to make matters even worse, I should think, prove you knew who it was by giving this person a large amount of money? If you are afraid of one of us, why do you go out of your way to give the murderer a real reason to want to do away with you?"

"I'm afraid I don't understand," said Hanna.

"If the murderer didn't know that you knew his—or her —identity before," said Sandy, "why do you tell us now?"

"But that's just the point," said Hanna. "One of you has been trying to break into my rooms all week!"

"Are you sure," said Theodora, "that it was one of us?"

"Yes, I know. I'm sure!"

"Did you see this person?" Vivian said.

"No. But I know! It started the first night. The night David was killed. It couldn't have been anyone else!"

"But perhaps it was," said Peter.

"Perhaps it was a thief." Theodora poured the last of the drink she had mixed into her own glass. No one seemed to care.

Hanna rose unsteadily from her chair and looked frantically around at her guests. "You're trying to trap me into saying who it was! I won't tell you! I'll keep my promise and I won't tell anyone if you'll only let me alone. Besides—it doesn't matter who it was. It could have been any one of you. You're all murderers! Every one of you wanted to kill David. I know because I watched you that night. One of you did it but the rest of you are all just as guilty.

"Maybe it was no crime to kill David. I think he must have hurt you all, or threatened to hurt you all, very much. At least, now that David is gone it wouldn't help to punish anyone—but why, now, do you want to hurt me? Why is it that someone who was innocent is always hurt more than anyone else? It's not fair! It only took a moment to kill David. You didn't hurt him at all. I don't think he even felt it. But the one person who just happened to be there you take days and weeks to kill! Please. Please! Leave me alone. I'm no danger to you. Can't you see that I don't want to hurt you?"

"I think we'd better leave," said Barton Zimmer. "She seems to have become hysterical. It's hardly our province anyway. It's a job for the police. Personally I believe she's made the whole story up."

"Do you think that she is really the one who killed him?" Sandy whispered, audibly.

221

"Possibly," said Peter.

"I think Mr. Zimmer is right," said Theodora, "we ought to leave."

Hanna stood beside her chair. Large, hot tears rolled down her cheeks. They were not tears of grief, or even of fright. They were the great, easy tears a child uses in moments of delicious self-pity. She was grateful to see that they were leaving. They went by themselves into the bedroom and took their coats. For one instant the murderer showed surprise and Hanna saw a hand clutch at the bulky package under the coat. No one else had seen. No one else knew that the money had been found. The next moment the murderer was again talking with the others easily. As her guests came back into the living room their figures appeared distorted through the film of tears.

One of them said good-by and the others mumbled something which Hanna took to be thanks. The murderer did not look at her, but as the group departed down the hall Hanna saw the hand touch once again the secret package under the coat. Hanna slowly went over and locked the door and looked with distaste at a room which was no longer completely hers.

Chapter 22

LESS than an hour later Hanna had succeeded completely in erasing all signs of her recent guests. She had cleaned the glasses, refilled the ice-trays and poured the rest of the liquor down the sink. She rearranged the chairs in her living room so that their position could not remind her of the people who had lately been sitting in them. Also, she had very carefully watered the philodendrons.

Now, for the first time, she could allow herself to remember what had happened. Had she convinced the murderer she was telling the truth? Yes. Now that she membered the conversation she realized that she must have done this. She had proved that no one could make her tell. The murderer knew now that there was nothing to worry about.

Hanna thought of David. Yes, he would understand. He would realize that revenge for the taking of his life could not bring him back again. David would see that she had had to do this. She felt that David was with her now and that he was watching over her. David wanted her to be happy.

Her drink had worn off almost as quickly as it had taken effect. It had left her body feeling a little numb and her mind drowsy. She would make herself a cup of tea in a little while and then, as a special treat, she would dress up as if she were going out and have Arthur bring her some dinner. For the first time in the last few days she remembered Arthur. Why hadn't he called to see if she needed anything? Arthur usually left her alone for several days if she didn't call him, but it was unlike him not to call for a whole week. She hoped he wasn't sick.

Yes, she thought again, David can't really mind if I've promised not to tell who killed him. In a way it had been his fault in the first place. He must have been the one who had told the murderer where she lived. While she was asleep in David's bedroom he must have told the killer that they both lived in the Hotel "38" or perhaps he had just said: "Oh, her name's not really Margot Case, it's Hanna Carpenter—you know, the Carpenter mining fortune. She's a neighbor of yours." That might have been the way it had happened. Later, when she had pretended to know who had killed David the murderer had grown afraid and had probably thought that Hanna had seen it all. Yes, in a way David was to blame for this as he had been to blame for everything else that had happened.

Perhaps she would never have known who was trying to kill her if she hadn't seen the picture in *Life*, but when she had read that the guest at David's party lived in her hotel, Hanna knew that this was the person David had said would try to kill him. This was the "neighbor" he had spoken of.

Now that she was safe again she could feel how terrible it all must have been for the murderer. Hanna did not know what David had done to bring such a terrible vengeance on himself, but the worst thing he could have done could not compare to the horror the murderer must have felt when Hanna had first announced that she knew who had killed David. Hanna realized now that this person must have suffered more than she had herself. At least, when she had been fighting to defend herself, she had had four walls around her. How terrible it must be, she thought, to have to fight for one's life out in the open where you could never tell who was coming up behind you; where every strange man on the street could be a policeman, and every smiling face could remind you that someone else knew your secret. Yes, she would keep the secret. No one would ever know what had happened and the murderer could take the money and go away somewhere.

Hanna felt exceptionally sad. She could go back now to her old life. She could settle once again into her familiar routine, and one day she would die here quietly and unmourned, but somehow she could not freely abandon thoughts of her life's greatest adventure.

The murderer would take the money and move away, perhaps to another country; to live alone, away from all friends and familiar scenes. Suddenly and quite implausibly, Hanna wished that she could go with her late enemy. Why couldn't she too travel to strange countries and see strange sights? It was silly of her to think of it, but she

224

began to imagine the two of them, grown to be friends, traveling on a caravan through Arabia, or riding in a coolie-borne chair up to the lamaseries of Tibet. In her mind she heard them calling each other by their first names and laughing at the strange things they saw together. They could do anything they liked and, together, they could build a world between them which would shut out all the horrible things of the past.

It was while Hanna was dreaming delightedly of these multicolored, joyous adventures that she heard a noise coming from her bedroom. It was nothing but a faint "tic-tic-tic-tic" and it took several minutes to realize that someone was chipping a hole through her bedroom wall.

Chapter 23

WHEN Kevin arrived at the Hotel "38" it was seven o'clock. He checked first with the guard outside and learned that the murderer had not yet left the hotel.

He avoided the clerk at the desk and went instead into the tiny dining room, where he asked to speak to someone who knew a woman in the hotel named Hanna Carpenter. He had learned, long ago, that hotel desk clerks, together with office managers and floor walkers, were about the least informative people in the world. Waiters, though they were often undependable about bringing food, were about the best source of information anyone could have. In a short time he was directed to Arthur, who was between courses and seemed very anxious to talk.

225

He explained immediately that he was a policeman and Arthur drew him nervously behind a white gauze screen which stood before the door of the men's room.

"Jesus, don't tell me something's happened to her. I knew it!"

"How did you know it?"

"Well, the old dame's always been queer, of course—off her rocker a little bit, but harmless—but I knew there was something extra the matter when I saw her coming in at three A.M. last week."

"Doesn't she usually come in so late?"

"Late! She don't usually come in at all! What I mean is that to my knowledge she ain't been out of here in over thirty years."

If Kevin hadn't heard Arthur reciting fluently the contents of an intensely French menu a few minutes earlier he wouldn't have believed he could do it. Arthur was one of the many people whose work, in catering to other people, required him to be excessively suave; so that, when speaking off duty, he was scrupulously careful to return to the language of upper Amsterdam Avenue.

"What night was it last week?"

"Last Thursday, or rather Friday morning."

"And she's never done that before?"

"I know her for thirty years, like I said, and I'd swear she hasn't been out once in that time. Afraid of her own shadow. I'm the only one she'll let in her door, and now maybe she won't let me in any more either."

"What makes you think that?"

"Well, like I was saying. I saw her get out of a taxi at three A.M. last Friday morning—I had a late shift that night and there's not much to do but sit around—so I figured maybe there was something wrong and I followed her upstairs.

"You know, I kinda like the old girl and she's always nice to me and the wife at Christmas—and that—so I wanted to make sure she was all right. I followed her up-

226

stairs—she walked up the stairs. She didn't seem to think she could use the elevator—and I just saw her close her door when I got to her floor so I knocked on the door to ask her if anything is wrong."

"You're sure she was the one you saw?"

"Sure. I seen her time and again. I even recognized the dress she was wearing because my wife bought the material for it. She was wearing those funny old-fashioned shoes too. I couldn't've made any mistake. So, like I say, I knocks on the door and there's no answer. I knew she was right there too because I could see her light under the door.

"Well, you know how it is. You go out of your way to help someone and you get called down for it right away. The old lady's pretty touchy and I knew she was busy hiding from something, like she does sometimes, and I didn't want to get in bad so I just left."

Arthur popped his head out from behind the screen and looked around the restaurant professionally. Then he returned to his conversation. He seemed relieved to be able to tell his story to somebody.

"Well, the next morning I got to thinking about her again and I thought maybe I scared her knocking like that in the middle of the night. You know, if it was a normal person you wouldn't get into a thing like that with them in the first place—so when something like this comes up you don't know just how to handle it. Anyways, I called her to tell her it was just me knocking on her door but she didn't answer. Then I began to think, Hell—maybe the old girl is sick and she tried to go out to get help or something. I swear I saw her dying up there with appendicitis and gallstones and I don't know what else. Still, on the other hand, I figured maybe she just wanted to be alone like she does sometimes."

"Garçon!"

Arthur made a face. "Listen to that! In French, garson means boy. Do I look like a boy to you? I'm old enough to be that bum's father.

227

"Oui, Miseu!" Arthur scurried around the screen and out onto the floor.

While Arthur rushed back and forth with the plates and while he tossed the salad and while he assured Miseu, the bum, that the duck was being prepared exactly to his taste, Kevin fidgeted unhappily behind the gauze screen. Finally Arthur came back, taking up exactly where he had left off.

"Still, by Saturday, I was pretty worried because I didn't hear from her. She's got some food up there in that kitchen, of course, and she can feed herself pretty well, but I had her *Life* Magazine that came on Friday and usually she's pretty keen on that. Well, I was worried and so Saturday morning I took a house key—no one ever says anything when I take a house key because I've been here so long—I took this key and went up to her room. I knocked a couple of times first but when I didn't get any answer I really got worried and so I opened her right up. The only trouble was that she had one of those night chains on the inside of the door and I couldn't get in any further."

Kevin waited impatiently for Arthur to finish. Now that he was so near to his goal it made him nervous to think that the murderer was still inside the hotel somewhere.

"Well, when there was no sound out of her I really began to get worried and I figured I had to get in right away. I was afraid she had died or something. Anyway I took a pencil out of my pocket and was trying to lift the chain when all of a sudden, like a ton of brick, this door came banging shut. If I'd had my hand in there I don't know what would of happened.

"Well then, I knew she was all right, you see, and the only thing I could think of after that was what a fuss she'd make if she knew I tried to break into her place. When they get like that, you know, it don't do no good just to say you was worried about them—so I cleared out."

"I don't understand, said Kevin. "If you were sure she

228

was all right, why were you worried just now that something had happened to her?"

"Because I didn't hear from her since. Last Sunday we had a fire, you know. It was just a toy fire in the stair well and if it had been anything big I would of got the old girl out, but there was no danger—though from all the commotion the Fire Department made and from the hell a lot of amateur firemen raised upstairs you'd of thought it was at least four alarms.

"Anyway, the thing that got me to worrying was that I didn't hear from her after the fire either. I expected her to call me one evening like she usually does for dinner. Then, when I took her dinner up I decided I would come right out and tell her that it was me who tried to get into her place. I don't know, I suppose I should of gone right up and told her or wrote her a note or something, but I was a little afraid of what she'd say, you see. Of course, I suppose I ought to of realized I'd have to tell her someday but after a while it seemed too late to go bother her just for that so I thought I'd just wait for her to call me.

"Oh yeh, and another thing that worried me was that some fellow from *Life* was around here asking about her. He spoke to the management, not to me—I wouldn't of told him anything. I know what it was about now. I see you got *Life*. You must of seen it too. Her picture, I mean. That was a lousy trick."

"Yes, I saw it. And she hasn't called you since?"

"No, sir, she hasn't. And now I'm beginning to get really worried. I was just thinking when you came in and asked if I knew her that if she didn't call today I'd go up and not leave until I made sure she was all right and I explained everything to her."

"I wish you had done that the first time," Kevin said.

"Then I was right, there is something wrong!"

"I don't know yet. I hope not."

"I'll show you her room if you want to go up now."

"Yes, I wish you would."

"Sure. Just let me get someone to take my table first."

Arthur hurried with Kevin to the door of the restaurant, where he stopped for a minute beside another waiter.

"Take over for a minute for me, will you, Mack? The old guy's the frogs' legs and his girl-friend's the medium-rare beef."

Chapter 24

KEVIN knocked sharply on Miss Hanna Carpenter's door.

Arthur was fidgeting beside him and Kevin knew that he was trying to think of a way to explain his actions to Miss Carpenter. Kevin could not subdue his own nervousness. He strained to hear the noise of footsteps on the other side of the door or the sound of a hand on the lock. If only he could be sure that the woman was all right, and that Arthur's fears were merely a reflection of his own guilt for having frightened her. He had no real proof that this was the person he was looking for, but his uneasiness grew as there was no response to his knock.

He hammered on the door again and the force he put into his doubled fist surprised even himself. From somewhere in the apartment he seemed to hear a faint rhythmic sound as if someone were softly pounding. The quiet persistence of this noise, which shivered the door faintly with each blow, made him turn savagely to Arthur and demand the key.

"I don't have it on me. It's downstairs." He added, in apology, "I can't carry a house key with me all the time,

230

I just said that I could get it if I needed to because I been here longer than . . ."

"Get it! Damn it. Hurry up!"

Arthur scurried down the hall, using the shuffle of a professional waiter, designed to cover short distances at great speed while keeping the hands and the upper part of the body perfectly level.

Kevin tried the knob of the door. It was locked. Suddenly he heard a heavy thud inside the apartment. The pounding stopped for a moment and then began again.

Although he'd never realized it quite, Kevin was intensely superstitious. He had long been convinced that there was such a thing as second sight and secretly believed that many events in his life were foreordained. Finding Miss Carpenter's picture in a magazine he seldom read was, for him, an example of this. Standing outside this door now, waiting to get in to see a woman who wouldn't or couldn't let him in herself, he was suddenly convinced that the situation called for an extraordinary action, and with perfect faith in his prescience Kevin turned from the door and ran down the hall.

He had remembered that the picture in *Life* had been taken from a fire escape. He ran up the stairs, three at a time, and in another moment he was before the door of the apartment directly above Miss Carpenter's. He knocked quickly.

"Come in!"

He burst through the door and found himself standing before a woman dressed in a negligee. She was seated on a couch and on a table before her were a cocktail shaker and two glasses.

The warm smile of welcome fell from her face. "Who the hell are you?"

Kevin pulled his police identification from his pocket and displayed it.

"I'm from the police," he said, uncomfortably. "I want to use your fire escape."

231

"Is anything wrong?"

Kevin didn't answer. He hurried to her window, raised it, and stepped out gratefully into the night air. He found the stairway down to the next floor and descended as quickly as he could.

When he reached the iron platform outside of Hanna's window he was dismayed to find his way barred by heavy metal shutters just inside the pane of the window. He squatted. One slat of the shutter was slightly bent and allowed him a partial view of the room inside. What he saw was in no way unusual at first glance and Kevin was about to turn around and go back, knowing that he had no legal right yet to disturb the privacy of this woman. Slowly, however, it came to him that this woman standing in the middle of the floor was frightened, terribly frightened, and that something she was watching, something Kevin could not see, was threatening her. As he watched she slowly raised one hand and pointed and her mouth seemed to be gibbering some half-formed words of pleading.

Kevin raised his foot and kicked in the glass. He unlocked the window from the inside and raised the frame, which still held jagged pieces of glass. As he reached inside to take hold of the shutter he saw that the woman was paying no attention to the noise he was making. She continued to point to the thing he couldn't see. Suddenly he was aware of a noise in the room. It was the pounding he had heard before, but louder now and accompanied sometimes by the high squeak of a nail being ripped from wood.

Kevin took the barrel of his service revolver and placed it in a crack between the shutter and the window frame. In the faint light which came from the room he could see that the hinges were old and rusted. He twisted the barrel of the revolver until he could get his hand into the crack. Then with his hands he began to pry the shutter away from the window frame. At first he felt he wouldn't be able to do it. He was in the wrong position to get any

232

leverage, but in a moment he felt the hinges begin to give.

Inside, he heard a loud, crumbling crash. The sound was familiar and he remembered that he had heard it once before when he and George were tearing down a small partition in their house. He realized now that a section of plaster had just fallen from one of the walls. Holding to the ledge of the window with one hand, Kevin strained his entire body against the shutter. It snapped off at the hinges and fell into the room.

What he saw inside was to furnish Kevin with nightmares for many years after. He had learned long ago not to be particularly squeamish and he was relatively impervious to what one human being could think of inflicting on another. For the first time, however, he felt as if he weren't dealing with a human at all but with an insane animal.

Following Hanna Carpenter's finger he saw Theodora stalking across the floor of the bedroom with slow, even movements—like a cat. Behind her he could see a gaping hole in the wall. Clouds of white dust were still thick in the air. Kevin moved over to Hanna's side to reassure her, but he was surprised to see that she showed no recognition at all that anyone else was in the room. She stood perfectly still, her neck slightly arched, staring ahead into the bedroom. Theodora approached the door of the living room, and Kevin noticed that her face was caked white with the dust of the plaster. In one hand she held a sharp chisel. Her hands were bleeding and Kevin could see that one of her fingernails had been ripped off. Although he stood beside Hanna, Kevin knew that Theodora as well was aware of only one other person in the room.

Kevin spoke, and his voice sounded hollowly in the room. It gave him the wild feeling that he was the only one here human enough to understand the words.

"Stop, or I'll fire!"

Theodora crept forward. Neither of the women had heard him. Neither one knew he was there. Kevin was not

233

ordinarily fanciful, but if he had looked around at this moment and had seen the heavy vegetation of a tropic jungle he would not have been surprised.

"Stop, damn it, or I'll fire!"

But these were only human words, to be learned centuries later after the steaming forests had dried up and withered away. The two creatures in the room could not understand him and would have laughed if they could.

Kevin stepped out before Hanna and grabbed at Theodora's arms. With one movement, hardly altering her path, she twisted and threw him to the side. If Kevin had been prepared for it, if he had been approaching a man of his own size, he would not have been set so easily off balance.

In that moment Theodora leaped at her victim and Kevin fired.

Chapter 25

ON THE long, molelike trip beneath the suburb of Queens, Kevin framed the report he would write tomorrow for Inspector Dayton. He knew that brevity was about the only thing the old man would value in the report. From what information Miss Carpenter had offered him after she had been given a sedative by the police doctor he could piece the whole story together fairly clearly.

Theodora had killed David Hammer because he wouldn't marry her. When he had heard all of the suspect's stories he had been fairly certain of this. All of the others had had a definite and very logical reason for wanting David out of the way, but in each case his death would have bared the very thing they wanted kept secret. There had been the possibility that they could have recovered the documents with which he was blackmailing them, but it was only a bare possibility, at best, and from what Kevin had seen of them there was little chance that any of them would have risked so much on this small chance.

Theodora Dennis, however, had risked no such dangerous exposure. What Hammer had done to her had already been accomplished and nothing could now alter it. Also, where the others had perfectly logical reasons for risking a return to David's apartment after the murder, Theodora had none—unless she was the murderer and wished to remove any evidence which would point to her. Theodora also was the only one who knew David well enough to realize that the others at his party probably had strong, traceable motives for killing him and that suspicion would fall equally on them. None of the others could be so sure of this. Each one would naturally suppose that he would be the only one to be suspected if David were to die.

All of this had made Kevin suspect that Theodora had done the killing, but even more important, to him, was the fact that Theodora appeared to him to be the only one temperamentally suited to do it. Both Boleyn and Zimmer were reasonable, calculating men who had risen to their positions because they used their minds as well as their emotions. If they had been the kind to make serious mistakes they would have done it long before this and would not have arrived at their respective positions of eminence. And certainly, committing this murder in a house full of people had been a serious mistake. If either one of them had done it they would have at least made certain that the documents they wanted were in David's possession.

Kevin had ruled out Peter and Sandy because he had felt that they were simply not capable of the kind of blind rage it must have taken to kill David without giving any thought to the consequences. Also, in spite of the fact that Peter had refused to pay David the money he had asked for, it was not conceivable to think that, with their tremendous wealth, they would balk for very long at paying a hundred thousand dollars if David's information were very dangerous to them. If Peter had chosen to kill David he would not have done it at a party—at any rate not a party at which his wife was present.

On the evening of the party, when Hanna had said that she knew who the murderer was, although she had only said it to frighten them, Theodora realized that she wouldn't be safe until she had destroyed Hanna also. During the time that the police had been searching for Margot Case, Theodora was also hunting all over the city for the one person who she thought could prove that she had killed David.

Hanna, in the meantime, remembering that David had told her that the murderer was a neighbor of hers, had found an article about Theodora and her sculpture in *Life*. The article had given Theodora's address and this was sufficient proof for her. Then she seemed to have decided that Theodora was trying to break into her apartment. Kevin had avoided telling her that the person trying to get in had really been Arthur. He had also thought it best not to tell her that she was partially responsible for the murderer's real attack because she had herself confirmed her knowledge by giving Theodora a packet of money.

Theodora's room in the hotel was on one of the upper floors. When he had gone up to see it Kevin had found the partly finished clay statue of David which he had watched Theodora making when he had interviewed her. She had evidently brought it to her room with her some time after he had seen it, for what reason Kevin could not know. Scattered on the floor beneath the statue, Kevin had found the money which Hanna had given. Some of the bills were torn into bits and one half of a hundred-dollar bill was stuck to the wet clay on the side of David's face.

The room next to Hanna's bedroom had been vacant for several days. The people who owned it had left shortly

236

after the fire and were planning to move out. After Hanna's party Theodora had evidently gone to her own apartment, taken a chisel which she used for wood sculpture and, returning to Hanna's floor, had opened the door of the neighboring apartment.

During the few hours that Theodora had lived after the shooting it was evident that she had gone completely insane. She had died thinking that she had killed Hanna Carpenter. In spite of the fact that he had been justified in shooting, Kevin knew that if he had been less clumsy he could have saved the woman. Although he was used to violent death, he had no liking for killing people, no matter what they had done.

He leaned back in the hard, wicker seat of the subway car and opened the *Life* which he had not yet finished. It would make the trip shorter. He wanted very much to be home.

Arthur carried the tray of empty dishes down the ninth-floor hall. Miss Carpenter had been placed in a new room until her own was repaired. She had surprised even Arthur when she told him that she had no intention of moving and that she hoped her apartment could be put back in order as soon as possible.

"I believe," she had said, when he came to pick up the empty dishes, "that I'll have my rooms repainted. Don't you think that would be nice, Arthur?"

"Yes, Miss Carpenter," he had said, quietly. When he had seen her after the shooting, she had been so hysterical that she hadn't even been able to talk until the doctor gave her an injection. Now, she was once again the polite, reserved woman he had always known. If anything, she looked even better. Her complexion had a better color and she didn't jump at all when he made a noise with a plate-cover.

"What would you say to pale rose with white woodwork?"

"Very becoming."

237

"Also I can buy some new furniture. Really, I think I can make it look very nice."

He had collected the dishes expertly on the big aluminum tray and had said, "Will there be anything else, Miss Carpenter?"

"No," she had said, "not really—except that I should tell you that there will be some evenings when I won't be eating in."

She had tried to be casual, but Arthur could see that she was very proud of what she had said.

He had taken her lead. "Are there any restaurants around here you like particularly, Miss Carpenter?"

"What? Oh, there's a very nice Schrafft's down the street. I thought I might go there occasionally."

"Yes," he had said, cautiously, "the food is wholesome and well prepared."

"I think so."

As he rang the bell for the elevator, now, he shook his head. Some people, he thought, cannot learn. What did all this prove but that the old girl should stay inside where she belonged? If she went out again something else would happen to her. Some people were marked for trouble. Why tempt fate?

nH8 P R